An Embarrassment of Itches

M.K. Dean

An Embarrassment of Itches

Copyright © 2021 by M.K. Dean

Published by REDCLAW PUBLISHING

Cover art by Melody Simmons, Bookcoverscre8tive.com

Edited by Phyllis A Duncan, Unexpected Paths Author Services

THERE ARE ALWAYS SO many people to thank for helping to bring a new story into the world. I couldn't do any of this without the support of my wonderful critique group, beta readers, editors, and cover artists. Special thanks to Claire M. Johnson for coming up with the clever title!

And as always, an extra-special thanks to my husband, who hears me muttering curses under my breath as I attempt to format something or wrangle something technical and, without asking, comes over to say, "What can I do to help?"

How did I get so lucky?

Contents

1. Chapter One   1

2. Chapter Two   13

3. Chapter Three   21

4. Chapter Four   41

5. Chapter Five   63

6. Chapter Six   77

7. Chapter Seven   89

8. Chapter Eight   100

9. Chapter Nine   113

10. Chapter Ten   121

11. Chapter Eleven   121

12. Chapter Twelve   121

13. Chapter Thirteen   121

14. Chapter Fourteen   121

15. Chapter Fifteen   121

16. Chapter Sixteen   121

17. Chapter Seventeen   121

18. Chapter Eighteen   121

19. Chapter Nineteen   121

20. Chapter Twenty   121

21. Chapter Twenty-one   121

22. Chapter Twenty-Two   121

23. Hyperthyroidism in Cats   121

24. About the Author   121

25. M.K. Dean Also Writes as McKenna Dean   121

Chapter One

THIS WASN'T SOMETHING I learned in vet school. As matter of fact, you don't learn a lot of things in vet school.

One of my friends once likened our veterinary education to the Rio Grande: four miles wide and two inches deep. That sums it up nicely. Professors throw facts at you at light-speed. Anatomy, physiology, pharmacology, parasitology ... If the word ends in "ology," chances are we studied it. But mostly what you learn in vet school is how to learn. How to study, how to look up things, how to find out what you don't know.

Anything beyond that is up to you.

Which is how I found myself standing in the middle of Ben's living room with his ball python, Dolly, wrapped around my body. I had her neck, if one could truly identify a neck on a snake, clamped under one arm so that her head came up to about chest height. I tried to ignore the fact that the bulk of her snaky body encircled my torso in a loving squeeze.

"Hand me the red rubber feeding tube, will you?" I said to Ben.

He passed it over and together we gently pried open Dolly's mouth. Snakes have fairly delicate jaw structures and we needed to avoid breaking her mandible. I began slipping the rubber tube into her mouth a little at a time.

"How do you know you aren't putting it in her lungs?" Ben asked.

The truth of the matter is that I wasn't entirely sure. This was the first time I had ever tubed a snake. But there was no one else in the area willing to help Ben and Dolly, and so I was giving it my best shot. I tried to sound confident when I replied, "It's not that easy to put a tube down the windpipe of a snake. Their esophagus is much bigger."

Ben nodded as if that made perfect sense to him.

Fortunately, Dolly remained fairly tractable to the procedure and we were able to place the pre-measured tube where I wanted it to go. "All right. See that syringe with the white stuff in it? That's the dewormer. Attach it to the end of the feeding tube and slowly push in the plunger."

Together we watched in quiet fascination as Ben administered the medication to his snake, Ben making sure that the syringe didn't detach from the feeding tube while I hoped and prayed that I was correct about the difficulty of getting the tube in the wrong hole.

Since Dolly showed no ill effects after receiving the contents of the syringe, I had Ben detach it while I kinked the feeding tube so it wouldn't leak much as I pulled it out of her mouth.

"I think that will do it. Hopefully that will take care of her parasites. We'll need to look at a stool sample in a week to make sure."

"Thanks, Doc. I sure appreciate you being willing to see Dolly. Most folks round here would rather take a shovel to her kind."

"No problem, so long as you realize I'm no expert. I consulted with an exotics specialist over in Charlottesville. Luckily, it turns out that you can use a certain kind of liquid dewormer for dogs in snakes. Who knew? Anyway, he told me what drug to get and how much to give based on her body weight."

"Well, I'm sure Dolly appreciates you taking such good care of her."

Ben started to unwind the snake from my body only she didn't want to go. Not only did she tighten her grip, but somehow during the deworming process, she had threaded her tail up underneath my sweater and had it hooked around my bra strap. I guess she liked the warmth? Either way, as Ben attempted to lift her off me, she pulled back and squeezed. I could feel the coil of her muscles clamp around me, and I admit to a little spurt of concern.

I like snakes in a mild sort of way. I don't mind handling them. I'm not afraid when I run across them in the yard. I respect them enough to keep my distance from the venomous ones, and then my primary concern is protecting my pets. But I also like mice. So, it's never really occurred to me to keep snakes since doing so involves feeding them live prey. And although Ben is a nice guy, it makes me just a little uncomfortable to be in his house. All those cages and tanks with heat lamps and a wide variety of reptiles and spiders. Not my thing.

But such is the nature of being a house-call vet. Often you are called to enter a wide variety of homes in all kinds of situations. I don't always have the luxury of taking someone with me, which is why I usually take my German Shepherd, Remington.

Not in Ben's house, however. I had visions of the big, young dog knocking over cages and releasing all kinds of creepy crawlies. Remy was waiting for me in the car, and I was alone with Ben and his too-affectionate snake.

"I'm so sorry." Ben struggled to remove the loops of snake. "She must really like you."

I managed a nervous chuckle.

Ben worked most of the snake off me, but her tail kept its tenacious grip on my bra strap. A frown creased Ben's face as he tried to determine what was preventing the snake from letting go, and he turned beet-red when a tug on Dolly resulted in me yelping and clutching my chest.

Before the moment could intensify further, Dolly suddenly released her grip. Ben draped her over his shoulders and cooed softly to her as he stepped back. From his constipated expression, he was trying hard not to laugh. I wondered how long it would take before my latest animal adventure made the circuit through the town gossip mill.

Manfully wiping the smile from his face, he asked, "What do I owe you?

I glanced at my watch. As usual, I was already running late. "Let me send you an invoice. I've got to get up to Amanda Kelly's place."

Ben lived in a single-wide trailer with aquariums in cages stacked along narrow walls. I shuffled down the passageway to the door. Ben followed behind me, carrying Dolly.

He paused at the door as I exited the trailer, squinting out into the chilly March day. "You going to the town meeting later this week?"

"I doubt it. Depends on if I have the time."

It was no secret that I had had my run-ins with the Town Council and its zoning policies. When I moved back to the area to take care of my family, I'd purchased a small piece of property with the proper zoning—agricultural—to open my own veterinary practice. Certainly, no one would ever buy the property for the house that was on it. Before I'd invested my life savings into the land, I'd gone to the planning office to make there wouldn't be any issues with my intentions. I'd been assured there would be no difficulties. Unfortunately, months later when I went to apply for a business license and to start building, I discovered a small clause in the zoning laws that required me to have a commercial kennel license in order to keep more than three dogs at that location. The land wasn't zoned for that, and none of my neighbors were keen on having a kennel of barking dogs next to them.

No matter that I didn't intend to board dogs and that the only animals there would be patients. Dozens of battles with the Town Council later, I was operating a house-call practice and living in a dump that I couldn't sell. Town meetings were a waste of my time.

Ben scratched the side of his chin. "It's going to be about that new development. You might want to come."

I shook my head. "The town's going to do what the town's going to do. Nothing we say is going to make one iota of difference. We all fought against the pipeline coming through here. They passed it anyway."

Ben shot me a grin, revealing a sad need for dental work he no doubt couldn't afford. "Yeah, but look what happened to the pipeline. We fought it so long it cost them too much money, so they bailed on it. We won in the end."

I cocked an index finger in his direction as I walked toward my car. "Point taken. I'll try to show up if I can."

"I just thought you might have something to say about the new lifetime dog licenses."

That stopped me in my tracks. "What are you talking about?"

"Mom got a notice in the mail the other day. She has to register Biscuit, but they want twenty-five dollars for a lifetime tag."

Biscuit was a lovely little spaniel that Ben's mother doted on, but she was at least twelve if she was a day.

"That doesn't make any sense. The whole point of dog licenses is that you can't get one unless your dog's rabies vaccination is current. So how are they going to police the rabies status of dogs once you buy a lifetime tag?"

A sour look crossed Ben's face as he shrugged. "I dunno. Feels like a money grab to me."

"It does to me, too." Frowning, I added, "Yeah, I've got a thing or two to say about that. I'll probably come to the meeting. Thanks for the heads up."

I opened the hatch on my battered Subaru Forester and stowed my bag in the rear compartment where my medical supplies stood stacked in plastic containers. Remy sat up in the back seat of the car and tilted his head to one side. Ninety pounds and sable in color, he resembled a large coyote. He should have been an intimidating presence. Perhaps he still was to some, but one ear listed to the side, giving him a kind of goofy look. He was more Scooby-Doo than Rin Tin Tin.

When I lost my last German Shepherd to cancer, I told myself no more big dogs. I no longer had the lifestyle to support their needs. I'd been twenty-four when I got Major, and I'd had him for fourteen years. When he was young, I'd been able to take him hiking twice a week, and we went swimming and camping. Even though I worked crazy hours at a busy veterinary practice, I still found the time and energy for him. I'd competed him in agility and rally obedience events. He'd gone everywhere with me.

But that's not my life now. Even though I'm my own boss, running your own practice means you're responsible for everything. It was hard to make time for the things I enjoyed, like hiking and horseback riding or training my dog. The plan had been to downsize to a smaller, less energetic dog. Or at least, it was until my mother had begun freaking out about all the times I went into people's houses by myself at all hours of the day and night. She wanted me to get a gun. The compromise was another big dog.

Unless I was being attacked by a bag of Scooby Snacks, I seriously doubted Remy would protect me. He was really a Labrador in a German Shepherd suit. Or a college frat boy. You could almost hear him asking where the keg party was.

When he realized he wasn't getting out of the car, Remy lowered his head back to the seat with a sigh. I got behind the wheel and waved to Ben and Dolly as I drove off.

The dashboard clock mocked my tardiness, but at least Amanda would expect me to be late. That was one thing I didn't regret by giving up the high-pressure appointment-every-ten-minutes practice where I'd worked when I graduated from vet school. Here, my clients knew if I was late to see them, it was because I had overstayed with the previous client, and I would also spend as much time with them as needed. The downside, of course, was being the sole generator of all income and the only one paying all the bills.

But when my dad had become ill, someone had to come back to Greenbrier and help my mom take care of him. Given the lack of job opportunities in such a small town on the border between Virginia and North Carolina, and the fact that my previous job had literally been killing me, I was the most logical candidate. My sister, Eliza Jane (Liz to her friends), and her husband both worked corporate jobs in Charlotte, North Carolina. Aside from uprooting their young children, they wouldn't have been able to find comparable jobs without a minimum two-hour commute.

As the unmarried daughter, I was the one with the most flexibility. Especially once I'd paid off my student loans. The irony was that at almost forty years of age, I was still living like a student. I'm sure I could have moved in with my mother after my father died. In fact, she'd asked me to do so. But I pointed out my coming and going at all hours, as well as the large number of animals in my personal care, dictated the need for a place of my own. Besides, I had hopes of dating again. Someday.

Because of the reptiles, Ben kept his trailer at the temperature of your average greenhouse. I had taken off my parka to enter his place, but now wished I'd put it back on before getting into the car. March in our little neck of the Blue Ridge Mountains could be extremely unpredictable. One day it will be nearly sixty degrees, and the crocus will be blooming. The next, the temperatures will have dropped thirty degrees with an ice storm rolling in.

Pewter clouds blotted out the sun as I cranked up the heat in the old car and drove along the winding roads to Amanda's place. Was that a fleck or two of snow coming down? Most likely.

I looked forward to my meeting with Amanda. I'd recently diagnosed her senior Siamese, Ming, with hyperthyroidism, a common disease in older cats. Today, I was taking her the initial medication for Ming, as well as some flea and tick preventative and dewormer for the small colony of feral cats Amanda fed. Okay, it was really *my* colony of feral cats. They just happened to live on Amanda's property. My place was too close to the road and Amanda was very accommodating about letting me relocate cats to her farm. I trapped, vaccinated, and had them spayed and neutered before taking them out to Amanda's place. So far, I'd kept the numbers low. We tamed and re-homed any young kittens. Most of the farm residents were older toms too wild to be rehabilitated.

As a house cat, Ming did not socialize with such scruffy ruffians as the ferals. And what a house he lived in. Sometimes it was hard not to be envious of Amanda's home. Perched on a hilltop, the house offered a stunning view of the Blue Ridge Mountains that stretched away across the valley. But she also had enough flat land to support a small barn and riding arena, and miracle of miracles, decent fencing. Amanda herself no longer rode, but she'd adopted several old rescue horses to save them from slaughter. I rarely had time to ride myself, but it was nice having a safe place to keep my horse. In exchange for looking after Amanda's old rescues, I got free board and hay for my horse. After I went over with Amanda how to medicate Ming and what to expect with his treatment, I'd stop by the barn to hand out apples.

I drove across the cattle guard into Amanda's property and up the long curving drive past the barn toward the house. Remy sat up when we bumped across the guard and whined with excitement. The closer we got to the house, the louder he became.

"I don't know, buddy," I said over my shoulder. "You know how Ming feels about you. You may have to stay in the car this time, too."

He yodeled as we drove past the free-standing garage, a little *whoo-whoo-whoo* as we approached the house. Amanda's little red Mini Cooper was parked alongside her green Jeep. It must be nice being able to have summer and winter vehicles. Actually, it would be nice to have *one* vehicle that didn't have over 200,000 miles on it. I would have to replace the Subaru soon, and I needed something with all-wheel drive. Unfortunately, another Forester wasn't in the budget.

I got out of the car and grabbed my kit from the back. Once the weather turned warmer, I'd reinstall the metal grill that would keep Remy contained but allow me to leave the back of the car open. Despite his friendly nature, no one in their right mind would try to break into a car with a German Shepherd inside.

"Wait here," I told Remy. His ears drooped as I shut the rear hatch. I swear it felt colder than when I left the house that morning. Given that I soon expected to be sitting Amanda's kitchen table, sipping a cup of chamomile tea, I decided to leave my coat in the car. As I stood on the doorstep waiting for a response to the buzzer, I regretted that decision. On the ridge, the wind blew constantly, stirring the large wind chimes hanging from a nearby tree into a sonorous murmur.

I glanced at my watch again. I wasn't *that* late. An artist, Amanda was an early riser. I hadn't seen much of her work, but the local library had one of her pieces on display, and I'd glimpsed various works-in-progress. Amanda Kelly was a gifted painter, and I suspected her art was the source of her money. It seemed kind of crass to ask if sketching flowers really brought in the kind of moolah it took to live as she did. What if she said no? The implication would be that she was born into wealth, and I was being nosy. And if she said yes, I would have regretted not paying more attention in art class. We were friends, but not watching romcoms in our PJs with a bottle of wine kind of friends.

Come to think of it, I didn't have any friends like that.

I glanced behind me down toward the barn, hoping to see movement there. A small herd of horses gathered around the paddock gate. If Amanda had already fed them, they would have drifted back out to the pastures to graze. The delay mildly annoyed me. Where the heck was Amanda?

Wherever she was, it was too cold to stand around waiting for her without a coat. I left my bag on the front porch and went back to the car. Maybe she was down at the barn and she didn't know I was here. I pulled my phone out of my back pocket and sent her a text.

I'm here with Ming's medication. Where are you?

Snowflakes flurried down out of the sky. The ground was too warm for it to stick, but between the snow and the wind, I was freezing. I opened the back door of the car to get my coat. Remy was on his feet, tail wagging, ears at half-mast, and tongue hanging out in a gleeful grin.

"Move." I shoved past him. "You're not getting out."

I leaned around him to grab my parka, but the hood hung on the gearshift. As I was trying to free it, Remy suddenly knocked me aside on his way out the car. Major *never* would have left the car without permission. He'd been an obedience champion. He'd gotten his

CDX—Companion Dog Excellent—title before I retired him from the show ring.

Remy's training left a lot to be desired. My fault, I know. But after working with other people's dogs all day long, sometimes it was hard to come home and train my own. Come to think of it, before my mother retired, she'd been a schoolteacher. That explained a lot about her child-rearing methods. I suddenly got a much better picture of why she was the way she was, and it made me shudder to think I might be following in her footsteps.

"Remy!" I bellowed. But it was too late. I saw the flash of a cream and chocolate colored cat dash around the corner of the house with Remy in hot pursuit.

Ming was out of the house!

No wonder Amanda didn't answer the door. She must be out looking for him. God only knows what would happen if Remy caught up with the ancient Siamese. Either Remy would lose an eyeball, or the poor old cat would have a stroke because of his thyroid disease. Abandoning my coat, I ran after my dog, shouting his name and the command, "Leave it!"

I rounded the corner of the house and stopped cold in my tracks.

Ming stood in the center of a picnic table with his back arched like a Halloween cat and his tail puffed out to twice its normal size while Remy barked cheerfully at him. Remy's hackles were up, but arousal is not the same as aggression. I could tell by the way he bounced in and out of the cat's reach that he thought this all a terrific game.

I needed to break it up, however. Ming looked sufficiently pissed that he would hurt Remy if he could. I was moving forward when something caught my attention out of the corner of my eye.

In an optimistic gesture for March, Amanda had already taken the cover off her swimming pool. Since it was heated, I might have done the same. It was one of those infinity designs, with the water spilling out over the far edge into a waterfall that then recycled back into the main pool. From the back of the house, it had the effect of appearing as if you were swimming out into the skyline. I'd taught Remy to swim in this pool, even as I'd worried about him getting too close to the far end. Steam rose off the water in lazy curls as the snow swirled down, and later I remembered thinking how bracing the contrast between the warm water and cold air must be. But my brain must have shorted out as I tried to process what I was looking at.

There was something near the bottom of the pool. A bundle of clothes? Some garbage that had blown in with the wind? I couldn't quite understand what I was seeing.

Until suddenly, I did.

No. Not a bag of clothes.

There's a lot they don't teach you in vet school.

Discovering the body of your friend at the bottom of her swimming pool was one of them.

Chapter Two

Time stopped.

At least, that's what it felt like. I don't know how long I stood there staring at the pool. It couldn't have been more than a few seconds. It could have been all of eternity.

Suddenly, I was moving. Without clear thought, but with definite direction.

I toed off my boots at the edge of the pool and dived in. I'm not a strong swimmer, and I broke the surface gasping for breath before I reached the deep end of the pool. Once there, I had to cling to the side and suck wind for a moment. The water was pleasantly warm. Every inch of exposed skin above the surface felt as though it was being seared off by the icy wind. The temptation to sink beneath the surface and not rise was strong.

Less than a foot away from me a pathetic little pile of items sat. A pair of shoes neatly lined up facing the pool. A wristwatch draped across the shoes. Nothing else, no socks, not even a ring. Just a pair of shoes and watch. As though they were waiting for their owner to return from a dip.

I took a deep breath and dived for the bottom of the pool. It was deeper than I had expected, and my ears popped with a change in pressure. By the time that my fingers brushed the cloth of Amanda's jacket, my lungs burned for air again.

Desperation drove me to dig my fingers into the jacket, and I twisted and kicked my way towards the surface, trying to pull Amanda behind me. I only managed to get her part way to the surface before I had to let go and scrabble to break through the water. Whooping in great gasps of air, I watched as her body rotated and slowly sank once more.

She was dead. There was no way she could be alive.

Drowning victims sink once their lungs fill with water. Sure, they'll rise again later, once decomposition sets in and releases gases, but that doesn't happen right away. All those fictional bodies you see in the movies, conveniently floating face down within easy reach? An actor holding his or her breath.

Even underwater, once I'd seen her eyes, I knew she was gone. That she had been gone for some time. The cloudy surface of her corneas was a dead giveaway.

A massive splash beside me sent a sheet of water cascading over my head. Startled, I lost grip on the edge of the pool and sucked in a mouthful of water as I flailed about. Choking and coughing, I couldn't even maintain a dog paddle, and a moment of panic overtook me.

But then Remy thrust his head underneath my hand, and I reflexively grabbed his collar. With long, sure strokes, he swam for the shallow end of the pool, dragging me behind him.

It was a game we had played when I taught him how to swim the previous summer. When I had first introduced him to the water, he was dangerous to everyone else in the pool. Until he figured out the mechanism of swimming, he tried to walk on top of the water and would climb up any person nearby. A ninety-pound dog trying to perch on your shoulders was a good way to accidentally drown, so I would go into the pool and call him to me while giving the command "rescue." Remy had learned to swim a circle around the "victim," who would grab his collar and be towed to safety.

He thought I was playing, but I accepted the ride with gratitude anyway. When we reached the shallow end of the pool, I dragged myself up the stairs, water pouring off my clothes that now seemed to weigh a ton.

In the short time that I'd been in the water, the flurries had turned to sleet. Ice crystals bounced off the outdoor furniture and tinkled on the tiled lip of the pool. I reached for my phone only to realize with dismay I'd never taken it out of my pocket, and now it was soaking wet. With shaking fingers, I took it out of the case and attempted to dial 911. I had to report Amanda's death.

No joy. A dead screen stared back at me, no matter how much I left streaky wet smears on the surface.

With cell reception being iffy up in the mountains, I knew Amanda still had a landline. Walking to the back door near the pool in waterlogged clothing was like trying to move through molasses. Isolated from the warmth of the heated pool, the frigid air penetrated my very bones. I couldn't remember ever being so cold in my life. My teeth chattered as I fumbled with the latch to the sliding glass door on the back of the house. Beside me, Remy leapt about in excitement, thrilled by the unexpected game and not at all fazed by the cold.

When I pushed back the sliding door, a blur of chocolate and cream dashed past me into the house. Remy would have followed, only I grabbed him by the collar.

"You wait here," I stuttered, and squeezed my way through the narrow gap in the doors inside, shutting the door in his face.

A very woebegone Shepherd looked at me through the glass. It couldn't be helped.

On the couch, Ming narrowed his slightly crossed blue eyes and licked his damp fur furiously.

I squelched my way across the thick carpet to the downstairs bar. It contained a nice selection of scotch and wine, but no phone. The only landline I could remember was upstairs in the kitchen.

Leaving a trail of water all the way up the stairs, I opened the door to the kitchen. It looked much the way it always did. I could almost imagine Amanda coming in from the living room with a smile to offer me a cup of tea. The realization she would never do that again punched me in the chest like a sledgehammer, but I made my way toward the avocado green phone hanging on the wall.

By the time the 911 operator answered, my teeth were chattering so badly I almost couldn't speak.

"911. What is the nature of your emergency?" The operator sounded calm and collected, exactly as you would expect from someone whose job was taking in bad news.

That settled me a bit. "My name is Dr. Ginny Reese. I'm a house-call veterinarian." I gave her Amanda's address. "I came here this morning to drop off medication for Amanda Kelly's cat. I found Ms. Kelly drowned in her swimming pool."

At least, that's what I thought I said. My voice broke and cracked and, at times, gave away entirely. Numb lips refused to form proper words. The operator asked me to repeat myself. Stuttering the entire time, I finally got the information out.

"We'll send someone right away. Please stay on the line until the Sheriff's department arrives."

I left the receiver dangling from its cord. I could hear squawking noises coming from the phone, much in the muffled manner of the adults speaking in a Charlie Brown cartoon.

I was freezing. I had to get warm. The danger of hypothermia was real. There was also the fact that Remy was loose outside. If I didn't get him back in the car soon, at best he would interfere with the deputies when they arrived; at worst, he would go down to the barn and harass the horses. I didn't need him getting kicked in the head on top of everything else this morning.

As I walked through the kitchen, I noted the corkscrew sitting alongside a half empty bottle of Merlot. No glasses, which struck me as odd. But then everything about this day had been odd so far. Perhaps Amanda had poured herself a glass and taken it into the living room. Unlike my own kitchen, everything had been cleaned and neatly put away, except for the wine. No kettle on the stove. No signs that breakfast had been made.

Leaving wet prints in my wake, I went out the front door. I left it standing open behind me. I know I wasn't thinking clearly just then, but for the life of me I couldn't do anything differently. I felt as though I were Anna in *Frozen*, touched by frost and slowly turning into ice.

Stumbling a little, I reached my car. You never knew what kind of gross filth you might encounter as a house-call vet, so I made a habit of carrying a spare set of clothing. Given how negatively an animal might react to the scent of another upset animal on your clothing, it paid to be able to change when needed.

The plastic trunk that contained my clothing was in the back of the car with the other storage tubs. Unfortunately, I had never refilled it after the last time I needed to use it, and what remained was a hodgepodge of odds and ends. A heavy sweater, but no turtleneck to go underneath of it. A pair of jeans but no socks. No bra or underwear either. Where were my boots? I opened and closed containers, shoving them around angrily until I remembered. Oh. Right. They were down by the pool.

I had to get out of my wet clothes before my brain shut down entirely.

The attempt to pull the soaked sweater over my head turned into a battle as I struggled to extract my arms from sleeves that didn't want to let go. I dropped it on the ground and my turtleneck and bra soon followed with a wet splat. I sat on the edge of the open hatch to tug off my socks and shimmied with difficulty out of my jeans. The cream cable-knit sweater from my trunk was definitely a backup option I rarely wore because it showed dirt and dog hair so badly. I scrubbed my legs with an old towel I found in the backseat. It wasn't very clean, and it, too, had its share of dog hair, but just then I wasn't picky.

The spare pair of jeans was another story altogether. I'm sure at one time they fit. They were *my* jeans, after all. But whether it was because my legs were still damp or because I had gained weight since the last time I put them on, I'd had less difficulty donning a pair of skintight surgical gloves. By dint of leaning back into the car and stretching my legs in front of me, I could pull them up over my hips and zip them closed.

Damp skin. It was definitely because of my clammy, damp skin.

Out of habit, I placed my useless cell phone in my back pocket. I'd just closed the back-hatch of the car when Remy came barreling around the corner of the house, his tongue lolling in a cheerful grin. In his mind, we were having the best day ever. He galloped toward me, and I knelt to embrace him in a fierce hug. It mattered not that he was still soaking wet. He was there, and I needed the contact.

I took hold of his collar just the same.

"Into the car with you."

I toweled him off and closed the rear door behind him. When I started the engine, the radio came on loud enough to make me wince as the speakers blasted a song that had been popular when I was in high school. I shut it off and cranked the heat as high as it would go, shivering violently as I held my hands in front of the vent. As I did so, I heard a car coming up the drive. Two SUVs, actually. Both from the Sheriff's Department and sweeping up the curving paved driveway at a good clip. It made me glad that Remy was safe in the car.

The shiny vehicles came to a stop behind me. Gone were the dull brown cars I remembered from high school. The Law had arrived in the form of stark white SUVs, with the county name and SHERIFF in bold blue letters. The doors opened on the lead car, and I recognized Deputies Holly Walsh and her partner, Frank Talbot, as they got out of the car together. It did not surprise me to see them. Holly and Frank were usually first on the scene whether you were dealing with a drunk from Lucky's Bar in town, a parking violation on Main Street, or hijinks from the high school kids on Prom Night. I'm sure they could handle more serious crimes and misdemeanors, but aside from the occasional domestic disturbance or drug-related arrest, crime took a leisurely tour through Greenbrier.

Seeing them was both reassuring and disconcerting. Somehow, I felt Amanda's death deserved more than the attention it would probably receive from these two.

I didn't have a clear view of the second SUV. It wasn't until the driver came around the back of the lead vehicle that I saw who it was for the first time.

You have got to be kidding me.

The man walking forward in the brown deputy's uniform, which fit his lean physique like a tailored suit, was none other than Joe Donegan, my high school boyfriend. Though twenty years had passed since

I had seen him last, there was no mistaking him. He had the same black hair in wild disarray. The same suggestion of a perpetual five o'clock shadow. Same hazel eyes that could never decide if they were green or brown. The same lean runner's body that had made him a track star in high school. Would he have the same lazy smile that declared his charm to anyone within a half-mile radius? I wondered.

What the hell was he doing back in Greenbrier? He left the town—and me, for that matter—years ago, making it clear he couldn't wait to shake the dust off his feet. Now he walked toward me, sheriff's hat in his hand, with his eyes narrowed as though he wasn't certain of his reception.

Damn straight, he shouldn't be sure. I wasn't the fair damsel needing to be rescued from the fire-breathing dragon.

Now I *was* the dragon.

And he was The One That Got Away.

Chapter Three

THINGS SEEM TO MOVE rapidly after that. Or at least, everyone around me did. I couldn't tell if I was the one moving in slow motion or if everybody else was running on fast forward. I suspect the problem was with me. Even the simplest sentences seemed to take me forever to process.

I got out of the car and shut the door before Remy could join me. My bare feet were like blocks of ice that might break off at any moment, and even standing on the cold asphalt felt like torture.

Deputy Holly reached me first.

"You okay, Doc?" Her obvious concern made me blink back tears. "Where are your shoes?"

Swallowing hard, I nodded first and then shook my head. Focus. What was she asking again? Oh. Right. Shoes.

"I think they're around back."

"What seems to be the problem?" Frank strode forward like a pouter pigeon, doing his best to sound authoritative but somehow coming off bored instead. Even at the best of times, Frank wasn't the sharpest tool in the shed.

It pissed me off.

"Did you even listen to the dispatcher?" My voice shook with either anger or cold. It was hard to tell. "Amanda is dead. She's in the pool."

Frank exchanged a look with Holly that somehow conveyed doubt that I was telling the truth. That I must have made some sort of mistake. That I was overreacting.

Joe picked this moment to join the party.

"Why don't you go check out the back, Frank?" he said, dismissing Frank without a second glance. That he reserved for me, giving me a look of narrow-eyed assessment before turning to Holly. "Do you have a blanket in the car, Holly? A spare pair of socks or a thermos of coffee? Anything hot. She looks like she's going into hypothermic shock."

"*She* happens to be right here in front of you." I managed to get the words out without a stutter.

He quickly suppressed the smile that twitched across his lips. Holly came forward with a blanket she'd taken out of the trunk of her car and dragged it around my shoulders. I clutched it with both hands and looked blankly at her when she held out a rolled-up pair of regulation brown socks like a fat bagel.

"You should sit down." Joe indicated the patrol car. "Holly can take your statement where you can stay warm."

Perversely, his order made me want to do the exact opposite.

"I'm fine," I snapped. "I'm not stupid."

His brows beetled together as he stared at me. "I never said you were."

"You were thinking it. I shouldn't have gone in the water after her. There was no way she could be alive at the bottom of the pool. But I had to know for sure, you know? If there was the slightest chance at all…"

His expression softened then. No attempt at being charming. No enforcement of his authority. Just a flicker of compassion in those hazel eyes, and then he said quietly, "Yeah, I get it. You had to know."

At that moment, maybe I hated him a little less than I had in the last twenty years. Only a little less.

"Go on." He nodded towards Holly's car. "Get in the car where it's warm. We'll check things out and then come back to you."

I started back toward the Forester, only to have Joe stop me with an abrupt command. I looked over my shoulder at him in some confusion.

"The patrol car, please."

I repeated his words back at him dumbly. "The patrol car? But I'm still damp. And my car is right—"

"This is a crime scene until proven otherwise."

"I agree. When you see Amanda, you'll—"

"Please get in the patrol car, Dr. Reese."

Well, that put my back up good and proper. I went rigid with outrage.

Holly shoved the socks at me again, and I freed one hand to take them when Frank came around the corner of the house. "Yep. Dead as a doornail. Probably offed herself sometime during the night."

I spun towards him so rapidly the blanket fell from my shoulders. "Amanda did *not* commit suicide." I stabbed my finger in his direction. "She had no reason to kill herself."

"Oh, honey." Holly tried to placate me, but I shrugged away from her comforting pat on my shoulder. "If someone is depressed, they don't need much of a reason to take their own life."

"No." I refused to believe it. "Look, her cat was outside when I got here. She would never leave Ming outside. Never. She loved that cat."

"I thought dispatch said there was something wrong with it. That's why you were here?" Ah. Joe being the voice of reason.

I whipped around towards him. "Ming has hyperthyroidism. One of the better old cat diseases to have because it often responds well to treatment. I'm telling you. She didn't kill herself because she was in despair over potentially losing her cat. And she would *never* have left him outside, no matter how upset she was."

Joe tried again. "Well, maybe the cat got out and when she couldn't find him..."

I couldn't deal with any of them anymore. I put my hand over my face and jumped at the contact of my ice-cold fingers. Before I knew it, Joe had his hands on my shoulders and was steering me gently toward the patrol car.

"Have you got anything hot you can drink? Anything with some sugar in it?"

"No." I started to cry.

His fingers tightened on my shoulders and then relaxed to rub them briskly. "Okay. We'll get you something. You sit here in front of the heater until we get back."

He opened the driver's door, and I sat down on the edge of the seat with my feet dangling out of the car.

Joe plucked the socks out of my hand, and before I could stop him, he knelt to roll them onto my frigid feet. Not being able to indulge in pretty clothes most of the time, I had a secret passion for outlandish nail polish, which I reserved for pedicures, since I had to keep my fingernails short for work. At the moment, I was sporting a black metallic polish with an iridescent green shimmer like dragon scales. Whatever was wrong with my brain made me focus on the unbearable warmth of his fingers on my feet, and the realization that the polish on my right big toe was badly chipped.

Grateful and mortified at the same time, I pulled my feet into the car and huddled beneath the blanket. My teeth began to chatter.

Joe stood and held his hand out toward Holly. "Keys."

She tossed her keys at him, and he caught them one-handed. Reaching around me, he put the key in the ignition and turned it. Still leaning over me, he said, "Stay here and warm up. Someone will take your statement as soon as possible."

He left me with my mouth open and my protest lodged in my throat as he shut the door.

At least I wasn't in the prisoner section of the patrol car.

With the engine running, I couldn't hear what they were saying, but having parked me on the sidelines, Joe had clearly taken charge. Frank went to Joe's vehicle and spoke to somebody on the radio. Joe said something to Holly, who nodded intently and called out to Frank. After stopping at their own SUV to gather supplies, Frank rejoined them to dole out gloves and booties. Joe cast a quick glance in my direction before the three of them went around the house to the pool area.

I waited for what seemed like hours. I held my fingers in front of the hot air blasting from the car's heater, but it felt like I was trying to stave off hypothermia with a candle. Remy got tired of waiting for me to return to the Forrester and finally curled up in the back seat once more, disappearing from my view.

Eventually, Joe came out the front door and hurried to his car. It surprised me when he headed my way carrying one of those tall insulated travel bottles. There was a weird dissociation as I studied his approach to the patrol car, like I was watching a movie instead of experiencing it in real life. He opened the driver's door and held out the mug.

"Relax." He lifted an eyebrow, presumably in response to my sour expression. "It's just plain coffee."

"Normal coffee or the high-octane jet fuel you used to drink back in high school? Have you started throwing VPCs yet due to the extra caffeine?" I reached for the thermos anyway.

"VPCs?" he asked.

"Ventricular premature contractions. Brought on by too much caffeine."

"Careful. You're starting to sound like your mother." The fleeting smile he shot my way indicted he was teasing.

"Them's fighting words."

"You must be feeling better." He made sure I had a good grip on the container before letting go of it. "I normally take it black, but I dumped a ton of sugar in it. You need something hot and sweet right now."

The urge to serve back a double entendre was so strong I worried for my sanity. What the hell was wrong with me?

The first sip brought back old memories of the first time I'd tasted real coffee, not that instant crap my mother made. It was like discovering the difference between a Formula One race car versus a Dodge Dart, or like the time I rode an Olympic-trained dressage champion instead of my childhood pony. I'd turned my nose up at coffee until I found out what excellent coffee tasted like.

Joe wasn't kidding about the sugar. He'd added enough to turn the brew into syrup, and I made a face and gagged as I sucked it down.

"Look out." His warning came with a crease of concern marking his brow. "Go slow."

Sleet continued to pelt down into his hair, which defied gravity as it had always done. Somehow, I wasn't surprised he hadn't put on his sheriff's Stetson. He'd always been a little vain about his hair. It was still as thick as ever and cut in the latest metrosexual fashion. I wondered who he'd get to trim his hair now that he was back in Greenbrier?

Certainly not Andy. Seventy if he was a day, Andy was the town's only barber. The local men went to him to get a buzz cut and have their beards trimmed.

His jaw had the suggestion of a five o'clock shadow even though it was only nine am. I found myself staring until I realized my thinking was still muzzy from shock.

"Well, don't just stand there getting wet." I tipped my head toward the house. "You're the Big City Detective, after all. Shouldn't you be investigating?"

"Who's to say I'm not?" The lift of his eyebrows paired with his slight smile was so familiar that it almost physically hurt to see it.

I'm sure his manner was meant to be disarming, but I was familiar with all of Joe's moves. So, I wasn't entirely surprised when he crossed to the other side of the car and got in on the passenger side.

Remy popped up from the back seat of my car, watching us through the window with the intensity that only a German Shepherd can muster.

"Nice dog. What's his name?"

"Remington."

"No way. You'd never name your dog after a gun. You *hate* guns." Joe leaned back slightly as though he'd encountered a Pod Person. "You can't have changed that much."

It had been one of many points of contention during our long-ago relationship. Joe had planned to go into law enforcement from the get-go. While I'd played around with theater and chorus in high school, I'd always known I wanted to be a vet. Every fall I'd go hiking, and Joe would go hunting with his buddies.

It didn't help that my mother was a vehement NRA supporter.

"When I started the house-call practice, my mother wanted me to carry a gun. I told her I had a Remington I took with me everywhere I went."

His bark of laughter startled me into a smile.

"That sounds like your mother all right. I was sorry to hear about your dad, you know."

I shrugged. "The cancer wasn't as bad as the dementia, until the very end."

When I'd first moved back home, I'd driven my dad around to every greasy spoon, every hole-in-the-wall diner, every Mom and Pop's place in search of the perfect chocolate pie, just like his mother used to make. I scoured the Church Ladies cookbooks and begged for recipes from every acquaintance. I'd never win awards for my baking, but for my dad, I learned how to use a double boiler and how to make meringue. All to no avail. The chemo had changed his taste buds. We probably came across the perfect slice of pie half a dozen times and never knew it.

An uncomfortable silence fell, only to be broken when I said, "I'm surprised to see you back here."

Ouch. That didn't come out right.

"I mean, given that your parents have moved to Florida. How are they, by the way?"

Smooth, very smooth, Dr. Reese.

He stared out the window as he thought about his reply. "They're fine. Loving the warmer weather. As for me, life in the big city wasn't all it was cracked up to be. Coming back felt right."

Time hadn't just been kind to him. It had made love to him and had his babies. Sure, he'd been good-looking in high school, but it had been in a half-formed, quasi-unfinished manner. Back then, some of the guys already had square jaws and chiseled cheekbones to go with their football uniforms. Many of them had peaked with high school graduation. Joe Donegan had only gotten better with time. Why couldn't he have shown up a few months ago? If we'd run into each other in a coffee shop downtown, I could almost imagine the two of us picking up a light banter, like in a rom-com. Oh. Right. Not.

"Coming back here was the second-hardest thing I've ever done in my life." I purposely didn't make eye contact.

Let him stew on what might have been the most difficult thing I'd ever done. Whatever. That door had closed, and I wasn't about to open it again, no matter how handsome the guy on the other side of it might be. There were more important matters at stake here.

"What happens now?" I asked.

His fingers beat a tattoo on his knee before he replied. "The coroner is on the way. He'll determine the cause of death and arrange to have her body taken to the morgue. Next of kin will be notified. You want to tell me what happened when you got here?"

I stared out the windshield at the splatter of ice crystals on the glass, noting how they trailed down the glass in a trickle of wet. The sleet was turning to rain. In an oh-so-casual manner, Joe flicked on the recording device on his smartphone.

"I recently diagnosed Ming with hyperthyroidism. As old cat diseases go, it has a good prognosis, but there are steps to the treatment. I had an appointment this morning to go over initiating therapy and what to expect in the first month of medication. If all had gone well, she probably would have opted for radioactive iodine therapy, which can be curative."

Ming's medical history was irrelevant to finding Amanda's body, and I suddenly had more sympathy for my clients who couldn't tell me why their cat was sick without explaining everything that had happened in the household for the last week. I lost track of my narrative and stalled out.

A slight frown furrowed Joe's brow as he nodded. "Then what?"

"She didn't answer the door. I could tell by the way the horses were milling about the barn they hadn't been fed." I indicated the horses down at the gate, huddled together in their blankets and looking a little miserable. "I rang the bell a few times and waited at the door, freezing my butt off before I sent her a text. I thought she might be down at the barn and didn't know I was here."

It was my turn to frown. "I went back to the car ... Oh! Right. I wanted my coat, so I went back to the car." I took a deep, shuddering breath. "Remy got out. He saw Ming and chased him around to the back of the house."

I turned to Joe and looked him dead in the eye. "Ming is never outside. Never. He's an old, pampered house cat. There are too many coyotes and feral cats around here. If he got out by accident, Amanda wouldn't have rested until she'd caught him again."

"Ginger—"

"Don't call me that," I snapped. He'd lost the right to call me pet names when he'd left for D.C. "And don't placate me. I'm telling you; something is wrong here."

"It looks like a suicide. She took her shoes off. She left her watch by the pool."

"I don't care what it looks like. Did you find a note? Don't suicides leave a note?"

He made a small noise of exasperation, and for the first time I noticed the fine lines around his eyes, and the touch of silver in his sideburns. He looked ... tired ... and the realization startled me.

"It's a myth that suicides always leave a note. Two-thirds of them don't." He seemed to sense my appraisal, and something in his face hardened. "Then what? What did you do next?"

I recited my next steps—chasing after the dog, finding Amanda in the pool, foolishly thinking there was something I could do, and then going off in search of a phone.

"Why didn't you use your own phone?"

I shifted off my hip to remove it from my back pocket. "I forgot it was on me when I went in the water. I'm hoping if I put it in a bag of rice overnight, I might be able to salvage something. What about Amanda's phone? Did you find it?"

Some indefinable expression I couldn't read flickered over his features. "I'm afraid I can't say."

"Can't or won't?" I would have said more, only he cut me off.

"This is a sudden death investigation. Until the coroner determines the cause of Ms. Kelly's death, the farm and everything on it is part of the death scene. I have to treat it as such. If this were an animal cruelty case, you'd know there are certain things that have to be done by the book."

"Fair point. But if her phone is on her body, doesn't that do away with the suicide theory?"

Joe's eyes narrowed briefly, as though he were trying to determine if I was somehow weaseling privileged information out of him. Then his entire expression relaxed. "Hardly. After all, you jumped in the pool without taking your phone out of your pocket."

"I wasn't trying to kill myself. And how does one fight the instinct for survival when trying to drown yourself anyway? Hanging, I get. One quick snap and you're done. Or you choke to death if you didn't set things up properly. Jump off a building and you have a few brief seconds to wonder if you made the right call. A handful of pills with an alcohol chaser and you just go to sleep. But drowning?" I shook my head. "Unless you swim out into the ocean so far you can't make it back, drowning yourself in a pool seems mighty hard to me unless you also took pills beforehand. What's to stop you from coming to your senses and swimming toward the side?"

Joe gave me the *Who the hell are you?* look again. "You seem to have given this a lot of thought."

"Not especially. I just know a lot about physiology. I'm telling you, none of this makes sense."

"Either way, it's up to the coroner now. Why didn't you stay on the phone with dispatch?"

"Huh?"

I must have looked terribly confused because Joe spoke slowly, as though managing a toddler, "You called 911. Dispatch asked you to stay on the line, but you didn't. Why?"

"Oh, crap." In my dismay, I brought my hands up to my face hard enough it could have passed for a slap. "I forgot to go back. I was so cold. I wanted to change out of my clothes and catch the dog. I didn't even think—I mean, I didn't hang up—I'm sorry."

He nodded as though he'd expected my answer. "Understandable under the circumstances. But you left the dispatcher wondering if something had happened to you."

I grimaced a second apology.

He held out his hand. "I'd like to have your phone, though."

My fingers closed over it reflexively. "Why?"

"It would be helpful to corroborate your statement. Besides, we may have better technology than a bag of rice to retrieve the information on your sim card." His charming devil smile made an appearance.

Fortunately, I was impervious to devils now. The law, however, not so much.

I handed the phone over. "My entire life is on that phone. Appointments, contacts, Plumb's, everything. I can't function without it."

He used a pair of blue nitrile gloves to accept the phone and slipped it into an evidence bag. At my sharp glance, he said. "Purely procedural. What exactly is a Plumb's?"

"A medical formulary this big." I spread my thumb and forefinger four inches apart. "Beats carrying around a book the size of the Encyclopedia Britannica."

"We'll get it back to you as soon as possible." He sealed the bag and placed it in his pocket. "In the meantime, I'm afraid I have to ask you to wait here a bit longer."

I glanced at my old Timex, glad that I hadn't given in to the smartwatch craze. "I've got patients to see. And I need to pick up a burner phone."

"Can't be helped." His shrug didn't seem particularly sympathetic. "You'll need to come down to the office and sign a statement when we're through here."

"I need to check on the dog soon. He probably has to pee. And I'm sure I have another pair of shoes somewhere in the car if I just look hard enough. If I could—"

"I can't let you in your car until it's been processed."

I know I must have goggled at him. "Processed? Joe, I run my business out of that car. My dog is *in* that car. How long is this going to take?"

"As long as it does. Sorry, Ginny, but an unexplained death takes precedence over your schedule."

"I'm not saying it doesn't," I snapped. "In case you haven't noticed, I want to know as much as the next person what happened to Amanda. Maybe even more so. But I have responsibilities as well."

"The sooner you cooperate, the sooner you can get back to them."

In the rearview mirror, I could see a black Taurus crawling up the drive, followed by an ambulance with the sirens off. Remy turned at the sound and woofed. His bark, normally deep and booming, was muted as though he were in a soundproof booth.

Joe started to get out, but I stopped him with a hand on his arm. He looked down at it in some surprise, and then shot me a glance that practically smoldered. Regardless of what he thought, my intention was only to get his attention.

"There are animals that need to be taken care of here," I said.

"That'll be up to the next of kin."

I shook my head. "One of the horses is mine. It's no problem for me to feed them and make sure everyone's okay—I do that when Amanda goes out of town, anyway. But Ming needs medication twice a day, and not everyone can pill a cat. He should come with me until Amanda's family decides who will take him."

Joe hesitated. His expression shuttered, and I couldn't tell what he was thinking. He glanced impatiently at the coroner, who was walking toward us. "Wait here. I can't let you back in the house until after the coroner views the body. I'll get Holly to bring the cat out."

I started to tell him why this was a bad idea, but he was already getting out of the car. "His carrier is usually in the hall closet," I called as he shut the door.

I watched as Joe shook hands with the coroner, and the two went round to the back of the house. My brain was coming back online after the hyper-sweet coffee and I reviewed my schedule for the day. I'd left myself plenty of time to meet with Amanda, knowing I'd want to visit with her before I left. I had nothing else scheduled until 2 p.m., when I supposed to do therapy on a dog we were managing conservatively for a torn cruciate ligament. After that, I had an appointment to vaccinate Waddles, an elderly pug. Surely, the police would release me before then. I might even have time to run by the house and change clothes. At some point, I'd have to pick up a burner phone for short-term use. I couldn't run my business without one.

The minutes crawled, and I grew increasingly restless. I wasn't used to sitting down except at the end of the day. Normally, if I had a few minutes between appointments I'd read, but the new urban fantasy I'd started was also on my phone. That's the last time I'd leave the house without at least one or two print books as backup.

Bugger this.

Holly had a notepad and pen in the coffee holder of her cruiser. Scratching out a quick note to explain where'd I gone, I left it on the dashboard. I winced my way over the frozen ground and found my spare boots under the passenger seat. Telling Remy to stay, I grabbed my coat and made my way down to the barn. With any luck, by the time I came back, I'd be able to leave with Ming.

I rushed through feeding the horses. I left the medications I'd brought for the ferals in the tack room. There was no point in trying to treat them today. The unusual traffic on the farm had most of them in hiding. Only Harley, the tamest of the wild toms, showed up when I shook the container of crunchies. I filled the bowls and climbed my way back up to the house at the top of the hill. At least it had stopped sleeting.

Joe waited by my car. His lips had flattened in a tight line and for once his eyebrows were neither flirty nor charming, but lowered thunderously instead.

"I left a note." I pointed to the car before he could speak.

It didn't help. His mouth tightened further, and when he spoke, anger clipped his words. "I told you your car was off limits. That the entire farm was a death scene investigation. I have a good mind to cuff you and toss you in the back of the patrol car."

I gasped. He wouldn't. Or would he? He looked pissed enough that I couldn't be sure. What would happen to Remy if I got hauled into jail? Would they call animal control and take him to the pound?

"I'm sorry. I wasn't thinking. Or rather, I was thinking the horses needed to be fed, and—"

"The damn animals always come first with you, don't they?" He took me by the arm and marched back toward the patrol car, dragging me in his wake.

His words were like a punch to the gut. Was *that* why he'd left all those years ago?

"Joe, please. I said I was sorry." I stumbled along behind him.

He wheeled on me, stopping so abruptly I almost ran into him. "How would you feel if you were prepping for surgery and someone breached your whatchamacallit—your sterile field? It's bad enough I have to work with people who don't have the sense God gave a goose, but you? I expected better of you, Ginny."

Ouch. That stung badly enough to make me wince. But instead of throwing me in the back of the patrol car, he began taking me toward the front door.

"Where are we going?"

He shot a seriously pissed off glare in my direction but never slowed down. "They can't catch the cat. Come with me."

As I followed him through the front door, the sense of loss hit me afresh. Amanda's personality spoke in the crisp, bright colors, the tasteful arrangement of furniture, and the vibrant artwork on the walls. My house was decorated in the Early Salvation Army Style, with a dash of Goodwill on the side. We passed through the living area and down the corridor to the kitchen. From within, I heard the low-pitched yowl of an angry Siamese. Before we reached the door, there came a crash, and vehement cursing.

"What on earth is going on here?" I demanded on entering the room. "Are you trying to *kill* the cat?"

Containers of flour and sugar had been toppled from their position on the counter, and their contents were scattered on the floor. Holly held the door open to a large cat carrier as though it were a sack she intended to use to scoop up a rabid animal. Frank, wild-eyed and disheveled, glared at the top of the cabinets, where Ming crouched, ears back and mouth open in a hiss.

Frank pointed vehemently at the cat. "That thing is a bloody devil."

Blue eyes in a chocolate face narrowed into slits, and the eeriest sound emanated from the cat. It started low, like the rumble of distant thunder, and rose to an earsplitting pitch that made the hair on the back of my neck stand up.

"He has a medical condition. His blood pressure is probably going through the roof right now." I pointed at Holly. "You. Put the carrier down. Everyone else—out."

Frank and Holly exchanged glances with Joe, who seemed to give them non-verbal permission to leave, an order they obeyed with alacrity, heading back down the stairs to the basement. Joe leaned against the island in the center of the kitchen with his arms folded across his chest. "Someone has to monitor your activity in the house."

Grown women don't stick their tongues out at the law, no matter how tempted. From the glint in Joe's eye, he could read my mind, however. I ignored him. I started for the cabinets until Joe clucked and handed me a pair of gloves. I slipped them on and opened several cabinets until I found what I was looking for: canned cat food. Amanda had placed an old piece of carpet inside the carrier to make it more comfortable, so once I could get Ming inside, we were good to go. After positioning the carrier with the door open, I popped the can's top and slid the entire can toward the far end.

Then I joined Joe at the island.

Ming had stopped snarling at the sound of the opening lid, and no sooner had I moved away than he leapt down from the top of the cabinets onto the counter. From there, he dropped to the floor and zipped into the carrier. I jumped forward and slammed the door. Inside, the sound of growling competed with the sound of a cat wolfing down his food.

"How'd you know that would work?" Joe asked.

After making sure the door was securely latched, I stood. "His condition makes him ravenous. He literally can't get enough to eat. That's why he needs medication."

Joe made no offer to carry the cat as he walked us back to the front door. When I would have reached for the medical bag I'd left there, he stopped me. "You'll have to leave that for now. I'll see that someone gets it back to you later."

"I can make do with other thermometers." Though I really didn't want to. The one in my bag was lightning fast and cost a bloody fortune. "But I need my stethoscope."

With a nod, he took out the pair of blue gloves again and retrieved the stethoscope from my bag.

"Hot pink?" He lifted an eyebrow as he passed it toward me.

Ninety-nine percent of every day was spent wearing colors that wouldn't show the blood, mud, or animal hair. The occasional splash of color was vital to my sense of wellbeing. He didn't need to know that, however.

"At least no one will mistake it for belonging to someone else." I hung the stethoscope around my neck.

The crime scene processors waited by my car. Suited up in white nylon outfits that covered them from head to toe, they reminded me of beekeepers.

"We've processed the exterior of the car," one of the CSIs said as we approached.

"Use the gloves I gave you." Joe nodded toward my car. "Get Remington out and keep him beside you."

I set Ming's carrier down and opened the driver's side door. Remy tried to shoot out—I grabbed his collar before he could escape—and I rooted around in the passenger's seat before coming up with his leash. He leapt out of the car with a painful *joie de vivre*, springing into the air all around me so that all four feet left the ground.

"Settle," I scolded, for all the good it did. He spied Ming in the carrier and dragged me toward it, jumping back when Ming struck at the door full force with a loud yowl of rage.

The specialists fell on the interior of my car en masse, liberally casting fingerprint powder in all directions.

I turned to Joe in outrage. "Do you have any idea how hard it will be to get that powder out of my car? Is it really necessary for them to open all my containers? I'll have to wipe down every vaccine vial, every bottle of medicine before I can use it."

Joe ruffled Remy's damp ears and gave that unsympathetic shrug again. "We have to prove Amanda Kelly has never been in your car. Speaking of which, we'll need your fingerprints for comparison, so when you come in to sign your statement, we'll take them then. We'll return your clothing once it's been processed."

By all rights, at this point Remy should have picked up on my intense loathing of one Sheriff Joe Donegan and bitten him on the leg.

Sadly, he looked up at Joe with canine adoration on his face and curled his entire body into a wag.

Traitor.

Just then, the rescue squad wheeled a stretcher around from the back of the house. Strapped to it was a body bag, like in the movies.

In a rare moment of solidarity, we watched them load the stretcher into the back of the ambulance. When they'd closed the rear doors and climbed into the cab, Joe spoke once more. "The coroner discovered evidence of blunt force trauma on the back of Amanda Kelly's head."

I was stunned. "I didn't see any blood."

He nodded in slow agreement. "Probably not the primary cause of death. Just hard enough to knock her out."

Gaping at him, I found myself stuttering again. "But that means…"

"Yeah." He gave me a long, cool, assessing look. It was unnerving. "It wasn't suicide."

Chapter Four

My visit to the police station didn't take as long as I feared, and after they'd taken my prints and brought me a statement to sign, I still had time to run by Bucky's grocery store to pick up a few things.

Until they'd built the supercenter over in Clearwater, twenty-five miles away, Bucky's had been the place where you went to get everything in Greenbrier, from cat food to bathroom caulking to a propane tank for your backyard grill. And yes, burner phones too. A member of the ubiquitous Linkous family, Bucky walked the fine line between charging what the market would bear and understanding sometimes it was worth paying four dollars for a box of saltines rather than to drive into Clearwater. We all gave a little sigh of relief when the supercenter provided Bucky with a little competition.

As luck would have it, I ran into the mayor and her son at the store. She spotted me a fraction of a second before I saw her, and I recognized the abrupt about-turn in an attempt to avoid a direct meeting. Hey, I'd been guilty of the same myself, bumping into chatty clients who wanted to talk about how their pets were doing when all I wanted to do was grab some grub and scurry home. So, I'd had a little sympathy for the mayor when I called out her name and saw her stop in her tracks and stiffen her spine before turning to greet me. Her son, a young teenager wearing ear buds, never looked up from the cell phone in his hand. From the way his fingers flew over the keyboard, he must have been playing a game.

Mayor JoAnna Austin was immaculate as always, facing me with a bright smile as she gave her bouffant light brown hair a pat and twitched her heavy wool skirt straight. She wore a matching blazer over a white blouse that peeked out of the end of her sleeves with frilly cuffs. I'd never seen her at less than her professional best, and given the way her smile had faded as she gave me a startled once-over, I probably looked as though I'd chosen my outfit from a garage sale. Her forced expression of cheerfulness gave way to real concern when she peered at my face.

"Dr. Reese, are you all right?"

I hesitated. If I told her the reason for my disheveled appearance, the news of Amanda's death would derail the conversation I wanted to have with her. But she was going to find out about it eventually, and it would seem odd that I hadn't said anything.

"Rough morning." I gave her what was probably a sickly smile. Lowering my voice with a meaningful glance at her son, I said, "I found Amanda Kelly drowned in her swimming pool when I went to her house this morning."

Mayor Austin gasped, and after noting her son hadn't even registered our conversation, tapped him on the shoulder. Startled, he looked up and popped one ear bud out.

"Wait here, Craig. I'll be right back."

He nodded and replaced the ear bud, returning to his game.

She left her cart to approach me. Grabbing my arm, she dragged me out of the flow of traffic in the aisle until my knees bumped up against the boxes of sugary cereal on the shelves beside us.

"Drowned!" She looked aghast as she let me go. Sparing a moment to glance around to see if anyone was listening, she asked, "What happened?"

"She didn't answer the door when I went there to meet her this morning. I found her at the bottom of the pool." No sense in giving her all the details. For starters, I wasn't sure Joe would be happy if I shared that kind of on-scene information.

"Oh, dear. How horrible." The mayor's face melted into a kind of standard political empathy. "So, suicide, then?"

It pissed me off. Why was everyone so quick to assume Amanda had killed herself?

I responded rather coolly, "That remains to be seen. The coroner will decide after an examination."

I'd leave that up to Joe to make public as he chose.

"Of course." The smooth way she delivered her agreement left no doubt she believed the coroner's assessment to be a mere formality.

I could practically see the wheels turning as Mayor Austin mentally prepared a statement to the press on the loss of a prominent member of the community. Before she could press me for further details, I added, "That's not what I wanted to talk to you about, however."

"Oh?" A look of wariness crept back into her eyes before she stiffened once more. "If it's about the zoning—"

"No, it's about this lifetime dog license. How did such a measure pass? It's stupid. Before, you couldn't get the dog tags unless you had documented proof of a current rabies certificate. Now, there's no guarantee that a dog wearing one of these lifetime tags is current on its rabies vaccination."

She looked at me as though I'd sprouted a second head. "You found a dead body this morning and you want to talk to me about rabies vaccines?"

Her voice carried to the woman shopping for granola behind us, and the shopper turned with a horrified expression on her face before hastily pushing her cart down the aisle.

"Besides, I had nothing to do with that measure." Her tone turned hard as she frowned, and I cringed a little inside at the voice of authority. "That was a decision made by the County Treasurer, not by the mayor's office or any member of the Town Council. So, you see—" She smiled as she thought of a clever quip, "—you're barking up the wrong tree."

"But your husband is the Treasurer's brother-in-law—"

The look of professional concern returned. "Why don't you go home and get some rest, Dr. Reese? It sounds like you've had a very trying day."

She collected her cart and briskly wheeled it off in the opposite direction.

What was I doing? The mayor was right. Focusing on the new ordinance was just my brain's way of shielding me from the bigger issue of Amanda's death. It wasn't the first time I'd fixated on smaller problems to regain control of my life.

So instead of chasing after Mayor Austin, I put a box of Cap'n Crunch in my basket along with the pre-paid mobile and the other impulse-buy junk food items I'd grabbed and headed for the checkout.

Next stop: a run home for a quick shower and to settle Ming before heading back out for my appointments. A glance in the bathroom mirror revealed that between the rain and the dive into the pool, my mascara had run into large black circles under my eyes, making me look like a wet raccoon.

Great. Joe's first impression on seeing me after twenty years was a dumpy, befuddled, clown-faced wreck of a woman instead of the independent, competent, professional I was. It had nothing to do with wanting to appear attractive, either, darn it. It had everything to do with needing him to know I'd done fine without him.

No wonder the mayor had looked at me as though I'd crawled out from under a rock.

Nothing I could do about it now. Thinking about Joe reminded me to call the sheriff's office with my temporary phone number in case they needed to contact me.

The hypothermic and emotional shock had left me as ravenous as Ming, but instead of eating a nutritious lunch of soup and salad, I wolfed down a plate of tortilla chips doused in hot queso sauce that I'd picked up from Bucky's. Yes, I know. Not exactly healthy fare. I didn't care. A shower hot enough to boil a lobster and a fresh change of clothes had me almost feeling human again, finally warm from the inside out.

My house was an old double-wide whose former owners had believed in making do or doing without. It had taken four layers of primer and hours of scrubbing the windows with vinegar water to remove the nicotine stains, but even the bright coat of paint couldn't improve the overall gloom within. The house was still as dark as the Black Hole of Calcutta, especially on a rainy day. I only had one spare room, where I locked Ming with a litter box, food, and water. He'd peered at me balefully from inside the carrier, his pupils dilated to the point all the blue had disappeared from his eyes, and I'd chosen to wait until later to attempt his first dose of medication. His growls followed me around the room as I sprayed kitty calming pheromones about and pushed Remy back out when he tried to shove his way in.

I hurried out to see the cruciate patient. Jake was a middle-aged Lab who'd partially torn the ligament in his stifle—or knee to you and me—and since stifle surgery could cost as much as three thousand dollars for a dog of his size, his owners had opted to go with conservative management first. His treatment consisted of rest, pain management, and twice weekly sessions of cold laser and acupuncture. After that, I vaccinated Waddles, only slightly behind schedule.

But now finished with the day's appointments and having some time to kill before meeting someone from the sheriff's office out at Amanda's to feed the animals, I couldn't delay the inevitable any longer.

I had to call my mother.

At five-eight, I towered over my mother's tiny bird-like frame. Julia Reese was pretty in an Audrey Hepburn kind of way, and I came off as a great hulking Amazon beside her. She still dressed in crisp polyester pantsuits made popular in the seventies, and her shining cap of auburn hair came in a box from the drugstore. A schoolteacher until they forced her to retire, she had her thumb in every pie imaginable—from organizing community literacy programs, to running a Sunday school class, to manning food bank drives. Charities loved her, administrators feared her, and I had always lived in her shadow that was much larger than her five-two frame.

She prided herself on her fierce independence and carried a gun wherever she went. I grew up hearing how I'd never been pretty enough to find someone to take care of me, so I'd better learn to take care of myself. I can appreciate the desire to raise a daughter who could stand on her own two feet. I really could. Unfortunately, according to her, I also wasn't smart, talented, or plain *good* enough, either. With an adult's perspective, I'd concluded it was neither rational nor personal. Liz, who'd married well, had children, and managed a successful career, came in for just as much criticism. Small wonder Liz hadn't wanted to move back home when Dad needed help.

Once, when I hadn't been back in town very long, I'd attended a veterinary association meeting in Birchwood Springs, the nearest large town about an hour away. I'd silenced my phone for the duration. When I arrived back at my dumpy trailer at nearly eleven p.m., my mother was waiting in my driveway. The first words out of her mouth were, "You need to call the sheriff's department and tell them to stop looking for your body."

There had been no emergency. She'd simply wanted to talk to me, and when she couldn't reach me for a few hours, her first assumption was that something terrible must have happened. Another time, when I planned an out-of-town trip for mandatory continuing education, my flight was scheduled for the tenth anniversary of 9/11. My mother called me every day for a week to ask me what kinds of funeral arrangements I wanted, and who did I want to take care of my animals? Did I have a spare key to my car? Because she was going to have to pick it up from the airport when I died. That sort of thing. I had to take a fistful of Xanax before I could get on the plane.

On meeting my mother for the first time, one of my friends from vet school had said, "Oh, my God. All these years we thought you were exaggerating."

Yep. That's my mom.

I half expected her not to answer the phone when I called, as she wouldn't recognize the number, but no such luck. She picked up on the third ring.

"Hey, Mom. It's me, Ginny. I had an accident with my phone today, and this is my new number for the moment."

I'd hoped the news of Amanda's death hadn't reached her yet, but no such luck there either.

"I heard about your friend's death, my dear. So sad. But then these artist types can be unstable. I suspect she lost all her money and was going to be forced to live in a garret."

And my dentist wondered why I ground my teeth.

"It wasn't like that, Mom."

"Well, what could it have been? It's all over town that she drowned herself. And you were the one to find her. I didn't want to say anything before, but I always questioned your friendship with her. The two of you couldn't possibly have had anything in common. What would a decent young woman be doing living all alone, anyway?" My mother sighed. "You know, if you would just start going to church again, I'm sure you could meet a nice man so you wouldn't be living alone, either."

A tic developed under my left eye.

For a split second, I considered telling her it wasn't a suicide, but she'd find out soon enough and jump to the conclusion it was murder instead of an accident. I really didn't want to have the "you need a gun" lecture right now. Navigating the waters to find a safe channel of conversation was always tricky with my mother. You never knew when you'd get bogged down on a sandbank of criticism or flooded when some gate of warnings unexpectedly opened. I didn't want to have the "nice man" conversation, either. For someone who was adamant I was too homely to warrant finding true love, she was very much set on my meeting the *right* kind of person and settling down now. I decided to fire a diversionary shot across her bow.

"Why didn't you tell me Joe Donegan was back in town? And don't say you had no idea he'd returned because you know everything that goes on in Greenbrier."

"How could you not know he was back? Ginny, they held a special election when Sheriff Linkous retired and everything. I assumed you *did* know."

I chewed on the inside of my cheek. She had a point. I paid more attention to politics these days than I used to, but I still hadn't heard. And I should have. How is it no one in the entire community had seen fit to share the juicy news that Joe was back—if nothing else, to gauge my reaction?

"I didn't see a single yard sign," I muttered.

My mother's exasperation came through loud and clear over the phone. "Because he ran unopposed. There was no need to campaign."

Huh. That was unexpected. A member of the Linkous family usually held some form of office in Greenbrier, but then again, perhaps they were all busy running the various family businesses. If you needed your heat pump fixed, some remodeling done, or a new well dug, you usually called a Linkous.

"Oh." That still didn't explain everything. "I'm surprised no one mentioned it to me, that's all."

"Well, I imagine most of the women in town saw you as potential competition and kept the news to themselves." She gave a loud sniff. "And any man interested in you—"

I cut her off. "*You* didn't bother to tell me either."

Like most tactics with my mother, this one failed miserably. "What would you have done differently had you known? Driven into Bristol for a decent haircut? Bought a nice outfit for a change? Made an effort to lose weight?" Her pause wasn't long enough for me to mount a rebuttal. "I suppose it's because you work with animals, so you haven't noticed the change in your appearance, but you *have* let yourself go, my dear."

At least animals don't run down a never-ending list of your failings every time you meet.

She continued with airy unconcern for my feelings. "At any rate, it shouldn't matter to you one way or another if Joe Donegan has returned to town. That chapter of your life is closed. Right?"

Funny how when she said it, I wanted to prove her wrong.

A second later, it hit me. Mom hadn't wanted me to know Joe was back. Interesting. I would have thought she'd have been all over the idea of a new eligible man in town for me.

Obviously, for some reason, Joe wasn't eligible in her eyes.

"Of course." Speaking with conviction would surely make it so. "Listen, when is the next town council meeting? I know it's sometime this week."

Curiosity sharpened the pitch of my mother's voice. "Thursday evening. Why? I thought you'd given up on the zoning stuff long ago. Is this about that new development people are talking about?"

"No. I found out today from one of my clients that the County Treasurer, in his infinite wisdom, has eliminated annual dog licenses. Now you buy a lifetime tag."

If disappointment could be measured over the phone like an earthquake, my mom would have hit at least a 3.4 on the Richter scale. She liked a good battle and frequently told me I'd given up too easily on my own zoning issue.

"I don't see the problem," she asked. "Won't people save money in the long run?"

"The problem is that before, you had to show proof of a rabies shot. Therefore, ipso facto, if a dog had a current license, it meant it was also vaccinated for rabies. That no longer holds true now. The whole point of licensing is not simply to generate revenue for the county—it's to make sure people vaccinate for rabies. That's just flown right out the window."

"You'll need some data to back up your case." You could almost hear my mother straining at the leash, begging to be released to tackle this problem. "I'll call Betty and ask her to do some research."

Yikes. The last thing I'd intended was for my mother to rustle up her dogsbody to look up information for me. Betty had been my mother's aide back when she was a teacher, and they'd both retired around the same time. I had no idea what my mom paid Betty to be at her beck and call twenty-four/seven, but it wasn't enough. And I definitely didn't want my mother coming to the council meeting on my behalf like bad legal counsel.

"I doubt there's any specific data available. It's more a case of pointing out to the Council the stupidity of the decision in the hopes they'll have some sway with the County Treasurer." I futzed about with my phone until it made a beeping noise. "Oh, I've gotta go. I'm getting a text coming in. Talk to you later."

I ended the call before she could think too much about who would text me on a new phone. As my excuse had been a complete ruse, I jumped when a real text alert came through.

I didn't recognize the number, but the text read: **Someone from the sheriff's department will meet you to feed the horses. What time will you be there?**

I glanced at my watch. It wouldn't get dark before almost seven p.m. now. Might as well get this over with so I could come back and eat something that resembled a proper meal for a change.

I can be at Amanda's in 30 minutes. That work?

I got a thumbs up emoji in response.

It wasn't entirely surprising to discover Joe's car waiting on the other side of the cattle guard. As soon as I pulled into the drive, he started his engine and led the way to the barn. I hoped when he assigned himself as my babysitter, he realized he'd have to meet me before and after work each day. I looked forward to telling him how early that might be.

"You look like you're feeling better," Joe said by way of greeting when I got out of the car, Remy at my heels.

"What's that supposed to mean?"

He'd been ruffling Remy's ears when my sharp tone made him glance up. "Nothing. You've got some color back now. You were white as a sheet this morning. Even a little blue around the edges."

"Good save," I muttered as I pushed past him.

Both he and Remy followed me into the feed room, where I collected several cans of cat food and a container of dry kibble. "The two of you should wait here. I'm feeding the ferals first, and they won't come out if you're there."

"No worries. I'll hang back enough to stay out of your way, but I need to keep an eye on you."

If I rolled my eyes any harder, I might develop vertigo. "How much longer are the restrictions on my accessing the property? Because the animals need to be fed twice daily."

"It's not up to me. The coroner has to determine cause of death and whether it was an accident. Once he releases the scene, I'll let you know."

"An accident, huh?" Something about that didn't sit right with me. "That is, if Amanda didn't give a hoot that Ming had gotten out, or that she decided to take off her shoes and then she slipped and fell into the pool. Striking her head on what?"

"You know I can't discuss the case with you except in general terms." My words had caused a slight glint in his eyes, as though they'd struck metal and created a spark. "But how well did you know her? She might have had too much wine. The tox screen will take a few days, but then we'll know."

He folded his arms across his chest and leaned into the doorjamb. "One would almost get the impression you *wanted* it to be murder."

I suspected he was deliberately rattling my chain, so I remained cool. "Of course not. I refuse to believe it was suicide. An accident would be tragic, but acceptable."

He gave a little snort of suppressed laughter and rubbed the tip of his nose.

I placed my hands on my hips. "And what, pray tell, is funny about that?"

"Nothing." He folded his lips inward, as though biting off a comment, before adding, "It's just you haven't changed a bit."

Huh. I could argue with him on that, and I was tempted to do so. Instead, I gave Remy a stay command and hoped for the best. Remy's stay was a bit wobbly at best, and he frequently oozed his way closer to me after only a few seconds. He might well still be technically "down," but there was a good chance he'd be waiting for me outside the feed room when I got back. I picked up the selection of cat food and headed out.

Joe trailed behind me, coming to a stop at the edge of the clearing, keeping his distance as promised. Harley, the fat black and white tom who was the tamest of them all, stopped dead in the middle of trotting up to greet me to fix Joe with a slit-eyed glare.

"Hey, cat," I said by way of greeting, and shook the container of dry cat food. Automatically, my voice shifted into the silly cat-speak I used when addressing the colony. If I'd burst into song, I would've sounded like Snow White. "Are you hungry? Pay no attention to the man in brown. He's not going to bother you."

After I doled out some dry food into the bowls stationed in various places, I popped the first of the cans and began dividing them as well. Harley wasted no time in eating. Through the dead grass and brush behind the barn, I saw a flash of white, but had I not known what to look for, I'd never have spotted Solomon. The brown striped tabby with the white bib blended perfectly into the weedy brambles. "Come on out, meow-meow. Dinner's waiting."

Seeing that he would not come any closer to the food bowls until I retreated, I rejoined Joe at the other side of the clearing. Solomon crept out to eat, one ear trained in our direction the entire time.

"Is that all of them?" Joe asked as we headed back to the barn.

I shook my head. "Blackjack didn't show up. Hopefully, it's just because you were with me, though it's not like him to miss dinner on a cold night. He's pretty shy, though. Also, there's a new tom that's shown up recently. I need to trap him as soon as the weather warms up enough that I don't have to worry about him freezing overnight. He's picking fights, and he needs to be neutered and vaccinated."

"I guess that's something the new owners will have to deal with."

Something I didn't want to think about right now. As expected, Remy lay half in, half out of the doorway to the feed room when we returned to the barn. His ears dropped to half-mast as I made a negative clucking sound and took him by the collar. Once I walked him back to the original spot where I'd left him, I set down the cat food and repeated the command to lie down and stay.

"Aw, do you have to be a such a stickler for the rules?" Joe chided from the doorway, where he leaned one shoulder against the jamb.

"You didn't know my last dog, but he was an obedience champion." I'd gotten Major when I went away to school and Joe was no longer a part of my life. "Major had a rock-solid down/stay. I could put him on a down outside the library, and he'd still be in the same spot when I came out." I gave Remy the hand command for "stay" for good measure, not breaking eye contact with him as I spoke.

"Maybe you shouldn't be comparing Remy to Major. Sounds like those are some big paw prints to fill." Joe's slow drawl made me snap my gaze in his direction. "This one looks like he's still got a lot of pup in him."

The nerve of that man. "Don't tell me how to train my dog, Donegan."

Joe levered himself off the doorjamb to place both palms up in a manner suggesting things were getting too hot to touch. "So, I'm Donegan now. That's a bad sign."

I ignored that observation as not being worthy of a response. "Look, it's not about an arbitrary set of rules. It's about safety as much as anything. If Remy is going to be safe while off-leash, then he must obey me. If I want him to stay put so he doesn't get kicked by a horse or hit by a car, then I have to teach him what the rules are. And I can't do that by being wishy-washy about them."

Remy cocked his head at my use of his name, and his not-quite-erect ear listed to one side.

"Okay, Remy," I said, giving him his release word.

Remy jumped to his feet and bumped up against my hand. I patted him absent-mindedly and plucked an old coffee can off the shelf to scoop some sweet feed into various buckets.

I almost missed the moment Joe's voice slid from friendly conversation into mild interrogation. "The new owners. You wouldn't by any chance know who that would be, do you?"

I blinked, caught off guard by the change of subject. "You mean Amanda's next of kin? She has a brother, I think. You can't find him?"

"We're having a little trouble pinning him down right now. Have you ever met any of her family?"

"She didn't talk about them much. I got the impression they lived out west. California, maybe?" Come to think of it, every time the subject of families had come up, Amanda seemed to redirect any discussion back to my relatives, of whom I was all too glad to vent. "Do me a favor, will you? Can you open the connecting gate between the pasture and the barn area? The horses normally show up for dinner about this time of day and will come in on their own."

Joe made as if to tip the brim of the hat he wasn't wearing and stepped out of the feed room. I continued setting up the buckets, measuring out the various supplements and the aspirin powder for Rebel, who had chronic uveitis.

I carried two buckets in each hand outside to the fence line, where hooks were attached to separate posts. Remy frisked alongside me, only to pause and lift one forepaw. I looked up to see a stranger standing on the other side of the gate. His appearance was so unexpected, I gasped, and almost dropped the bucket I'd been about to attach to the fence.

Dressed in a business suit with sun-bleached hair slicked back from his forehead, the stranger removed his sunglasses and placed his fists on his hips. "Who the hell are you and what are you doing on this property?"

"I could ask the same of you." I clipped the bucket in place and grabbed Remy by the collar. This had the effect of making him pull against me, and to the untrained eye, made it look as though Remy wanted to get at the stranger. He did, if only to leave muddy paw prints all over the man.

Just then, the horses came trotting in from the pasture, squealing and nipping at each other as though they were vicious monsters. Given they were still wearing blankets, this was largely for show. They splashed through puddles of standing water and each horse went to its usual station, attacking the scant amount of grain in the buckets as though they'd just returned from a Mongolian campaign.

Joe followed behind them.

"Good." The stranger nodded toward Joe and raised his voice. "Deputy. This woman is trespassing."

Joe didn't alter his pace but continued to move toward us in his usual saunter. He came to a halt beside me before speaking. "And you are?"

"Brad Taylor. The deceased was my sister."

The deceased? His sister was dead, and he referred to her as the deceased? How cold was that?

"Ah. Sheriff Donegan, sir." Joe nodded thoughtfully and rubbed his chin. I shot him a glance—he seemed to be playing the part of a small-town sheriff a little too convincingly. I half-expected him to quote Andy Griffith. "We've been trying to get in touch with you. I didn't realize you were in town."

"Yes, my secretary forwarded your message to me, and I contacted your office as soon as I heard."

"So, you were already in town to see your sister?" Joe's smile remained friendly.

"Yes, we had a business matter to discuss." Brad's brow furrowed as he glanced in my direction. "I take it this woman is one of your deputies?"

"No." I broke in before Joe could speak for me. "I'm Dr. Virginia Reese. I'm here to see to the horses."

The lines on Brad's forehead relaxed, and a hearty grin lightened his expression. "Well, there will be no further need for your help in that matter, Miss Reese."

"Doctor Reese," I said. I rarely correct my clients when they persist in calling me Miss or by my first name instead of my title. But this man wasn't a client, and he got my back up. "And why is that, Mr. Taylor?"

I might have emphasized the "mister" ever so slightly.

He shrugged as though it were self-explanatory. "Simply because they won't be here for much longer. I've arranged for someone from

Ringbolts to pick them up in a day or two. They have pasture and access to water. They'll be fine on their own for that length of time."

"Ringbolts? You called Ringbolts?" I released Remy's collar and headed for the gate. Remy looked at me in some confusion and fell in beside me. "That's a slaughterhouse! Your sister loved these horses."

Joe made to grab my arm, and I shot him a stare that would have been lethal had he made contact. He withdrew his hand and held it palm up in a gesture of peace. I continued to the gate and began working the catch.

"Look, I'm not the bad guy here. I have a limited amount of time to make decisions regarding my sister's estate, and that includes disposing of her animals."

I lifted my eyes off the stubborn gate latch to bore holes in him.

"Okay, perhaps dispose is the wrong word. But look at them." He gestured to the horses, which had finished eating their small amount of grain and now milled about the paddock area. "Nobody wants them. I tried a rescue group but they're full up. And the handicapped riding program couldn't use them either. They're older than Methuselah and are fit for nothing but rendering. All except that brown one there. He'll bring in more than the others just because he's so damn big."

Making an inarticulate sound of rage, I gave up on the latch and scaled the gate. Brad backed up a few steps, alarm creasing his brow. Dropping to the ground made my knees hurt, but I stalked past Brad to my car as though it didn't.

"That big bay horse is a mare. And she happens to be *mine*."

"Oh?"

Maybe I was just pissed at him, but I could have sworn a flicker of disappointment crossed his face before his nostrils flared.

"Can you prove that?" he asked.

Flames surely shot out of my ears then. "Yes. I can."

I rooted around in my glove compartment until I found what I was looking for. I held up the sheet of paper. "Coggins papers. For that horse. Listing me as the registered owner."

Grabbing my checkbook out of the glove compartment as well, I slapped it down on the hood and took a pen out of my back pocket.

"What are you doing?" Curiosity made him lean closer to see what I was writing, but when I glanced up, he tilted back again.

I dug the pen so hard into the pad, it nearly tore the check. "The going price for horsemeat is fifty to sixty cents a pound. Let's say Amanda's three horses average eleven hundred pounds each." I was being generous. Rebel couldn't have been more than eight hundred. "The best you can hope for is six-sixty a horse. I'm making out a check to you for three thousand dollars." I ripped the check off the pad and held it out. "That's a thousand per horse, more than you'll get anywhere else. I'll be back with a trailer in the morning to take them away."

"Hold up here." Joe had gotten the gate open, and he and Remy joined us. I noticed Remy stuck by Joe's side instead of going over to eviscerate Brad. Where was a vicious attack dog when you needed one? "Ginny, you don't have to do this right now. There's such a thing as probate, you know."

His drawl was so laid back, every syllable dripping with Good Ol' Boy tones that I suspected the act was for Brad's benefit.

Brad snatched the check out of my hands as though I might change my mind. He stuffed the check in his wallet before returning it to his pocket. "I spoke with Amanda's lawyer in California earlier this afternoon. She left no will. As I am her next of kin, everything comes to me anyway. I figure it will take a matter of weeks to settle things here, but you can see I couldn't leave things as they were with livestock involved."

"Yes, you're a regular St. Francis of Assisi."

Brad's puzzled look said he clearly didn't understand the reference or the sarcasm. The smile he gave me was purely perfunctory as he turned to Joe. "If I could trouble you for the keys to the house and cars..."

"Well, about that." Joe scratched the back of his neck. If it hadn't been so muddy, he would have probably dug a toe in the ground. It wouldn't have surprised me in the least if he'd said, "Aw, shucks, mister."

But he didn't. A hint of a devilish smile brushed his lips as he spoke. "I'm afraid this is still a crime scene. Which is why I'm escorting Dr. Reese here. Truth is, you can't be here without an escort, either. But I tell you what. You come down to the office in the morning. We'll have a little chat about this business of your sister's that brought you to town, and I'll see about getting those keys to you. In the meantime, I'd sure appreciate it if you gave me the name of the place you're staying."

Brad knew when he'd been outmaneuvered. Mouth tight with annoyance, he gave Joe his local address—the B&B at the Mossy Creek winery. After agreeing to come down to the sheriff's office in the morning, he drove off with a cascade of gravel spinning out from under his wheels.

"You're letting him go?" I asked as soon as Brad was out of earshot.

Joe lifted a quizzical eyebrow in my direction. "No. You heard him. He'll be by the office in the morning."

"And you're taking his word for it? When he's obviously hard up? Mark my words: this business matter he needed to speak with Amanda about had to do with getting money out of her." I made finger quotes over the words *business matter*.

"First, he's hardly likely to cut and run given he expects to inherit. Second, if he does, we know who he is and where to find him. He's not going anywhere. Third, have you considered maybe you're seeing conspiracies where none exist?"

"Come on, Remy." I threw open the car door and waved him within. He leapt into the car in one fluid motion. I got in behind him.

Joe came to lean on the open door, one hand on the roof and the other on the frame. "Where are you going?"

Tugging on my hair briefly provided no relief whatsoever. "I'm going to transfer funds from my credit card to my checking account before that jerk tries to cash my check. And then I need to find a place to move the horses and beg, borrow, or steal a trailer to move them in. I can't take a chance that Ringbolts might not show up here first thing in the morning."

I would *not* cry, darn it. It's just that getting really pissed made me weepy. If the steering wheel had been Brad Taylor's neck, I'd be up for manslaughter.

"Okay, look. I can't help you with the trailer—I don't have a rig yet—but you can move them out to my place."

"What?"

What was he talking about? His parents had sold their farm when Joe had decided to go into law enforcement instead of running the dairy, and it had been turned into a housing development years ago. Meadow's End was wall-to-wall ranch houses and duplexes now. Joe's folks were living the good life in Boca Raton.

He scratched the back of his neck again, but this time, his discomfort seemed real. "I bought a piece of land near Potter's Mountain. No house there yet, and the drive is iffy in bad weather, but I've got a barn and fencing up. You're welcome to keep the horses out there for the time being. You know, until you can find some place better."

I wasn't going to find a better offer any time soon. Few places in the area offered pasture board alone, and stall board for four horses would be the equivalent of monthly payments on a new Subaru four times over.

He let go of the door as I pulled it shut. "Give me your number so I can call you once I line up transportation."

"You already have it. I texted you earlier this afternoon."

With another tip of his imaginary hat, he walked back to his car.

Chapter Five

IT'S A GOOD THING I'm a problem-solver.

After I'd made an online cash advance on my credit card (wincing at the new total on the bill), I deposited the money into my checking account and called my old horse show buddy, Deb Hartford. As soon as she heard what was going on, she volunteered not only the use of her van, but also to help me move the horses. I gratefully took her up on her offer and then called those clients I could remember being on the books to reschedule their appointments. I knew I was forgetting something or someone, but it couldn't be helped. From now on, I'd maintain a written schedule in addition to the calendar on my phone.

I then texted Joe. He sent directions to his place and arranged to meet us there at noon the next day. He'd send someone else to supervise our presence on the property when loading the horses in the morning.

Fortunately, Ming's drive to eat made him unlikely to check treats for medication, and he wolfed down his first anti-thyroid pill as though it were cat candy. I decided until the therapy started to work, it would probably be best if he remained isolated in the spare room for the time being. Having him stroke out because he was furious with Remy would be icing on a terrible cake. He seemed calmer than he had after being manhandled by the deputies earlier in the day, and I rubbed his bony body when he bumped up against my legs.

Kneeling, I scratched him behind the ears. His disease was causing him to waste away because of an excess of thyroid hormone, but treatment had a good chance of reversing his symptoms. I knew Amanda had been interested in sending him off for radioactive iodine therapy once he'd stabilized, but that wasn't likely to be something I could afford, especially not after having bought Amanda's horses.

"We'll figure something out, old man."

Ming began making biscuits on my knee, which caused me to hiss in pain. Another symptom of hyperthyroidism was excessively thick claws. I tried to withdraw, but one of his claws had hooked into my jeans, and I had to grab his paw to work it out. Naturally, this pissed the short-tempered cat off. A low-pitched growl emanated from him as I unhooked his foot. It was only then I noticed the dried blood.

Scooping the cat up, I carried him to the bed and switched on the lamp on the nightstand so I could get a better look at his paw. Mashing his foot to make him spread his toes and extend his claws, it appeared as though Ming had bits of flesh sticking to them.

It wasn't mine. Ming hadn't scratched me *that* hard.

Exactly how had Ming gotten out of Amanda's house, anyway?

I pulled the burner phone out of my pocket and started to call Joe, only to hesitate. He'd only come back into my life this morning, and already I had his personal phone number and was moving my horse—now horses—out to his property. I'd just texted him a little while ago. If I called him now, would he think I was trying to rebuild our old relationship?

And worse, would he be right?

No. That had nothing to do with it. I had information that might be relevant to the case, and he needed to know.

He answered on the second ring. "Ginger. What's up?"

"I told you not to call me that."

"Old habits die hard." His voice, whiskey-smooth, sent a little frisson of warmth through me.

"Yeah, well, I was medicating Ming when I noticed he had blood on him. On his paws, that is. I think he's scratched someone."

"Frank referred to him as The Incubus. I'm not surprised."

"I'm surprised Frank would even know what an Incubus is."

"You can learn a lot from slasher flicks. So, the cat scratched someone. You're calling me because...?"

Oooh. Exactly the attitude I expected. "I'm calling you because you're in charge of this case and this might be vital information as to who Amanda's killer is. Can't you run DNA on it or something?"

He made a noise that is usually described as a long-suffering sigh. "What kind of budget do you think the sheriff's department has? Who's to say where the blood came from? Maybe he killed a mouse. Not to mention, if it *is* human blood, there's a good chance it's Frank's. So, unless you have another reason for calling me—"

"You know what? Never mind. Forget I ever called."

"Ginge, don't be like—"

I hung up before he could complete his sentence.

"Okay," I told the cat. "That was a bit rude. Especially given the fact he's being so nice about the horses. But he's wrong. This is a clue, and we need to preserve it."

I went off in search of a pair of thumb forceps and one of the specimen bags I used when shipping samples off to the lab. Ming was surprisingly tolerant when I put on a pair of surgical gloves and held him in my lap to pick flesh from his claws. He even began purring.

Holding up the bag to the light after the collection was complete, the sample seemed pathetically small. Yeah, they could extract DNA from mosquitoes, but no one had successfully cloned a dinosaur yet. Perhaps Joe was right, and I was barking up the wrong tree.

Regardless, preserving the evidence felt like the smart thing to do, but I needed a place to store it. The fridge seemed the wisest receptacle, and opening it reminded me I hadn't had much to eat all day. At almost eight p.m., the thought of deciding what to make for dinner and actually cooking it seemed like too much work, so I had a bowl of cereal. Cap'n Crunch, dinner of champions.

Remy was intensely interested in the "visitor" living in the closed guest room, and I had to call him twice to come to bed before he abandoned his vigil of lying with his nose pressed up to the crack beneath the door.

The next morning, I met Frank out at Amanda's place. Frank looked less than thrilled to be our supervisor for the morning, and after escorting me to the barn, sat in his cruiser drinking coffee while Deb and I worked.

Deb was the only person I knew who drove an old-style van that could hold up to six horses. The red and white truck with its familiar lettering: CAUTION: HORSES was a welcome sight as I drove up to the barn. Thankfully, neither Brad nor the Ringbolt's truck were anywhere to be seen.

When I hurried to feed the cats, I was relieved to spot Blackjack among the crew, and scolded him in a silly voice for worrying me while I fed them.

I started bringing the cans of grain out to the van while Deb stuffed hay nets. "I really appreciate your help, Deb. Thanks to you, we can make the move in one trip."

Anyone looking at Deb would peg her for a horsewoman right off. She was lean in a tough, wiry kind of way, with arm muscles that would rival a rock climber's. She wore her thick hair back in a braid and was tanned from spending hours in the sun teaching riding lessons. She tied up the last of the hay nets and then swung the fifty-pound container of grain onto the rig as though it were a carton of milk. "I can't believe Amanda's brother would be such an asshole as to sell her horses for meat. Or maybe I can. Word is around town he's been a real jerk there too."

"Oh?" I placed my tack trunk on the edge of the van floor with a slight pang of regret. Another year had passed without me reaching the goals I'd had to compete my mare. Maybe I should accept the fact that it wasn't something I was ever going to do. "What are people saying about him?"

Deb took the trunk and hefted it up into the hold behind the driver's seat. "Well, at first he was just the uppity stranger staying at the B&B, you know? Nasty to waitresses, and a poor tipper. But I heard he was rude to Miss Ellie."

"What?" Miss Ellie was a fixture at the local library. Already gray when I was a kid, she dominated the library much in the way my mother dominated the town. Except in a kinder, gentler way. No one was mean to Miss Ellie. "Whatever for?"

"He wanted some information she couldn't get for him, so he got ugly with her, according to Donna."

As Donna was the assistant librarian, the source was a good one. "What was he looking for, do you know?"

Deb shrugged. "No idea. But that's no excuse to be a jerk about it. What are you going to do about the cats?"

"I don't know." I sighed and rubbed my forehead. "I've got to come up with something before Brad calls animal control. I can hardly dump them on Joe, and I can't really bring them home with me. They aren't going to be happy being moved, either. I have to figure something out soon, though. No doubt Brad will refuse to let me back on the premises once he gets control of the property."

"Joe's being very cool about taking the horses." Deb had the grace not to smile, but I could hear it in her voice. "I'm sure he would take the cats, too."

"They would probably be safer there than out at my place. But it could take me days to catch them, especially if the weather doesn't cooperate. I'm going to have to come back tonight and try. After I ask Joe about taking them, that is."

"What about Ming? You already have him, right?"

I blew my breath out. "Yes, but I'm not saying anything about Ming just yet, and between you and me, I'd like to keep that quiet. I don't want Mr. High and Mighty Taylor to demand custody of the cat. He'd probably order Ming euthanized."

"Not if he had to pay for it. He'd just drop the cat off at the pound."

"You're probably right. He couldn't take my check for the horses fast enough."

Which was food for thought. Was that why he'd come to town? He was hard up for money and had hit Amanda up for some kind of loan? Maybe the two of them had gotten into an argument, and—

"Earth to Ginny."

I became aware Deb was speaking to me. "Huh?"

"I said that should be everything. All we need to do is wrap and load the horses."

It would have taken me forever without Deb's competent efficiency. I didn't have enough leg wraps for Amanda's three horses, but fortunately, I found shipping boots for them in the tack room. I still used the old-fashioned cotton padding and flannel wraps on my own horse, as they provided superior protection.

Getting the shipping wraps out, however, cued my mare into the fact Something Big was going on. At seventeen hands tall with a jet-black mane and tail, during the summer show season, Scotty was a magnificent sight to behold. Now, having yet to shed her shaggy winter coat and wearing a muddy blanket, she looked more like a moose than a competition horse. I could see why Brad had lumped her in with the others. To him, her worth could be measured by the pound.

As I put her in the crossties, she snorted and blew as though she heard the foxhunting bugle or the start bell at a racetrack. I managed to get her bell boots on to protect her hooves while shipping, but she continued to shift in place, making it hard to wind the nine-foot-long flannel wraps over her legs. If it hadn't been for Deb's stern eye, I might have been tempted to use the less protective shipping boots myself. Four tabs to Velcro in place and you're done.

Having already determined the order in which to place the horses on the van based on their weight for the best distribution, Deb didn't wait for me to finish wrapping, but began loading the other horses without me. It took both of us to get Scotty on the van, as she refused to go up the ramp without a lot of encouragement. As soon as we got her in the van and buckled into her slot, we put up the chest bar to lock her in and hoisted up the ramp.

No wonder Deb was built like a rock climber. Everything with horses required some serious muscle.

We waved to Frank as we left. He saluted us with his travel mug and a yawn.

Joe hadn't been kidding when he'd said his drive was iffy in bad weather. The long winding road into his property had been graveled at some point, but rain had washed a fair bit away. Serious potholes forced us to creep along the drive. I followed behind the van in my car and watched as tree limbs scraped its roof.

The bulk of the van blocked my view until the trees opened up, and suddenly we were in a large bowl of land with a nearly three-sixty view of the Blue Ridge Mountains. Whereas Amanda's house was on a ridge, Joe's property was flatter, but still high enough for breathtaking scenery. A neat, newly built barn stood to one side. A stack of treated lumber was visible beneath a blue tarp, but a fair amount of fencing had already been finished, along with a run-in shed. No automatic waterers, but a brand-new water trough stood under a spigot that had been built into the fence line. There was no house either, but a foundation had been dug, and cinderblocks lined the sides.

An old RV stood near the barn. The awning was up, creating the effect of a porch, and a beat-up lawn chair resided in the relatively dry space beneath. An electrical cord snaked its way into the barn. He must have had a 30/50 amp hookup installed to power the RV when needed.

As we pulled up in front of the barn, Joe came out carrying a bale of hay. He was dressed in a blue-check flannel shirt, jeans, and cowboy boots, and wore leather gloves to protect his hands from the baling twine. Seeing him like that took me back twenty years in the blink of an eye, when he'd used to work on his daddy's farm.

He set the bale of hay down and came over to greet us.

Deb, as usual, said exactly what was on her mind. "Nice place. Must have set you back a pretty penny."

"You're asking how I could afford it?" His smile showed no offense taken. "My share of the proceeds from the sale of my dad's property. He made a killing when they turned the dairy into a sub-development."

He gave us a quick tour of the barn to show us where to store the feed and supplies and then explained the layout of the pastures. "I only have so much fenced in right now. Eventually, I plan to put in an arena, and keep at least one field for making hay, but they can go in the field by the barn for now."

Since Deb would not see anything unusual in his living arrangements, I had to ask. "Are you living out here in the RV? Why build the barn first? Why not the house?"

"Now that the days are getting longer, I can work here in the evenings. I spent more than one night camped out at the station this past winter, that's for sure. As for building the barn first..." He shrugged, making a non-committal sound that could have been a laugh. "The house is going to take me a while. I thought it would be nice to get a horse to ride up in the mountains on the weekends. If you come across a nice little Quarter Horse or Anglo Arab, let me know. Something quiet. It's been a while since I last rode."

At the rate he was going, it would take him years to build his house. "Yeah, not much opportunity to ride in the Big City, I guess."

I hadn't meant for my statement to come out as snide as it did.

Joe took it at face value. "Middleburg isn't that far from D.C., but they turn out more fancy dressage horses there than they do cow-ponies."

That was another thing different about the two of us. I trained in the English sport of eventing: dressage, cross-country, and stadium jumping. Joe rode as well, but in the Western style: reining, cutting, and at one time, barrel racing. It might not sound like a big difference, but it's a gap as wide as the gulf between someone enjoying Top 40 versus country. They're both styles of music, but the tone, rhythm, and typical message are as different as can be.

"Wade Harris has a horse you might want to look at," Deb volunteered. "Nice blue roan. Good feet. Good temperament. Bought it for his daughter to show in Western Pleasure a few years ago, but she started college last fall. He's looking to sell. The best part is now you'll have other horses to keep it company."

"Temporarily." I stressed that point.

She and Joe discussed the particulars of the blue roan as he helped us unload. We ended up with a pile of dirty blankets and wraps as we stripped the horses and turned them out into their new surroundings. They squealed and ran about briefly, but except for Scotty, they were all senior citizens who quickly decided they'd rather eat the bright green grass coming in with the change of seasons than run about like lunatics. Scotty trotted around the perimeter of the field in great, floating strides before hearing the siren call of the grass herself.

We watched them until they settled to make sure no one was going to do something stupid, like try to run through a fence. Joe asked for the rundown on each horse, and I shared their history. Rebel, the little chestnut Arab, who needed daily aspirin for his chronic uveitis. King, the flea-bitten grey who was practically white with age. And last, but not least, Sherlock, the big, homely chestnut who was swaybacked, and would crib if given the chance. Cribbers grabbed hold of any stationary object with their teeth and pulled back while sucking air, making a noise like a giant bullfrog. The habit was as addictive as smoking cigarettes, since it created an endorphin release. Unfortunately, they did marked damage to fences and stalls. He would have to wear a cribbing muzzle until Joe could run a strand of hot wire up along the tops of all the fencing, something he assured me he was planning to do anyway when I insisted on paying for it.

Joe indicated Scotty as she lifted her head and flared her nostrils, testing the air. "She's gorgeous. What's her breeding?"

I couldn't help a little puff of pride. She wasn't a fancy sport horse, but she had the potential to be a great competition horse just the same. "Clydesdale crossed with a Thoroughbred."

The draft horse in her gave her the shaggy feathers on her legs and the white blaze down her face. In the summer, she'd shed out to a rich mahogany, as shiny as a new penny.

"Like the Budweiser horses?" He shook his head with a little laugh. "Well, you always did like them big."

Deb released a braying laugh that sounded exactly like a dying donkey, and I shot her a dirty look. With a bright-eyed look, she wandered away to pick up the wraps, whistling innocently.

Ignoring her, Joe lead the way into the feed room, where we'd set up aluminum trashcans for mouse-free grain storage.

"Since I'm staying out here now, I'll feed the horses and check on them twice a day."

I didn't argue. Coming out to this place twice a day would have added a significant amount of time to my already jam-packed schedule. I went over the feed amounts and how to administer the various medications, and he gave me the key code to the gate at the end of his drive, which would be locked whenever he wasn't there. It reminded me of the situation at Amanda's.

"I've still got to go out to Amanda's twice a day to feed the cats until I can get them moved. And I don't have a place to move them yet—then there's the matter of catching them. I'll have to set traps on the nights it's not too cold."

I had to remind myself he was doing me a big favor by taking the horses when he sighed. "Can't you put out a feeder or something? Set them up so no one needs to go out there for a few days?"

"First, putting out self-feeders only attracts wildlife, like skunks and racoons. Second, if I don't come out regularly, they may disperse, and then I'll never catch them."

He didn't say that might not be such a bad thing, so I didn't punch him. As I would have, had he said it.

"All right. I'll assign someone to meet you. But once the scene is released, it won't be up to me anymore. You'd better move those cats as soon as you can."

I bit my lower lip. It wasn't meant as a display of feminine wiles. I simply didn't know how to broach the question. But he picked up on it anyway.

"Aw, c'mon, Ginge. You're not seriously asking me to take the cats, too."

This time I didn't chide him for using an old nickname, as it wouldn't have furthered my goals. "Short-term only. Just until I figure out what to do with them. As you pointed out, as soon as Jerkface Brad gets control, he won't let me back in. And who knows what he'll do with the cats, given his decision about the horses."

Joe grimaced and rubbed his forehead with a gloved hand. "I'm going to regret this, aren't I? Okay. You can bring them out here. But only until you find another place for them. I may be set back off the road, but there're coyotes out here, you know."

We're not huggers in my family. Growing up, I didn't receive a hug unless someone died, so it had negative connotations. But the memory of being hugged by Joe suddenly surfaced: how it felt to be engulfed in his arms, to lean into his chest and smell his clean, rich scent. It had felt like safety and love. For a split second, I wanted to throw my arms around him and give him a squeeze.

Yeah, right. When Hell freezes over.

Instead, I said awkwardly, "Thanks, Joe. I know this is a big imposition. I'll try to find another place to board the horses as soon as possible, too."

I left him standing there with a frown as I rejoined Deb to finish putting away the gear. I found her lifting the ramp to the van by herself and rushed over to help. She'd already swung the monster ramp into place and thrust the holding pins down before I got there.

"I hung the blankets in the barn so they'd be dry the next time you use them. Hosed off the shipping boots as well. I left your wraps so you could take them home and wash them."

"You're a lifesaver, Deb. I appreciate this more than you could know."

She waved off my thanks, got into the van, and drove off. I collected the dirty wraps and threw them in my car. Joe came over as I was getting in.

"You headed out?"

I got behind the wheel and left the door open so I could reply. "I'm actually ahead of schedule for once, thanks to Deb. I'm going to go home, grab some lunch, pick up the dog, and head out for my afternoon appointments."

He nodded. "They should be done with your phone if you want to go by the office and collect it."

"Really?" I was pleasantly surprised. "You got it working?"

A brief smile touched his lips. "Yep. Plumb's and all."

A momentary panic hit me as I wondered what kinds of private information he might have had access to, but then I gave a mental shrug. No sexy selfies to share with a BF. No thrilling text conversations or arrangements for clandestine meetings. Mostly a lot of photos of animals, many of which were work-related, and therefore kind of gross. Scheduling appointments with clients. Reminders from the dentist and eye doctor. My life was an open book so dull it could be used to treat insomnia.

"Glad to hear it. It's funny how dependent we've become on our phones. I'm going to do a better job of keeping a paper record in the future. I hate feeling as though I've forgotten to do something." I hesitated and then rushed on. "Thanks for letting me park the horses here, at least for the time being. It's a huge favor. I owe you big time."

He glanced around the property, as though seeing it for the first time. He took a deep breath and let it out with a satisfied sigh. "I don't mind. Like I said, I was planning on getting a horse soon, anyway, and you can't have just one horse. You've got the gate code now, so come out whenever you like. It's pretty isolated, though. You sure you'll be okay out here on your own if I'm not here?"

"You're forgetting. I'm a big girl now, and I have a big dog." I hadn't brought Remy this morning because it had been easier to deal with the horses without his youthful energy.

That drew a snort out of Joe. "Your Canine Marshmallow? He's a pushover."

Ugh. He sounded like my mother. "While it's true Remy has never met a person he didn't like, he looks like he would protect me. And that's what counts with most people."

Though, to be fair, Remy's easy-going nature had me doubt whether he would protect me in a pinch as well.

"Still, do me a favor and send me a text when you're headed out this way and when you're leaving. For my peace of mind."

I *really* didn't want to do that, but it was his property. Besides, after a few early morning messages, he'd probably ask me to stop.

The drive back into town was pretty, but long. The inconvenience of not being able to pop into the local grocery or having to go into work in bad weather was probably worth it, though. I envied Joe his little slice of heaven, even as I wondered how long he would stay this time.

Chapter Six

ONE THING LED TO another, and it was almost time for dinner before I made it to the sheriff's office to pick up my phone. I saw a litter of snotty-nosed kittens and vaccinated Hank Davis's new working Great Pyrenees puppy. The giant fluff ball looked like a cuddly polar bear baby at nine weeks of age, but by the time he turned a year old, he'd be a massive, aloof member of the flock, ready to protect Hank's sheep from all predators. I filled prescriptions, unpacked a box of vaccines I found waiting for me on the porch that had to go in the fridge right away, and caught up on records. It wasn't until I glanced at the clock that I realized it was almost time for dinner.

A quick check of the fridge revealed nothing inspiring. I tended to make something in the crock pot once a week and live off it three meals a day until it was gone, but aside from my quick run the day before, I hadn't made it to the store recently and was low on everything. Running into town to pick up my phone would give me the excuse to grab something from Sue's diner, and then I could swing by the store on the way home. It was a good plan. I could offset the guilt of an old-fashioned cheeseburger and fries by loading up at the grocery with vegetables that would likely rot in the crisper drawer of the fridge.

Belatedly, I remembered the cats at Amanda's. I'd ask someone from the sheriff's department to meet me there when I picked up my phone. A check on the weather showed it would be mild enough for the next few nights I could risk putting out traps, so I stuffed my live traps into the car, whistled up the dog, and drove into town.

It was a relief to get my phone back. When had we become so dependent on the pesky things? Joan at the station desk told me to call when I needed someone to meet me at Amanda's, as she had no one available she could assign to that duty then. I took my phone back to the car and powered it up.

Surprisingly, the phone didn't blow up with messages when I turned it on. That's when I realized that Joe, or one of his people, had listened to them all. Rattled, I hoped I didn't overlook any as a result, as I always left my messages marked as unread until I dealt with them. I nearly thumped my fist into my forehead when I read the text from Andrea Chapman asking where Bluebell's medication was. I *knew* I'd forgotten something. I texted back explaining the issue with the phone and promised to phone the prescription for Bluebell's heart medication to the pharmacy at once. I completed that task before doing anything else.

There were a slew of voice mails as well, most calling to request refills, set up appointments, or reschedule existing appointments. My mother had been nagging me to set up a website or a phone app where most of these communications could take place online, and I admit, it was looking as though she might be right. I didn't recognize the number of the five remaining messages waiting for me, but I decided they could wait until after I'd eaten. As usual, I was starving.

Though it would be light for several hours yet, it was close to dinnertime, and the streets became more crowded as people sought their evening meal. Most of the stores on Main Street would be open until nine p.m., though it wasn't unusual to see a sign posted saying a store had closed early for the day. Once the weather warmed up, we'd get more tourists and day-travelers passing through, but I honestly wondered how most places stayed in business during the winter months. Greenbrier was the kind of town you stopped at on your way to somewhere else.

Though if it turned into the bedroom community suggested by all those new sub-developments, downtown Greenbrier might become rejuvenated. That is, if new businesses didn't wipe out the downtown area altogether. Main Street had its charm in a fashion reminiscent of the fictional town of Mayberry. It seemed a pity we couldn't capitalize on that fact somehow.

A delicious scent of frying meat wafted out of the little Greek restaurant sandwiched in between the bakery and the used bookstore. I was tempted, but I had my heart set on a cheeseburger. If you didn't want chain fast food or pizza, the only choices in town were *Calliope's* and Sue's diner at the end of the street. I would not find better parking than I already had, so I cracked the window and told Remy to wait in the car.

Poor Remy hadn't been out for a good run in days. I'm lucky he wasn't the type of dog to eat the upholstery in the car because his energy levels were climbing. Which was probably why he chased Ming the day before. The temptation was too irresistible.

As I passed *Calliope's*, I noticed Brad sitting at a booth near the window, sharing a glass of wine with a striking woman. Her blonde hair was cropped in a sleek, asymmetrical bob that angled down from the back to swing below her chin, and she was dressed in Manhattan-chic—or at least what I imagined Manhattan-chic to look like—in a smart black suit with a blood-red blouse to match her lipstick and nails. They appeared to be examining the contents of a large portfolio-type folder with great animation on the table between them. Drawn despite myself, I couldn't help slowing down to glance at the papers in the folder. If I wasn't mistaken, they were drawings from Amanda's sketchbook.

Brad looked up sharply, caught my interested gaze, and slapped the folder shut.

The phrase "if looks could kill" suddenly took on personal meaning.

He made as if to rise, but the New York City woman laid a restraining hand on his arm, even as she cast a piercing glance in my direction.

I couldn't help but stare back at the two of them, but even as I started to turn away, a man in an expensive suit stopped at their table. You didn't see many people wearing suits in Greenbrier outside of a funeral home, and certainly no one around here wore anything that fit like it was tailor made.

Brad broke off glaring at me to shake hands with the newcomer, and realizing I'd pushed the bounds of politeness, I pretended I hadn't been staring.

Thankfully, my phone rang, giving me a legitimate reason to look away. It was the mystery number again. Hoping to avoid another confrontation with Brad, I answered it as I hurried down the street.

"Hello. Dr. Reese here."

"Dr. Reese." The gentleman's voice on the other end was tinged with relief. "This is Lindsay Carter over in Clearwater. I've been trying to reach you."

Clearwater was a bit outside my practice range. When I'd first started my business in Greenbrier, I hadn't been too proud to drive a long way for a house call, but now I could afford to be a little choosy. If only because I no longer had the time to drive all over the state.

"I apologize, Mr. Carter. There was a mishap with my phone. I only now got it working again, and I haven't had a chance to listen to my messages. What can I do for you?"

"It's what I can do for you, Dr. Reese." He sounded pleased with himself now. "I'm the lawyer handling Ms. Kelly's estate. We're holding a reading of the will this evening in my office, and I would strongly suggest you make every effort to attend."

"Wait. What?" I stopped dead in my tracks, causing a pedestrian to mutter as they almost ran into me. Mouthing "sorry" at them, I stepped close to the buildings to be out of the foot traffic. "I thought Amanda died without making a will. At least, that's what her brother seemed to think."

"Yes, well, he would be wrong. Ms. Kelly may have chosen not to use her family's law firm for personal reasons, but she did, in fact, write a will. I've been trying to get a hold of you ever since the news of Ms. Kelly's death was made public. The reading is at 7 p.m. I realize that's an unconventional time, but—"

"In Clearwater, you say?" If I skipped dinner, I could make it with time to spare. I could grab something at a drive-thru and eat on the road. As I debated the best course of action, the door to *Calliope's* opened, and Brad and his mystery date stepped out onto the sidewalk. She walked away without looking back, but Brad appeared to fixate on my location and began stalking toward me.

I glanced in both directions and cut across the street to head back to my car.

"Do me a favor," I said as I darted in front of a passing car, giving the driver a cheery wave to show thanks for not running me down. "I'm not in a position to take down your address right now, so could you please call me back and leave the location of your office on my voice mail? I need to hurry if I'm going to get there on time."

Mr. Carter agreed and ended the call. When my phone rang again, I ignored it, allowing it to roll over to voice mail so Mr. Carter could leave his message. I was just about to click the key fob to unlock my car when I heard Brad behind me.

"You," he said, not bothering with any sort of salutation. "I don't appreciate you spying on me."

I turned to face him. He stood with his fists clenched and his brows beetled together as he leaned toward me in a belligerent manner.

"I think you're mistaken." I kept my expression as bland as possible. When dealing with a dog that is thinking about biting you, the best course of action is to remain calm, not make any sudden moves, and above all, do nothing to escalate the aggression. "I wasn't spying. I merely realized that I recognized you, and my attention focused on you as a result."

As tempting as it was to tell him he was overrating his importance to me, I thought it would be best to remain silent on that front. Also? Probably not the best time to bring up the feral cat situation. I noticed he was carrying the portfolio I'd seen on the table, and involuntarily, my gaze fixed on it.

He caught the direction of my stare and shoved the large folder under one arm. Taking a step toward me, his radiating anger forced me back until the car's door handle was beneath my fingers. "If you know what's good for you, you'll mind your own business."

Sometimes when you're dealing with a threatening dog, you try to calm it down. Sometimes, however, your best move is to redirect its attention. "Aren't you going to be late?"

He blinked at the question, and then frowned. "What are you talking about?"

"The reading of Amanda's will in Clearwater. Traffic on the interstate at this time of day can be bad."

His eyes widened and his nostrils flared. Interestingly, he took hold of the portfolio as well, gripping it even as it remained clamped under his arm. "What do you know about that?"

"Same as you, I imagine. Mr. Carter invited me to the reading as well."

Well, that did it.

"Why the hell would you need to be present at the reading of my sister's will?"

If I'd thought he was angry before, he was about to blow a gasket now. His face had turned beet-red, and the tendons in his neck stood out like a weightlifter under a heavy strain.

"I realize you didn't know she had even written a will in the first place, but I'm sure my presence at the reading has something to do with finding homes for her animals."

He seemed someone mollified by that, but I didn't like being pinned in so close to my car. I held up the key fob and pressed the button. The door locks disengaged, and Remy sat bolt upright in the car's backseat. I didn't give Brad time to think. I opened the door. Remy pressed his way through the front seats to drop his head and peer out.

Brad stopped in his tracks and cleared his throat. "I thought that was the sheriff's dog."

"Nope," I said cheerfully. "Mine. He goes everywhere with me."

I left Brad on the sidewalk, swallowing hard, as I shoved Remy aside and got in the car. I rolled down the window and gave him a friendly little wave. "See you at the reading."

The confrontation had driven all thought of grabbing dinner out of my mind until I took the Clearwater exit. Larger than Greenbrier, the town offered much more in the way of shopping and restaurants. Any other time, I would have enjoyed browsing through the local artisans shops or a leisurely meal at the Barn Door, but I didn't have time tonight. Though I probably could have picked up a burger and fries from one of the fast-food chains, the idea of bolting down greasy junk food prior to rushing over to Mr. Carter's office turned my stomach. Hopefully, the reading wouldn't take long, and I could get something on the way back.

Since I had a few minutes, I pulled over and listened to the phone messages from Carter's office. The first four were polite requests from a woman for me to contact the office, starting out at my convenience and escalating to a taut "as soon as possible". The fifth was from Mr. Carter himself, presumably to lend weight to the previous requests. The sixth was Carter calling back with the address.

My phone's GPS guided me to a quiet, tree-lined street where the former first-family homes had been converted to professional offices. Carter, Beasley, and Worth hung a shingle on an old Victorian-style house complete with a turret.

I parked in the small paved lot behind the building and cracked a window for Remy. "This won't take long, I promise."

I'd been saying that a lot lately, and it was utter crap. At some point soon, I'd have to make time to get him out for a long run in the woods. For both our sakes.

An older woman with her gray hair styled in a severe bob greeted me. "Dr. Reese. So glad you could make it. You're a difficult woman to get a hold of."

"Sorry." I wasn't sure what I was apologizing for, but authoritative women had my number, something no doubt a psychologist would have a field day with, should I ever seek counseling. "My phone was out of service until today."

"No matter." She ushered me down the hall. "I'm just pleased Mr. Carter was able to get in touch with you. If you'll wait here, he'll be with you in a moment. There's coffee if you'd like a cup."

I entered a meeting room to find a stylish woman with bright scarlet hair cut in a super-short afro seated at a large table, nursing a cup of coffee. Dramatic eyeliner made the most of her gorgeous eyes. She wore a small nose stud and a black leather jacket and skirt. My gaze was drawn to her hands, where vibrant, cobalt blue nail polish flashed as she broke off a piece of cookie from the stack resting on a napkin in front of her.

"Oh, my God," I said as soon as the assistant had left. "Please tell me there are more of those somewhere."

Smiling, the woman indicated the side table, where a carafe of water, a coffeemaker, cups, and a plate of cookies stood.

I rushed over and selected an assortment: chocolate chip, sugar cookies, and the cheap cream-filled knockoffs pretending to be Oreos. It was a bit late in the day for coffee for me, if I had any hope of sleeping, but I poured myself a steaming cup just the same.

"Hungry?" The woman at the table grinned when I took a seat across from her.

"Always. Never time for a decent meal, either. I'm Ginny Reese, by the way. Amanda's veterinarian."

"Ah." The woman nodded as though this made perfect sense to her. "Laney Driver. Amanda's agent."

We fell silent for a moment, as if remembering why we were here. The siren call of the cookies prevented me from becoming maudlin, however. "I didn't know she had an agent. Though that only makes sense. She was really talented. She had a gift for making her drawings seem almost alive."

"That she did," Laney agreed with a heavy sigh. "It's hard to believe she's dead. That there will be no more work by her hand."

"What will happen to her art now?"

Laney shrugged, somewhat angrily, I thought. "It will depend in part on her will. I guess her brother will get the rights to everything. Which sucks because he wouldn't know a hawk from a handsaw."

I recognized the Shakespearean quote but said nothing, choosing to munch on my cookie instead.

"Her work belongs in a museum," Laney continued. "Her jerk of a brother will probably sell it to the highest bidder."

Brad's defensiveness in light of his dinner with Miss New York made more sense now. It was always possible Brad was making deals before he had the legal right to do so.

"Did she have any other family?" I asked, surreptitiously brushing crumbs from my sweater.

"Not any immediate family that I'm aware of. Her mother died of cancer a few years ago. Her father is gaga, from my understanding, and Brad runs the family business in his place. Something out west. I'm not sure what."

I polished off another cookie in two bites so I could speak. "How is it her brother has a different last name?"

"Oh, that." She made a dismissive gesture with her hand. "Amanda Kelly was her artist's name. Kind of like a pen name for authors. She didn't want anyone connecting her to her family's wealth, I guess."

Huh. That answered the question about the source of her income, at any rate. Weird to think the woman I knew as Amanda was someone else altogether. Brad's refusal to call her by name made more sense now, too. It must have grated on some level that she'd chosen to live under another identity.

"I guess it's hard to make a living as an artist."

"Normally, I'd agree." Laney leaned forward and tapped the table-top with a shining blue fingernail. "Amanda was truly gifted, however. Also? She knew how to market herself. Have you ever seen her work?"

I nodded but added a qualifier. "Only what she had at the house or in town."

Laney sighed again, as though contemplating the loss to the art community. "She was brilliant. She did her drawings and paintings on commission, but she had a whole series of children's books that rivaled Beatrice Potter for their sheer appeal. She also maintained an Etsy shop where she offered adult coloring books of her drawings, and sold plushies, calendars, and the like."

Amanda had sketched a picture of Remy with a butterfly on his nose that had captured his innate gentleness and goofiness, and I'd been meaning for some months to have it framed. It was bound to still be in the safe place I'd put it, if only I could remember where that was. "Wow. I had no idea. But then again, I didn't even know her real name."

"Samantha." Laney's face fell with her words. "Her name was Samantha Taylor."

The door opened, and a man I'd never seen before blew into the room like he owned it. If Brad was the epitome of the California Surfer Dude forced to work in an office, then this guy was Brooklyn Bad Boy personified. Dark hair shone with some sort of styling gel, and he appeared to be sporting at least two day's growth of ferocious stubble. He wore a battered bomber jacket that had probably set him back at least five hundred bucks, paired with distressed jeans and black motorcycle boots.

The glance he flicked in my direction dismissed me instantly as not being worth his time. He cast a similar look at Laney, and all but sneered before taking a seat at the head of the table between us. "Ladies. Are they going to get this show on the road or what?"

Hah. I'd been right on the accent. His words were flat, as though his tongue were at the back of his teeth. I half expected him to throw his thumbs to the side and say, "Aaaay" like the character in that old *Happy Days* sitcom my dad had liked to watch.

I suppose had the new arrival not bruised my ego with his dismissal of my charms, I might have seen his appeal. In many ways, he was a grittier, edgier version of Joe, and Lord knows, I have a type. But Joe had ten times the animal magnetism of this guy, more so because I suspected this guy often felt the need to beat his chest.

The door opened once more, this time as the assistant ushered in Brad Taylor. He scowled at us all on entering and made a beeline for the coffee.

"Hey," Brooklyn called out as the assistant was shutting the door. "How much longer is this going to take?"

The assistant fixed him with a steely eyed glare. "Mr. Carter will be with you shortly."

Brooklyn made a sound of disgust, took out his phone, and began scrolling. Brad, having poured himself a cup of coffee, seemed undecided where to sit, and finally took a seat between Brooklyn and Laney.

Pausing only to shoot me an unfriendly glare, Brad gave Laney a brief smile, as though they'd met before. Then he turned to Brooklyn and spoke in his stuffiest voice. "And you are?"

Brooklyn looked up from his phone with a wolfish smile. "I'm Derek Ellis. Samantha was my wife."

Chapter Seven

AND THAT, AS THEY say, put the cat among the pigeons.

"She was *what*?" Brad sputtered, even as Laney's eyes popped wide open and she gasped, "No way!"

"You heard me." Ignoring Laney, Derek responded to Brad instead. "I'm Samantha's legal husband. Which means all her stuff comes to me, not you."

Brad half rose out of his seat. "Impossible. My sister never would have married the likes of *you,* and she wouldn't have kept it a secret, either."

"Don't be so sure about that, pal. Who do you think gave her the idea to cut you guys out of her life? Go to New York and make a new life for herself? Me, that's who." Derek shot Brad a withering look that made him sink back into his chair.

"But that was at least five years ago." Brad had the poleaxed expression of a man who'd just received word of a terminal disease. "She would have said *something* before now."

Laney piped up. "She left New York a long time ago. Where have you been all this time? I've been Amanda's agent for the last four years, and she's never breathed a word about your existence."

"Yeah? Well, she never mentioned *you,* either." Derek lifted his lip in a perfect sneer.

Brad's brows pulled together in a sudden scowl. "I'm not buying it. Sure, Sam abandoned her family—left me to run the company while still benefiting from the dividends—but we'd mended our fences. And she never said a word about being married. Prove it."

"Prove what?" Derek leaned back in his seat and rested his elbow on the back of the chair. "That I'm her husband? Yeah, I thought you might want to see the certificate." He pulled a folded document out of an inner pocket of the bomber jacket.

Brad made to snatch it away, but Derek whipped it out of reach and held it open. "Look but don't touch."

He positively gloated as both Brad and Laney craned forward to examine the unfolded certificate.

Brad made a noise of disgust and slammed back into his own seat. "That means nothing. So, you got married. There's nothing to say you're *still* married. You could have gotten divorced."

"She didn't divorce me." The statement was delivered in a cold, flat tone that raised the hair on the back of my neck.

"Yeah, well, we'll see about that." Brad pushed his hand through his hair angrily in a gesture that screamed his uncertainty.

Derek's smug smile returned; there wouldn't be any record for a divorce filing.

"Suit yourself." Derek shrugged with a curve of his upper lip. "No matter what you think, I'm the legal heir." He shot a malevolent glance at Laney. "Which means you can both stop panting over her crappy drawings. They're mine, not yours."

"If her work is so crappy, why do you care what happens to it?" I broke off a piece of cookie and popped it into my mouth.

Derek's eyes went hard and still, like chips of flint. A wave of hostility emanated from him. If Brad had made me uncomfortable earlier in the evening, Derek triggered all my alarm bells.

"I'd lay off the cookies if I were you, sister." Derek's smile was toothy as he patted his stomach. He let that sink in a moment before adding, "Who the hell are you, anyway?"

"I'm the vet." Somehow my mouth kept running even after I should have shut up. "You know, the one skilled in castration and euthanasia."

Brad's coffee cup hit the table with a clatter, splashing coffee on his sleeve, which he mopped up with a napkin, cursing under his breath. Laney's eyes went wide with suppressed glee, and she sat with the lively expression of a cat watching two mouse holes at once.

"Zat so?" Derek half-closed his heavy eyelids. "I'm thinking you're the woman who needs to shut up."

Okay, so he didn't say "woman." He called me a term for female dogs seldom used outside of a kennel. And like any female dog that had been insulted, my hackles went up.

Stop provoking him.

Odds were, he was going to inherit Amanda's estate. I needed to cooperate with him for the sake of the animals. If I'd thought Brad was bad—the cats didn't stand a chance around Derek. Another horrible thought occurred to me: what if she'd left the horses to Derek? I couldn't afford to buy them a second time. So, as tempted as I was to tell Derek to stuff it, I finally came to my senses and bit off my next angry words.

Fortunately, Mr. Carter chose that moment to enter the room, followed by his assistant.

"Thank you for gathering here on such short notice." He glanced around the table, took a seat at the opposite end from Derek, and laid his folder in front of him. His assistant checked the supplies on the coffee cart, straightened the plate of cookies, and poured a glass of water to set beside Mr. Carter's right hand. She then came to stand behind her boss like a kind of watchful Doberman.

Derek had slid back into his too cool to care persona, lounging back in his chair as though king of the room. I half expected him to put his boots up on the table. Brad didn't look exactly rumpled, but his chairman of the board impression was marred by beads of sweat that had gathered around his temples. He took out a handkerchief and patted his brow. Laney cupped her coffee mug in both hands and stared down into its depths as though it held the secrets of the universe.

"Before we begin, I have a letter to read at the specific bequest from the deceased, Samantha Marion Taylor. Also known as Amanda Kelly." Mr. Carter put on a pair of reading glasses and undid the string on a manila envelope. A single sheet of paper slid out, and he picked it up to read.

"A chance conversation a few weeks ago with my veterinarian and friend, Dr. Ginny Reese, made me realize I had not left my affairs in good order should something happen to me."

The eyes of everyone in the room except for Mr. Carter shifted toward me, and I smiled weakly.

Mr. Carter adjusted his glasses and continued. "Subsequent events brought home the need to write my will to prevent my worldly belongings—but most especially my animals—from being assigned to people who do not deserve them, nor would take care of them according to my wishes. Likely at the time of my death, I will have a considerable net worth. I know that money brings out the worst in people, which is why I requested the law office of Carter, Beasley, and Worth to expedite the formal reading of my will as soon as possible after I'm declared dead, in order to prevent the vultures from descending."

Mr. Carter paused to clear his throat. Derek's eyes narrowed unpleasantly, and his hand clenched where it rested on the table. Brad mopped his brow again. Laney slew her gaze in my direction and raised her eyebrows. I pulled my lips down in a brief grimace in response.

Paper crackling in his hand, Mr. Carter finished reading Amanda's statement. "I know people and situations may change over time. Ten, fifteen, or fifty years from now, I may re-write this will to reflect my current status and connections. But for the record, know that at the time of writing this will, there is one thing I wish to make crystal clear: If at the time of my death, I am still legally married to Derek Antonio Ellis, he is not to benefit in any way, shape, or form from my estate. He knows why."

The term for a female dog exploded again from Derek's lips. "If she wasn't already dead—"

"Mr. Ellis. Some decorum, if you please."

Mr. Carter's prissy tone sounded so much like my fifth-grade teacher that I half expected him to whip out a ruler and smack Derek on the hand. I would have helped hold Ellis down if he had.

Mr. Carter opened another sheaf of papers. "Now, for the terms of the will itself."

His dry voice plowed through the opening paragraphs of the will, stating the sorts of legalese that made my eyes glaze over. I started paying attention again when he began listing Amanda's various holdings and accounts. Sheesh. Besides the mountain home in Greenbrier, she had a condo in Hilton Head that was under the management of a rental company, save for the times of the year she took up residence there herself. There was also a sizeable chunk of change in an annuity, as well as an IRA, a money market account, and other investments, including her holdings in her family's company. And then there was the body of her work, which had been valuable before but now would likely skyrocket in price because of her death.

"I won't itemize the works by name, but please understand, there is a detailed list of art by title and catalog number listed with the company that insures them, as well as licensing agreements for the prints, T-shirts, mugs, etcetera, sold through the KellyArt LLC." Mr. Carter flicked a glance around the table. "To ensure counterfeit works don't start flooding the market with Ms. Kelly's death, or should there be a question about provenance of a particular piece."

That felt like a statement aimed at a particular person in the room, but darned if I could tell where it was aimed. It could have easily applied to anyone. Maybe even me.

Amanda's net worth was a total I could only imagine. At nearly forty, having spent over a decade paying off student loans in a profession that notoriously underpaid its members and working for myself in a rural community, I couldn't even dream of retirement. I envisioned a future where the cats and I shared the same can of food.

It made sense why Brad was anxious that Derek did not inherit Amanda's fortune, even though the Taylor family probably had more than enough money to live comfortably. I didn't want to see Derek benefit from Amanda's estate, either. As Mr. Carter droned on, Brad stopped sweating and the tension melted out of his shoulders. Apparently, Amanda's letter had reassured him she'd never allow Derek to inherit.

Or was it something else that eased Brad's concerns? It seemed to me it was the recitation of Amanda's holdings that soothed her brother more than her letter declaring Derek a non-starter in the inheritance stakes.

Finally, it came down to the bequests. She'd left tidy sums to various people in her life, including twenty-five thousand to Laney, for being the first person to take a chance on her art. The bequest included a statement that she held Laney in absolute trust and that anyone managing her artwork after her death would be wise to continue to use Laney's expertise and services. Laney knuckled a tear from her eye a moment later.

Amanda bequeathed a couple of specific pieces of art to various organizations. The nicest bequest was a painting of the Blue Ridge mountains in full autumn color to be donated to the local library. I knew the piece—they already hung it in a place of honor as a loan in the library—and I also knew it was a personal favorite of Miss Ellie.

"As for the re-homing of my animals," Mr. Carter began, and I leaned forward to listen. "Should my Siamese cat, Ming, still be alive at the time of my death, I ask that he be given to Dr. Virginia Reese. I can't think of anyone else better suited to care for him for the rest of his life."

"That mangy cat is still alive?" Derek's interruption was as unexpected and unwelcome as a heckler in a comedy club. "I would've sworn—"

He closed his mouth abruptly, and his lips pressed together in an ugly, tight line.

Mr. Carter chose to ignore him and continued reading. "It is my wish that Ming receive radioactive iodine treatment for his thyroid condition, providing he proves to be a candidate for the procedure. As such, I will award three thousand dollars to Dr. Reese for the cost of this treatment."

I certainly hoped my relief wasn't visible, but I suspect it was. At least now, if Ming passed all the criteria for therapy, I wouldn't have to withhold it based on cost. Laney gave me a subtle thumbs up from her side of the table.

"As for the horses, Rebel, King, and Sherlock—the document here provides descriptions of the three animals—should they still be alive at the time of my death, I also place them in the care of Dr. Virginia Reese. I know she will take care of them as she would her own."

I shot my most evil glare at Brad. He'd had no right to sell the horses to Ringbolt. Moreover, I shouldn't have had to buy them from him to prevent them from going to slaughter. Mr. Taylor and I were going to have a little conversation about that when this meeting was through.

Mr. Carter paused and took a sip of water from the glass provided by his assistant. "Now, while the next part of this will contains statements at the behest of Ms. Taylor, I assure you, everything regarding the terms of this will are legal and binding, even if some of the wording included here is less than orthodox."

I exchanged another glance with Laney. She lifted her eyebrows again and gave an infinitesimal shrug.

"As for the bulk of my estate, I imagine my brother, Bradford Wayne Taylor, is assuming he will inherit it all. He assumes incorrectly. Brad has the resources of Taylor Industries behind him. He has more than enough for his needs. He did me a favor when he bought out my controlling share of the company and advised me to 'go play with my paints', as I would have made a lousy CEO. However, I made a rather excellent artist, and I do not intend for him to benefit from my hard work. Thank you, Brad. I wish you well."

Whew. I had no idea Amanda could be so vindictive. She'd always struck me as a quiet, contemplative sort of person. I guess there was something about the idea of being dead that had allowed her to speak her mind.

I glanced at Brad to see the blood drain out of his face, leaving it a ghastly white, only to have the color rush back in red blotches across his cheekbones. "This is preposterous! I'm her brother! Her only relative who is mentally competent. If she's not leaving her money to me, and she's made it clear that *he* isn't getting a penny of it—" he wagged a finger in Derek's direction, "—then who inherits?"

"Ah, yes. That." Mr. Carter adjusted his glasses once more and continued reading. "I hereby bequeath all my worldly possessions as laid out in the previous articles to Dr. Virginia Reese. I know of no one else who is as hardworking as she is, with so little reward for her compassion and dedication. She deserves to have a comfortable place to live, the facilities to keep the horses, and the means with which to open her own clinic, should she choose."

"What?" I squeaked, unable to believe my ears. It was the last thing I expected.

Brad exploded out of his chair and slammed a fist down on the table. "Undue influence! I'll contest this will on the grounds of undue influence." He wheeled to glare at me. "I have an entire bank of lawyers at my disposal. Unless you are prepared to sink everything you own into defending this ludicrous bequest, I will have you and this penny-ante lawyer for breakfast." His sweeping gesture included Mr. Carter as well.

"Undue influence?" I pulled my head back in consternation. "Wherever did you get such a crazy idea? Based on what?"

"You—you—you *seduced* her." Brad pointed at me now, flecks of spittle flying from his lips as his rage frothed within. "You and this dyke here."

"Excuse me?" Laney sat up in haughty outrage, her eyes flashing fire.

"Hey, that's a good one." Derek snapped his fingers and pointed at Brad. "I'll contest the will on the same grounds."

"What grounds?" I sputtered. "If you're implying that I somehow conspired with Ms. Driver—who I met tonight for the first time—to persuade Amanda to make me her sole heir, you're nuts."

"And why would I be a party to something like that? What could possibly be in it for me?" Laney put her palms flat on the table and leaned forward to burn holes in Brad with her eyes.

"Twenty-five thousand dollars for one. And a probably a commission on every painting you sold for *her*." The sneer he aimed in my direction left no doubt who he was referring to.

"This is ridiculous." Laney stood up and collected her purse. "I don't have to sit around and be insulted like this."

"Ladies, gentlemen." From the look Mr. Carter cast at the men, I assumed he used the term "gentlemen" loosely. "I assure you, this will is legal and binding. Ms. Taylor was of sound mind when she outlined her requests, and neither Mr. Taylor nor Mr. Ellis have grounds to dispute it."

Brad flushed so deeply, I wondered if he had hypertension, but it was Derek who spoke first. "What happens if we can prove the will was made with whatchacall'em, under duress or something? Won't that invalidate the will? That would mean Sam died intestate, so everything would come to me, right?" He fixed the kind of sly smile on me that one associated with small boys possessed by the devil in a horror film. "Even the cat."

If blood could freeze in one's veins, mine momentarily did. When my heart started beating again, it was in triple time.

"First, there is a no-contest clause in the will, which automatically disinherits challengers." Mr. Carter wrapped his authority around him like a mantle and took charge of the room. "Second, you have no grounds to contest the will, and any lawyer worth his salt will tell you that up front. But they will be happy to take your money, I'm sure. So, by all means, challenge the will. You have three months in which to file your motion or produce a will that was written after this one."

Derek wasn't done, however. He indicated me with a lift of his chin. "What happens if she dies? That voids the will, right?"

Oh, lovely.

Mr. Carter's patience seemed to be wearing thin. "No, Mr. Ellis, it does not. Should Dr. Reese die at this very moment, you would have to take up the matter with her heirs."

"Given that I'm not in the will in the first place, I have no problems challenging the no-contest clause or the whole damn document." Brad tugged viciously at his tie to loosen it and stood. "I'll see you both in court."

He was headed for the door when I stopped him. "What about the three thousand dollars you owe me? You made me pay for horses that were already mine, that weren't yours to sell."

Brad pulled up as though I had shot him. He took several deep breaths, his spine rigid with anger, before he turned to respond. His eyes narrowed in a glittering fury until his expression smoothed into one of preternatural calm. "I'll return the money for those nags if you renounce the estate."

"Never mind. If you contest the will, I'll bring it up in my countersuit." I pretended to examine my nails. "I imagine the courts might find it interesting that the CEO of Taylor Industries is so hard up for cash he'd sell his sister's horses to a slaughterhouse on the same day as her death." Looking up, I met his gaze. "Maybe the Securities and Exchange Commission would be interested to hear that, too, while we're at it."

It was literally a shot in the dark. A pushback for his appalling behavior. But damn if something in his expression didn't smack of an arrow winging its way straight into the bull's-eye.

Chapter Eight

THE GATHERING BROKE UP shortly after that.

Brad left without another word, in a fugue of fury so hot you could almost see steam rolling off him. Derek seemed to have accepted there was nothing he could do at the moment about the terms of the will, but the glower he gave me on leaving clearly said he didn't consider the matter closed, not by a long shot.

I remained behind to speak with Mr. Carter. He assured me the executors of Amanda's will would begin the probate process as soon as they received a death certificate, but that even with no one contesting the will, it could take six months or more to probate an estate the size of Amanda's. If they challenged the will, I could be looking at a lengthy process—even years in the making. We discussed what defending the will might look like in court, and the possibility of a long battle draining the estate of all its worth.

He also advised me to make a will if I hadn't already done so. Thanks to my mother wishing to plan my funeral a few years ago, I already had a will in place, but it would need updating now.

Before I left, Mr. Carter handed me a sealed envelope. "Ms. Taylor left this with me to give to you. Perhaps it will answer some of your questions."

I took the envelope with some misgivings and stuffed it into my oversized bag. What on earth had Amanda been thinking? Hopefully, the letter would explain.

For all practical purposes, nothing had really changed. The horses might as well stay with Joe for the time being. Ming was already in my care. If they did not give me access to the property after the coroner released his report, I'd move the ferals to Joe's place as well, and hope they'd hang around for him to feed them.

Which reminded me, I needed to get back to Greenbrier to feed them tonight.

To my surprise, Laney was waiting for me on the porch when the assistant escorted me to the door.

"You want to grab a drink?" She thumbed over her shoulder in the general direction of Main Street. The exterior light of the law office cast a pool around her like a stage spotlight.

"Maybe tomorrow?" I hesitated, then explained about the cats.

Laney shook her head. "I'm planning to head home tomorrow. Sorry, not a fan of small towns."

"No apology necessary." My stomach growled, and Laney pressed her fingers to her mouth to hide a grin. "On the other hand, I was planning to grab some food before I headed back. Tell you what. I'll call the sheriff's office and see when they could send someone out to Amanda's. If the timing works, I'll get something to eat with you."

The dispatcher seemed a bit disapproving when I told her I'd been held up and wouldn't be able to go to Amanda's place for a couple of hours. After grumbling about the inconvenience, the dispatcher told me to call when I had returned to Greenbrier and they would send someone to meet me, provided there wasn't a conflicting call for the deputy on duty.

"We're set," I told Laney as I pocketed the phone. "There's a bar and grill on 5^(th) Street, if that works for you."

We arranged to meet there, and I let Remy out to pee before stuffing him back in the car again. Poor dog. He really deserved more of a life than he had with me.

There was a church lot that was open to public parking in the evenings a few blocks from the bar, so we parked there and walked the short distance.

"Where is home for you?" I asked Laney as I opened the door into the bar. The noise of happy customers, along with the odor of BBQ and fried onion rings, blasted us as we stepped inside. At the far end of the room, a few patrons were playing pool. The area near the bar was crowded, but I led the way to a side room where half a dozen tables were set up. We grabbed a table and took our seats.

A server quickly handed out a pair of menus and asked what we'd have to drink. As much as I wanted a beer, as little as I'd had to eat all day, I knew that would be a mistake, so I settled for water. Laney chose an IPA and waited until the server promised she'd be right back with our drinks before answering my question.

"You asked where I'm from? I'm based in Atlanta." She smiled as I helped myself to the dish of peanuts in the center of the table.

"Sorry. I'm starving."

"So, I noticed. I guess your job keeps you on the run until all hours?" She opened a menu and frowned as she glanced down at the options.

"Given the nature of a house-call practice, which means I'm not equipped to deal with anything that needs hospitalization or surgery, I'm pretty busy most days, but the evenings are usually my own." I didn't need to look at the menu. I knew what I wanted to order. "To field phone calls, triage emergencies, catch up on paperwork, inventory, and the minutia of running my own business, that is. If I'm not too tired by the end of the day, I might watch a little television or read a book. If you want a glamorous life, look no farther than veterinary medicine."

The startled look on her face was akin to someone expecting a Dalmatian puppy and getting Cruella de Vil instead. "But being a vet is extremely rewarding, right? And fun. All those puppies and kittens."

If only it were all puppies and kittens. I looked into her eyes and saw yet another person who'd dreamed of becoming a vet when she was a child. I decided not to disillusion her more than I already had.

"Oh, yes. Very rewarding. But it can be—" I struggled for the right words, "—emotionally challenging, too. When you have to deliver bad news, that sort of thing."

Her frown lightened, and she nodded. "Of course, yes. I can see that."

I let it go. For her, my job would still be primarily taking care of puppies and kittens. She'd never know the cost of not knowing what is wrong with someone's beloved pet and being unable to fix it. Or worse, knowing how to fix it, but also knowing they wouldn't be able to afford the treatment. At least with a house-call practice, I didn't have the added pressure of making life and death decisions every ten minutes because some corporation deemed the speed at which I saw clients was more important than the care I delivered.

I still had nightmares about my first couple of years in practice.

On the other hand, I loved being able to walk my clients through the pros and cons of decision-making with their pets. One of the best things about being my own boss was the freedom to take all the time I needed to explain a medical condition or the best course of action to a client.

Puppy and kitten visits were pretty awesome, too.

To my relief, Laney dropped the subject when the server returned with our drinks and took our order. I got the BBQ pork with sweet sauce, hush puppies, and coleslaw. After much wrinkling of her nose and flipping the single page of the menu back and forth, Laney ordered a tuna salad.

When the server left, I snagged another handful of peanuts. "I hope you know that salad you ordered is going to consist largely of iceberg lettuce."

Laney shrugged and took a pull from her bottle of beer. "I suspected as much. At least the breakfast at the B&B where I'm staying has been decent."

I squeezed the slice of lemon provided into my water. "You're at Mossy Creek? Isn't Brad Taylor staying there too?"

She made a face. "Unfortunately, yes. Though I didn't realize who he was until today."

"Word around town says Brad is generally unpleasant to be around, even when he isn't actively fighting to inherit his sister's estate."

"I don't know him well enough to say, but it wouldn't surprise me. Though he was nice enough when he met me." Laney shot me a wry smile over the lip of her bottle. "Of course, he still thought he was the primary heir at the time."

Made sense to me. If he'd found out Laney was Amanda's agent... "Did he approach you about Amanda's work? Her legacy?"

"Legacy is a good way of putting it. She was *that* talented." Laney's brown eyes went cold for a moment. "Neither one of us knew who the other was at first. Not until news of Amanda's death came out. When I realized he was Amanda's brother, I introduced myself to offer condolences. It took him less than a minute to switch from bereaved brother to wanting an estimate of Amanda's worth."

It was funny how we both kept calling her Amanda, but then again, that's the name we knew her by.

"Sounds like a real charmer, all right." Curiosity made me ask. "Do you know how long he's been at the B&B?"

Laney set her beer down and leaned back in her chair. "Not really. I got in late on the 12th. He was at breakfast the following morning when I came down, but I don't know when he checked in. It could have been earlier that day or that week. Why?"

I'd discovered Amanda's body the morning of the 13th.

"Just that something's been bugging me. Before the reading tonight, I saw Brad at a restaurant in Greenbrier. He was showing a sophisticated-looking woman a portfolio. It occurs to me he might have jumped the gun on Amanda's drawings and was trying to sell them. Granted, at the time, he probably thought he'd inherit, but—"

"Wait. What did this woman look like? A blonde Morticia dressed in Prada?"

"That's scarily accurate. Remind me never to ask you to describe me to anyone. Do you know her?"

"It sounds like Liv Markham. She runs an art gallery in Manhattan and has a reputation for being a bit of a ghoul. Always the first to show up at a funeral." Laney called Brad a highly uncomplimentary name, the sort of thing my mother would have punished with a lecture and a bar of soap. Somehow, I liked her even more for it. "I wouldn't put it past her to read the obituaries and contact heirs the moment the news dropped."

Given that any sale of Amanda's art that didn't go through her agent would effectively take a commission out of Laney's pocket, I could understand the harsh language.

"But Brad's plans to sell anything would be nipped in the bud, right? It sounds like Amanda kept tight control over her inventory."

We paused our conversation when the server showed up with our order, shouldering a huge tray that contained half a dozen meals. With a deft hand, she swung the tray down to an empty table, and began doling out the dinners to the surrounding patrons. Laney and I got our food last. As predicted, Laney's tuna salad rested on a bed of limp lettuce. My BBQ sat nestled in a plastic basket lined with red-and-white checked paper. Crispy hush puppies lay tucked alongside the sandwich. The harried-looking server left a selection of brown and red sauces in plastic dispensing bottles and hurried off to fill the next order.

I removed the top bun from my sandwich and drowned the pork with red sauce before replacing the bread. Not caring how messy it was, I took an enormous bite, barely refraining from letting out a moan of pleasure.

"Yes and no," Laney said, answering my question from before as she poked at her salad without enthusiasm. "As a rule, Amanda was very good about cataloging her work. She was far more organized than the average artist I work with. But she didn't update her files daily. More like once a month. So, anything she was working on recently might not be on the official list."

I nodded, chewed, and swallowed. "That makes it more likely what I saw was Brad showing drawings from Amanda's sketch pad. How much would one of her sketches go for, anyway?"

"Hard to say." Laney continued to move her tuna salad around without eating any. "All of her art would be worth a pretty penny now because of her death. Some subjects would fetch a higher price than others."

I stuffed a hush puppy in my mouth and nearly wept at the sublime combination of flavors. The deep-fried cornmeal was utterly perfect. Of course, in my ravenous state, I would probably have said the same of shoe leather. "What about a drawing of a dog? Off the top of your head, what would that bring?"

Laney took a small bite of her salad and laid her fork beside her plate. "Her animal drawings definitely are worth more than, say, her flowers or trees, though perhaps not as much as her landscapes. A cute dog done in charcoal? Probably around five."

"Huh. I guess she'd have to do a lot of drawings to make any money at five dollars a pop." It was good to know that framing the image of Remy would cost more than the drawing was worth. Somehow that made me feel better since it was lying around my house somewhere. I tried to recall if I'd ever seen Amanda at the local craft fair, where artisans would gather for a weekend of food, live music, and to show off their wares.

Laney lifted her eyebrows at me with a gentle smile. "Not five dollars. Five hundred. Five hundred dollars."

A crumb of hush puppy went down the wrong pipe and I coughed and wheezed, only to stop when I took a big slug of water. "I own a drawing worth five hundred dollars?"

The couple at the next table turned to look at me in curiosity, their eyes wide and eyebrows raised.

"That's just the charcoal sketches. A limited run print might go for two or three thousand a piece. Her oils and landscapes are worth far more. Twice a year she went to Hilton Head or the Keys. Her seascapes are extremely popular, though she thought them crass, commercial images. Don't get me started on her Ireland series. People snapped them up like candy. She was planning to go to Wales this summer, and she would have made a killing on those paintings. Then there's the merchandizing, too." Laney tipped the neck of her beer bottle in my direction before taking a sip. "My dear, you own it *all*."

"Well, but most of it's sold already, right?"

Laney nodded. "The commissioned work and the limited-edition prints, yes. But you own the rights to anything unsold, the prints, and anything currently hanging in a gallery or museum. Don't discount the plushies, coloring books, and mugs, either. A twenty dollars purchase may not sound like much, but sales at her site are consistently in the thousands each month. You could live on that alone if none of the other assets were yours."

Appetite effectively quashed, I pushed the basket away from me. "About that. Amanda and I were friendly, but never in my wildest dreams could I imagine being her beneficiary." I thought about the sealed envelope in my bag that I had yet to read. Would it provide any answers? "You've known Amanda longer than I have. Why on earth would she leave everything to someone like me? If she didn't have any close friends, why not the library, or a charity?"

"I'm glad you said something. I wondered myself. You had no idea? You looked shocked at the reading."

"I *am* shocked." That was an understatement. "Don't get me wrong. I liked her. We had some interesting conversations about art and books when I went to her place. We both liked animals, and she was glad to have someone who knew something about horses look after the ones she'd rescued. I usually wound up staying longer than I should while we chatted, and she showed me what she'd been working on. But we were hardly BFFs. Why make me her heir? And why now?"

Laney hunched her shoulders and turned her palms face up in the universal gesture of 'haven't a clue.' Her expression grew thoughtful, and she glanced around as though concerned someone might overhear her.

"I think something spooked her. She called me out of the blue and asked me to come see her, and Amanda wasn't the type to use the phone when she could email. She wouldn't say why, either, only that she needed to see me as soon as possible." Laney eyed my basket with longing. "Are you going to finish that?"

I wiped hands on my paper napkin and pushed the basket toward her. "Have at it. What kinds of things would she have needed to discuss with you? Urgently, I mean?"

Laney snagged a hush puppy and bit into it, closing her eyes and humming with delight. "Why is it carbs taste so darn good?"

"Because life is stressful, and God knew we'd need something amazing to make up for it."

Laney laughed; a warm, rich sound that made me wonder if she sang. She had the voice for it. "While also making it a sin if we overindulge? Sounds about right." She finished the second bite and wiped her fingers as well. "As for needing to see me, most of our communications could be handled by email. Contracts, museum loans, gallery tours and sales, that sort of thing. I came up to see her once or twice a year, and only then because she was by far my best client. But counterfeit artwork or copyright issues—anything of a legal nature, for that matter—might warrant a face-to-face meeting."

Ice shifted in my glass as I took another sip of water. "So, she might have wanted to see you about the will, then?"

Frowning, Laney shook her head. "I don't think so. The will had already been drawn up by that point. If she'd wanted to consult with me about her estate, she would have contacted me weeks ago. No, I think there was something else going on, and having met Derek, I think I have an idea now."

"Oh? I thought you didn't know about him."

Laney tapped a long, blue fingernail on the table. "Not about him, per se, but I had a feeling someone like him existed. Amanda took being the reclusive artist to a whole other level. No headshots circulating of her online. No public appearances. Even her bio contained false details about where she actually lived. I think she was hiding from Derek."

"Yeah, I got that vibe, too. If she built a new life with a new identity for herself, I could see where she might have been afraid to file for divorce. But would she have called you about something like that?"

"Maybe." Laney grabbed another hush puppy. "If he found her, yeah. She might have been thinking about disappearing again."

That was a staggering thought. I slumped back in my chair. "How awful. She told me when she first moved here that her cat had been injured in an accident and had to have his jaw wired. Do you think—"

"I wouldn't put it past him. I know the type. You'd better watch your step."

In my experience, men who hated cats—not those with a preference for dogs but actually *hated* cats—also hated women. Time and time again, I'd seen the pattern. The things they claimed to dislike about cats, their independence and their "slyness," proved to be code for the things they wanted to quash in women. It was all about control with these men, and as you know, no one controls a cat. Not to mention, anyone who'd deliberately hurt a pet wouldn't hesitate to hurt a person, either.

"I hear what you're saying. But Derek has no reason to hang around. Amanda's dead, and she made it clear he's not getting anything from her estate." A sense of unease spread over me just the same. Time to wrap up dinner and get on the road. The cats needed feeding, and I no longer felt comfortable leaving Remy in my parked car.

"Does he need a reason?" Scorn cut through Laney's melodious voice. "He's a man thwarted. First Amanda got away from him, and now she's made sure he won't inherit any of her wealth. He could transfer all that hostility toward you."

"Cheerful thought, thanks."

"I didn't mean to scare you, but I think you should be careful." She scrubbed a hand across her short curls. "I hate this. I hate all of this."

"I know what you mean." Trying to lighten the mood, I added, "If it's any consolation, I think Brad's a bigger threat than Derek right now."

Her pupils widened. "Right? He looked so pissed at the reading. If looks could kill, we'd be holding your funeral next. You know, if you're right about him trying to sell Amanda's drawings, that could be why she asked me to come up. Maybe he's tried this before."

"Or maybe he was hitting her up for money. There has to be a reason he came to town. Derek, too, for that matter. How did he know where to come?"

"Derek, you mean?" Laney winced. "That may be my fault, unless he already knew where to find her. When I heard about Amanda's death, I notified some buyers and galleries. I also sent out press releases to several of the major news outlets. I included a pic I'd taken of her last summer on her back porch. It was a terrific photo, and I didn't see the harm now that she was dead. I wish I hadn't. I should have known she'd had her reasons for maintaining a low-profile."

I wished she hadn't too, but saw no point in making Laney feel worse about it. "You meant well. And nothing can hurt Amanda now."

Laney finished my hush puppies. The server came with our tickets, and when we declined letting her box our leftovers, told us to pay at the bar. I insisted on picking up Laney's tab. We engaged in some mild argument over that, as one does in those circumstances, but Laney's position was weak by virtue of the fact I was the local who'd picked the bar.

We walked back to the parking lot together. When we reached our cars, I asked for her email so we could keep in touch. As she dug a card out of her purse, she said, "I'm going to do a little digging around to see if there's any hint of Amanda Kelly art being up for sale."

"You don't have to do that." I pocketed the card and glanced at my car. Thankfully, Remy sat up in the backseat, proving my fears about leaving him unattended to be mere paranoia.

"Actually, I do. I have to make an accounting of her holdings—at least as far as the LLC is concerned—for the executor of the will. If someone is trying to sell her work without permission, they'd naturally want to hide it from me, if nothing else, to avoid paying my commission."

Made sense to me.

"Besides, if someone is stealing from Amanda's estate—and we all know by 'someone', I mean Brad—then he's stealing from you now." Laney unlocked her car door and shot me a grin. "I'll put you in touch with the people running Amanda's Etsy shop. I imagine for now, they'll just keep operating as before, as long as they get paid. How does it feel to be a millionaire?"

"My dinner wants to come back on me if I think about it too hard." I pressed a hand to my stomach and grimaced. Laney laughed and waved as she drove off.

There in the dark parking lot, a disturbing thought crossed my mind. Would Laney have been so friendly had I not been Amanda's heir?

Chapter Nine

DEPUTY LINKOUS MET ME at Amanda's place just after 9 p.m. Green as grass, and obviously having taken lessons from Frank on how to be a pompous ass, the former sheriff's nephew, Rusty, was inclined to give me a hard time about being called away from more important duties to watch me feed a bunch of mangy cats until I asked him how his mother's dog was doing. He unbent enough to admit Little Bit was feeling much better since I'd recommended the elimination of all table food and put him on a low-calorie kibble. Between the weight loss being kinder on his joints and the control of his chronic pancreatitis, Little Bit was much more his feisty self these days. Which meant he'd probably bite me during his next exam, but a return of surly behavior was a good sign in my book as far as Little Bit was concerned.

It took some doing to persuade Rusty to wait by the barn for me to feed the cats, but I explained things would go faster if he did. No doubt, duty warred with a desire to go home and catch a late dinner, so after making a show of checking out my car and the containers of food, he allowed me to go to the feeding stations without him.

As I expected, Harley was the only cat who showed up at this late hour, despite my calling "kitty, kitty, kitty" in a loud voice. I suspected he recognized the sound of my car engine, for he never failed to appear when I came to put out food.

Given the results of the reading of the will, I decided not to set the traps that evening. If I was the presumptive heir, most likely I'd be given access to the property once the investigation had finished. If not, I could always trap the cats later.

"That didn't take long," Rusty said when I returned to the barn. He watched as I tossed the empty cans in the trash and replaced the container of kibble on the shelf in the feed room.

"As promised." I glanced at my watch. With a little luck, I'd be home by ten. Amanda's letter was burning a hole in my purse, but I didn't want to read it until I was home and settled for the night. I wasn't sure what kind of can of worms it might open. "Shall I call the station in the morning to arrange for someone to meet me here? How much longer are we going to have to keep this up, anyway?"

In the powerful light of the feed room, Rusty looked distinctly uncomfortable, no doubt weighing how much he could tell me without getting into trouble. Shuffling his feet slightly, he said, "Word has it the coroner will release his report soon. So maybe not much longer."

"Good." Coordinating my ever-changing schedule with the sheriff's department was a pain in my butt I didn't need. "I probably won't be out here tomorrow until late morning. I don't have anything scheduled before eleven a.m."

"Must be nice." He escorted me back to our cars. "Being your own boss. Deciding when you want to work."

"Sure is." I agreed. "I love constantly worrying where the money is going to come to pay the drug supply company, whose prices go up constantly, while I'm trying to keep my fees the same. And having to pay my own health, liability, and disability insurance. No paid time off, no sick days, no vacation..."

Rusty's eyes widened and his brow furrowed. "Here, I thought you vets were making money hand over fist."

Tempting as it was to enlighten Rusty on how, despite having a medical degree, I was making less money than I had as a new graduate, it wasn't worth the battle. In a profession that was notoriously underpaid for the level of education it required, new graduates could spend a decade or more paying off their student loans. I certainly had. Yes, it is possible to make a good living as a veterinarian. But the big salaries rarely exist outside of the metropolitan areas with the high cost of living to boot. Unfortunately, drugs, equipment, and supplies to practice quality medicine tends to cost the same, regardless of species. Which is why the only place I could cut costs was by shaving off professional fees where I could. I couldn't discount supplies, but I could discount my skills. Yeah, I know. It's a lousy business model. I probably shouldn't be my own boss but when you live in a farming community, you charge what the market will bear. There were few enough stand-alone small animal clinics these days. Most were operated by corporations now, and the veterinarian had no say in how much to charge.

"Look, I bet people think your job is glamorous and exciting, right? Catching the bad guys, putting them away in jail?"

Rusty snorted. "Breaking up bar fights and handing out traffic tickets is more like it."

"Well, it's the same with being a vet. It's not that I don't love it, but it's never as cool as other people think it is."

He nodded at that and waited until I got in my car before he got into his. He followed me out of the driveway, but turned left onto the main road when I turned right.

If I really got that inheritance, I wouldn't have to work at all.

It was a seductive thought. I could sit on Amanda's back porch, drinking herbal tea as I watched the sunrise. Remy could run to his heart's content all day on the property. I could sleep as long as I wanted, and ride Scotty whenever I felt like it. I even had a condo in Hilton Head, within walking distance of the beach. Heck, I could travel. See parts of the world I'd only read about.

But who would take care of the animals?

Part of the reason the house-call practice worked in Greenbrier was because there were so few options for pet owners in the area. The existing practice in town was run by Amos Smith, who had to be pushing eighty. On nice days, Doc Amos was out fishing more often than not. I think he was happy to have me take the load off him, as I suspected the only reason he hadn't retired was because he didn't want to abandon his patients, either. Only with his reduced hours and his decision to no longer perform routine surgeries, our clients either had to drive to the single practice in Clearwater, or they could head almost an hour north to reach Birchwood Springs, a town large enough to host multiple vet hospitals and an emergency clinic. If they were looking for more specialized services, they had to cross over into North Carolina. I tried to envision elderly Mrs. Beasley getting on the interstate with her cat, Muffin, yowling in distress for the entire drive.

Okay, but with the inheritance from Amanda's estate, I could start my own veterinary clinic.

That had been the dream for a long time, hadn't it? I could buy Doc Amos out. He could retire with dignity, though practicing medicine in his ramshackle building that had gone through at least one incarnation as a Pizza Hut and another as Blockbuster Video, with a struggling second-hand clothing store in there somewhere, wasn't what I had in mind.

No. I would build from the ground up. I could hire someone to do the surgeries, as it had been so long since I'd picked up a scalpel, it was not something I wanted to do myself. With an associate on board, I could have regular days off. I could even take a vacation if I wanted. The thought made me giddy.

But quickly behind that fantasy came the realization of all the work that would be involved in pulling that dream off. Battles with the Zoning Commission. Regulations and licenses. Consultations with contractors. It was almost too much to contemplate, particularly coming at the end of several emotional days. If this was something I was going to even consider, I would probably need to take at least a month off before I could tackle it. Which put me back to: who would take care of the animals?

A month wasn't the end of the world. My clients could get by without me for a month, couldn't they? I hadn't had a vacation in years. The idea of having an entire month off almost made me weep. I had so many choices now; it was an embarrassment of riches. My fingers practically itched to get started.

Who was I kidding? Brad was going to fight me tooth and nail for Amanda's estate. Even though, according to Mr. Carter, I had an unimpeachable position, Brad could still bleed the estate dry before giving up. No point in planning my veterinary clinic before my monetary chickens had hatched.

The full moon rose like a great golden disc among the trees as I came around a bend in the road. I slowed the car for a better look. Part of me wanted to pull over to the side and snap a picture with my cell phone, which was stupid. Those phone images never lived up to the glory that was the actual thing being photographed. And when did we become so obsessed with documenting the moments in our lives instead of actually experiencing them? I leaned forward to peer out the windshield at the glorious sight.

Headlights in my rearview mirror reminded me to move along and not block traffic.

I'd already sped up, but scarcely between one breath and the next, the headlights lit up my rear window. As they approached, they suddenly switched to high beam.

Oh. One of *those* jerks.

The winding road was too narrow for me to pull over and allow the car behind me to pass. The blinding light filled my car, causing me to squint as my concentration bounced from the car behind to the road ahead. I toggled the angle of my rearview mirror so that it pointed down, minimizing as much of the glare as possible. Whoever it was behind me was just going to have to wait. I wasn't driving that slowly, for heaven's sakes. Tempting as it was to consider slowing down to a crawl, the driver behind me was already being enough of a jerk that I didn't want to piss him off further, so I resumed my normal speed.

The roar of a sudden acceleration made me look up in alarm. The headlights loomed even closer than before. My hands tightened on the wheel as I pressed on the gas. I'd been driving these back roads since I was a teenager. I knew every curve like the back of my hand. Shifting gears like a Formula One driver, I saw the needle on the speedometer climb to forty-five, then to fifty. That may not sound fast if you're used to interstate driving, but when you're looping turns on a mountain road at night at that speed, it's like riding a roller coaster.

The headlights behind me fell back, and I eased up on the gas when I took a corner tight enough that the car swayed as though it might roll over. Remy sat up and thrust his nose between the seats.

"Not now, Remy. Lie down." I snapped out my order with no thought of reassuring him. When I cornered another turn too sharply, his shoulder slammed into my driver's seat, and he withdrew.

The road opened up into an open straightaway, and I slowed down. There still wasn't any good place to pull over, but if this idiot wanted to pass me, now was his chance. The view ahead was unobstructed, and there were no headlights coming from the opposite direction. As expected, when I decelerated, the car behind me sped up. Its headlights filled the interior of my car again as the car behind me loomed ever closer.

The hair on the back of my neck rose when I realized the driver had no intention of passing.

You can always tell. The aggressive, impatient drivers in their pick-up trucks will roar into the opposite lane well before they reach your car to pass you on one of these back roads. Too late, I realized the car racing toward me had something different in mind.

The engine screamed as I stomped on the gas and delayed shifting gears as long as possible to allow my car to shoot forward. But the Subaru isn't built for racing, and mine was loaded down with equipment. The car behind me had the prior advantage of traveling at speed, and I braced for impact as it bore down on me.

The thump of contact with my rear bumper was hard enough to snap my head back, but I retained control of the wheel. We were rapidly running out of straight road, and while I couldn't maintain this kind of speed on the curves, I thought I might be the better driver there. My phone was still in my back pocket instead of sitting in the hands-free bracket where it was supposed to be, so I couldn't even call for help. I was on this ride to the end, whatever that end might be.

I drove even faster.

A pair of green-gold glows by the side of the road caught my eye, but instead of braking as I'd normally have done, I laid on the horn and mashed the gas pedal to the floor. As soon as I'd passed them, I slowed and flipped up the rearview mirror.

Silhouetted in the glare of the headlights behind me were the forms of several deer leaping across the road. My pursuer slowed at the sight of deer crossing ahead of him, but sped up as soon as the deer were on the other side of the road.

But I knew something the other driver didn't or had forgotten in his eagerness to run me off the road.

There's always one more deer than you think there is.

The final deer, lagging behind the herd, stepped out in the middle of the road. Blinded by the oncoming headlights, it froze, staring in the direction of the car bearing down on it.

Tires squealed behind me as the driver slammed on the brakes and twisted the wheel, throwing the car into a spin. As the headlights flashed away from the road out into the open field, the deer sprang away in a bounding leap. The car slid into the ditch, but it wasn't steep. I knew if the driver was good enough, he could probably get out of it on his own.

Which is why, heart pounding in my chest like a bird trapped in a room full of glass windows, I didn't wait to see if the driver was okay. I gunned the engine and drove away into the night.

Chapter Ten

My hands were still shaking when I got home. Remy sprang from the car when released and raced up the stairs to the front door, leaping and corkscrewing in place while he waited for me. I climbed the stairs like an old woman, clinging to the handrail for support. Not enough of the right kind of food and too much emotional drama these past few days. My blood sugar had to be in the gutter.

When I unlocked the door, Remy bolted within, headed for the kitchen. The sound of lapping water reached my ears before I'd even closed the door, and then the clatter of Remy chasing his metal bowl around the linoleum. Dinner was later than usual, and he wasn't shy about letting me know he was starving to death.

Ming's yowls from the back room demanded I feed him as well. No sooner did I glop his canned food into his dish than he attacked it like a wolf going after his kill. I tiptoed out of the room while he growled and ate.

After he inhaled his kibble, Remy parked himself outside Ming's door like a sheepdog guarding the flock. He made snuffling noises with his nose pressed to the crack until a chocolate paw snaked out to bat him. Chastened, he flopped down with a heavy sigh a foot away from the door. I couldn't decide if he thought Ming was part of the flock or a predator lurking at the boundaries. My guess was the predator.

I spent the next hour tearing up the house, looking for Amanda's drawing of Remy. I finally found it sandwiched in between two pieces of cardboard for safety, and still protected as such, placed it in the car so I'd remember to take it to the framers in the morning.

By this point, my stomach was growling again, reminding me I hadn't finished dinner. It was too late in the evening for anything substantial, so I made myself a stack of cheese and crackers, poured a glass of wine, and settled down at the kitchen table to read Amanda's letter.

I'm not sure what I expected. Certainly not what I read.

Dear Ginny, it began.

If you're reading this, then I must be dead, and Mr. Carter has given this letter to you. I can only imagine the confusion, surprise, and disbelief you must be experiencing right now. I can picture the look on your face and the exact expression when you turn to the nearest person and ask, "Why me?"

The reason is simple, really.

I was born into wealth, and for the longest time, didn't know any other life than to ask Daddy for whatever I wanted: money, a car, a ski trip, tuition for art school in Paris—it was all the same to me. Even when I went out on my own and refused to enter the family business, I still had more than enough resources. I was comfortable.

But there was also a period in my life in which I lost almost everything. I know how hard it is to have to make it on your own. Samantha Taylor had to die so that Amanda Kelly could be born. And now, apparently Amanda Kelly is dead, too. That can't be a coincidence.

You probably don't remember, but a few months ago, we had a conversation about you being the executor of your father's estate, and how grateful you'd been that he had his affairs in order before his dementia set in. You said something that struck me at the time: how you'd made your own will, not because you had anything of value to leave behind, but because you wanted to spell out in writing your wishes for what happened to your animals in the event of your death. You made me realize I needed to do the same. Not only regarding my animals, which I entrust to you as the only person I could imagine taking care of them for me, but because I **do** *have things of value to leave behind, and there are people in my life that don't deserve them.*

I think you deserve them, Ginny. I've never met anyone as selfless as you have been, returning home to take care of your ailing father, giving up your life and income in the city to eke out a living at a much lower salary than you had before. I've seen you with your patients, and I know how often your big heart tempts you into discounting your fees or waiving them altogether. I know your dream is to start a real clinic, so you don't have to run all over the county at all hours of the day and night. I want to be a part of something lasting, something good for a community that has been nothing but kind to me, even if I'm no longer here to see it.

The gift of my estate comes with no strings attached, however. If you decide you'd rather sit on the couch reading books and eating bonbons all day, or take Scotty to Prix St. George or whatever the highest level of competition the two of you can attain, then go for it with my blessing.

I can almost hear your protests, that you don't deserve this, that you hardly knew me at all. I think that is precisely why I wish to make you my beneficiary at this time. You expect nothing from me.

I must have sat in stunned silence, re-reading the letter I don't know how many times, until Remy thrust his head under my arm in a demand to go outside. When we came back in, I half-expected to be unable to sleep, but between the wine and the adrenaline crash, I was out like a light the moment my head hit the pillow. I didn't even notice when Remy left his perfectly good dog bed and crept up on the mattress with me where he didn't belong.

My dreams were the twisted stuff of anxiety. I was being chased; I was lost. I couldn't find something I needed. At one point I saw Amanda standing on her back-deck waving at me, but every time I tried to reach the house, the path changed, a fence went up, or a canyon opened at my feet. When I started awake, my pulse thundering in my ears, it was good to reach out and stroke the silky coat of the warm dog curled beside me.

Even if he took up most of the bed.

Dawn's early light streamed around the edges of the blackout curtain in my bedroom. A faint, persistent sound drilled into my head. Remy got off the bed, padded out of the room, but soon came back. A long snout with a cold, wet nose nudged my elbow. Groaning, I jerked my arm back under the covers. Something depressed the mattress near my head, and I opened my eyes to see Remy resting his chin on the bed, staring at me with a bright, alert expression. As soon as my eyelids lifted, his tail began to wag.

The persistent sound transformed itself into the piteous cries of a cat locked in a bedroom while starving to death, and I dragged myself out of bed. Small wonder Amanda had realized something was wrong with Ming. The cat was a bottomless pit. Hopefully, the anti-thyroid medication would begin working soon. I think Remy's insistence on my getting out of bed was just so someone would shut the cat up.

After feeding the animals, I took Remy outside and inspected the car. Though the back bumper was dented and compressed, the damage didn't look too severe. Was it worth reporting the accident to insurance and paying the deductible to have it fixed? I wasn't sure.

No sense in counting on Amanda's money until it was sitting in my bank account. In the meantime, I had to operate under the assumption I had to continue pinching pennies until Lincoln burped.

The fields behind my house stretched toward the ridge where Amanda's house sat. I couldn't see her house from mine, but I knew it wasn't far, as the crow flies. But the woods between her place and mine were nearly impenetrable, thanks to the greenbrier that gave the town its name. It was a pity I couldn't just zip over and feed the cats without having to go through the rigmarole of having an escort.

I'd just about resigned myself to taking Remy for a walk on my property, the way I usually did, when a cool breeze ruffled my hair, bringing with it the scent of rain. You know what? Screw it. There was nothing on the books until late morning. I could feed the cats at Amanda's before my first appointment. I whistled up the dog and loaded him into the car.

It had been too long since I'd taken the time to go hiking, but the morning was more or less open, so after bumping our way up the rutted service road to the trailhead, Remy and I set off for Lizard Rock. It was still chilly in the shade, but I stuffed my jacket in my backpack after we got going and my muscles had warmed up.

Remy's delight was a sight for sore eyes. Guilt stabbed at me even as I smiled when he ran big looping circles around me, leaping fallen tree trunks and splashing through puddles with the abandonment of a puppy. Periodically, he zipped up to me to make sure I was still there, and I acknowledged his check-in with praise and a treat.

Too long. It had been too long since we'd shared this simple pleasure.

When we climbed to the top of the ridge and reached the big, flat rock that gave the trail its name, I tossed my backpack on the rock and clambered up beside it. The sun wouldn't hit this west-facing ridge until late afternoon, which meant we would miss any basking lizards today. I didn't mind. After admiring the breathtaking view of the valley for a moment, I sat cross-legged on the rock and pulled a breakfast bar and a bottle of water out of my backpack.

The distinctive cry of a red-tailed hawk made me look up, and I spied the bird of prey riding the drafts overhead. The wind murmured through the pine trees like a woman sighing. I traced the pale green lichen on the stone with my fingers, marveling at how firmly attached it was. A chipmunk, not realizing I was there, popped over the lip of the rock for a moment, then flicked its chestnut tail with a sharp chip of alarm and scurried away as Remy bounded through the woods behind.

My mind emptied of thought as I became one with the rock, the wind, and the view.

Eventually, Remy climbed up on the rock beside me, looking like Rin Tin Tin as he stared off into the distance. Stealthily, I snuck my phone out of my pocket and angled the camera so I framed his head against the backdrop of the distant mountains, their hillsides dotted with pink and white of blooming redbud and dogwoods. I took three pictures in rapid succession before he turned his head toward me at the sound of the clicking shutter and came up to lick me in the face. Laughing, I buried my chilly face in his thick ruff.

I'd needed this. More than I'd realized. Time spent grounding in nature wasn't just a pleasant activity for me. I needed it like a plant needs sunlight and water, and yet too often, I let other demands on my time override the need for self-care. A vision of myself as the dried-up and wilting orchid my mother had given me for a birthday gift came to mind. I had so many things to take care of on a daily basis. Houseplants, like myself, came last on the list.

Even now, when I would have liked to sit on the mountaintop for longer, the pull to be up and about my responsibilities was strong. If I did take time off as a result of Amanda's bequest, I'd need at least two weeks to unwind from a knee-jerk reaction to get up and do something productive.

Stuffing the water bottle in the backpack, I said, "Come on, boy. We need to get back to work."

On the way back down to the car, my mind wandered, as it did in the rare moments when I let it idle. It kept circling around back around to Amanda's letter.

What had she meant by "that couldn't be a coincidence"?

The question nagged at me the entire way back to the car.

My phone began blowing up with messages as soon as I hit the main road again. This time, I'd remembered to put it in the clip attached to my dashboard, so I could see that I'd received several calls from the sheriff's office, as well as a text from Joe. Like the night before, there wasn't a good place to pull over right away. That didn't stop me from worrying, though. A problem with one of the horses, perhaps? There was always a risk when you moved them to a new location that they'd find the one piece of barbed wire that had been overlooked for the last century. Or maybe it was good news about Amanda's property. Maybe the coroner had finished with the exam and I'd be able to feed the cats without a babysitter.

There was a little scenic overlook farther down the mountain, and I pulled into it and parked the car.

The text from Joe was a simple: **Where are you?**

I ignored that for the moment and replayed my voice mail. The first was a polite but generic request for me to contact the sheriff's office at my convenience. A slightly more terse request that I come to the office as soon as possible followed. The third voice mail was from Joe, though I could hardly credit it. He introduced himself as Sheriff Donegan and stated I needed to come to the office at once.

What the hell?

I punched in the number for the sheriff's department and got Joan at the front desk. Since we were being all formal now, I said, "This is Dr. Ginny Reese. I've received several messages from your office. Could you tell me what this is about?"

"One moment, please." Joan put me on hold, and a second later, Joe came on the line.

"Where are you?"

I knew that tone. Pissed, and doing his best not to show it in front of other people.

"Good morning to you, too."

"I'm serious, Dr. Reese. I need to speak with you immediately. We've been trying to get a hold of you all morning."

Dr. Reese?

The formality triggered a red flag, and my eyebrows lifted in response.

"I went hiking. I must have been in a dead zone between cell towers. What's wrong?" His tension had bled over the phone and infected me now. "Look, if this is about the incident last night—"

"What incident last night?" The sharpness of his voice could have cut glass.

"Er, nothing. Just a little thing with someone trying to run me off the road on the way home from Amanda's last night."

"Did you report that?" His voice rose as he spoke, and I winced.

"I'm reporting it now." Although the way I ended that sentence, it could have been interpreted as a question as opposed to a statement.

Was that grinding noise in the background the sound of Joe's teeth?

"I need you to come in for further questioning regarding Amanda Kelly's death. While you're here, you can make an official report as to this traffic incident."

"There hardly seems any point to that. I can't give you a description or a license plate." I glanced at my watch. "I can come in this afternoon. I have an appointment at eleven, and I still have to feed the feral cats. As a matter of fact, if you could—"

"Where *are* you?"

The interruption was another bad sign.

"Right now?" Okay, his attitude was pissing me off. "Currently sitting at the overlook near Lizard Rock."

There was a pause while he presumably calculated the time it would take me to get back to town. "Fine. I expect you here at the station in an hour. Don't make me send someone to pick you up."

"For crying out loud, Joe." Alarm coursed through me now. "What on earth is going on?"

"I'll tell you what you need to know when you get to the station."

He did *not* just hang up on me. He merely broke off the conversation. But I was mad enough that I didn't immediately get back on the road and head toward the sheriff's office. Joe could darn well wait until I got there.

Instead, I sat in the wayside and checked my email. I quickly deleted the bulk of the promotional emails, keeping only the ones relevant to a house-call practice. I fired off a response to one hopeful looking for work that while I wasn't hiring at this time, I would keep them in mind for the future—something that wasn't necessarily a white lie for a change. I left the request for a transfer of records as unread until I could deal with it in the future and moved on to the email with "Amanda Kelly Property" in the subject line.

That was an eye-opener. One that I would also have to put on the back burner for the time being.

I'd just put the car in gear when I received another text from Joe.

Are you on your way yet?

Ugh. As if he had the right to act as though he still knew me.

By the time I reached the station, I'd built up a good head of steam. I stormed into the station with enough force the door almost bounced back in my face, which would have spoiled my perfectly indignant entrance. Joan looked up with raised eyebrows as I stalked up to her desk.

"Please tell *Sheriff* Donegan I'm here to see him." Two could play the formality game. "As summoned."

"Dr. Reese." Joe's voice behind me, cool and clipped, not sounding friendly at all, made me whip around. "If you'll come with me."

Fuming the entire way, I followed him into his office. He beckoned for me to shut the door behind me and take a seat. I did so, only to gape when he switched on a recorder on his desk and began reading me my rights.

"Joe, what is this all about?" My anger evaporated with the sudden blast of alarm.

"Dr. Reese. Do you understand these rights as I have given them to you?"

It was like looking into the eyes of a stranger. Joe stood with his arms folded across his chest. An impenetrable wall had lowered over his features, and the man I thought I knew was nowhere to be seen. His blank expression, so different from his usual smirks and laid back friendliness, made me swallow hard before replying.

"I understand my rights. What I don't understand is why they were read to me."

A flicker of something indefinable reached his eyes, but he quickly snuffed it out.

"Am I to understand that Amanda Kelly made you the beneficiary of her estate?"

"Is that why you're mad at me? Because you had to find out from the community grapevine? Heck, I'm still processing that information myself. I only found out last night." I narrowed my eyes as an additional thought occurred to me. "I certainly didn't tell anyone yet. Not even my mother. So how it is that it's common knowledge already?" I snapped my fingers. "I get it. Brad has probably been complaining to anyone who'd listen."

"Mr. Taylor has certainly been... vocal... about the terms of the will."

I relaxed into my seat. "Well, there you are. I had nothing to do with Amanda's decision. And I certainly would have told you about it the next time I saw you. So why insist I come down to the station?"

He hesitated for a fraction of a second before speaking in a steely kind of voice. "Because the coroner has completed his examination. He's ruled that Ms. Kelly died of blunt force trauma to the head in a manner that could not be accidental or self-inflicted."

"You mean—she was murdered?"

That odd look was in his eyes again, as though he were pleading with me to understand or recognize something. In a flash, it disappeared, and the Sheriff was back again. "Yes."

"I *knew* it." It was odd to feel triumphant over something like this, but I knew there was something wrong with the scene as I'd found it. If Amanda had taken off her shoes with the intention of swimming, then why leave on her clothes? And if she'd accidentally fallen in, why take off her shoes and watch? Someone had read too many mysteries and had made a clumsy attempt at making her death seem like a suicide.

Joe glanced at the recorder and seemed to repress a sigh. "Ginny."

His correct use of my name pinged my attention like an intruder triggering a trip wire. My mouth opened and closed helplessly as words failed me.

Joe, however, had no such problem. Speaking carefully, as though for the recorder, he said, "This has officially become a homicide investigation. And you are the number one person of interest."

Chapter Eleven

The questioning seemed to take forever.

Joe allowed me to reschedule my morning appointment and sent a deputy out to feed the feral cats over my objections. We went over the same material again and again. I recognized Joe's technique from my own when taking a history on patients from clients. Sometimes asking the same question in different ways elicited information the client had forgotten about, like when Jesse Simpkins forgot his grandson had fed LuLu bacon over the weekend and that might be why she was vomiting three days later.

"Did you have the code for Ms. Kelly's alarm system?"

"Well, yes. As I mentioned before, I took care of Amanda's animals when she went out of town. If she left Ming behind, which wasn't often, I went up to the house to feed him as well."

Joe could have been a Grand Inquisitor for all the friendliness he conveyed during my questioning. "How is it you didn't disengage the system when you called 911?"

I blinked at that one. "I... I don't know. I mean, I didn't think about it. To my knowledge Amanda didn't arm the system when she was home, so it never occurred to me I might trigger the alarm when I went in. I'm afraid I wasn't thinking very clearly at the time."

He seemed to let that slide, although he made a note on the yellow legal pad in front of him.

"Do you have a key to her house?" Cool and clipped, Joe's question was like a dash of ice water to the face.

"Er, yes."

Clear hazel eyes, the color of a hawk's, seemed to search my face before he spoke again. "You didn't disclose that information yesterday."

"It totally slipped my mind. Finding a friend dead in her swimming pool will do that to you."

He held out his hand. "I need the key."

He watched in stony silence as I pulled my key chain out of my jeans pocket and flipped through half a dozen keys before I found the one I wanted. I worked it off the ring, but instead of placing it in his waiting hand, I slapped it on his desk and pushed it toward him.

He left it there to tap his legal pad with his pen a few times before he met my eyes again.

"Are you sure you never went into Ms. Kelly's bedroom?" Joe was still in interrogator mode, but seemed to be trying to tell me something with his eyebrows. Unfortunately, I wasn't well versed in eyebrows.

"I can't think of any reason why I would go into Amanda's bedroom." I frowned as I considered his question. Snapping my fingers, I added, "Oh, wait. There was that time I had to help her get Ming out from under the bed."

"Perhaps it would be easier if you told me which parts of her house you've never been in."

I shrugged helplessly. "I'm not sure I can remember. Amanda has been a client for years. We were also friends. I helped out with her rescue horses, and she invited me to swim in her pool. She let me board my horse on her property, and I took care of her cat. I was in and out of her house a lot."

Joe's shoulders relaxed infinitesimally at this declaration, and I decided I was on the right track with my non-specificity. Honestly, the only place I could think of I'd probably never entered at Amanda's place was the master bathroom, but something told me not to share that little tidbit. Generalities seemed safer than absolutes.

"Let's talk about this friendship." He made it sound as though he'd put finger quotes around the word "friendship." He toyed with the pen again, tapping it on his notepad as he spoke. "Is that normal? That you make friends with your clients?"

After what felt like hours of this same line of questioning, my irritation levels rose once more. "Define normal. I work ten to twelve hours on any given day. Where am I supposed to make friends outside of work? I liked Amanda, and we had common interests. How is becoming friends a crime?"

"It isn't unless there's a suspicious death and a large fortune involved."

"One I never expected," I snapped.

"That remains to be seen."

"I can prove it." I reached for my bag but faltered when I realized I didn't have Amanda's letter with me.

"Yes?"

There went those eyebrows again, but instead of advising me to be cautious, they seemed to taunt me now.

"After the reading of the will, Amanda's lawyer gave me a letter that she'd written. In it, she explained why she'd chosen me to inherit her estate." I indicated my bag. "I thought I had it in my purse, but I left it at home."

The tapping pen went still. "What did the letter say?"

I hesitated, conscious of the heat that entered my cheeks. "She thought I was some kind of damn hero for coming home and taking care of my dad. Giving up Manhattan for *Green Acres*, that sort of thing. She said I deserved something for that, and she didn't want anybody in her family to inherit. I guess I'd talked about my hopes of building a clinic one day often enough that she liked the idea of being a part of that if something happened to her." I leaned forward to tap his notepad with one finger. "She also said she didn't think it was a coincidence that Samantha Taylor and Amanda Kelly were both dead now."

"I need to see that letter."

"Of course." I eased back in my seat. "Something else you should know. I got an email from those developers—Riverside—this morning. I'm guessing they found out from Brad that I was the legal heir now. They certainly wasted no time contacting me."

"Oh, really?" Joe cast aside his pen and leaned back in his seat to cross his arms over his chest. "What did they have to say?"

I leaned forward to rest my elbows on the desk and steeple my fingers. "They wanted me to know they had an agreement with Amanda to sell her property to them and wanted to be sure that I would honor that arrangement."

He frowned at that. "You sound as though you don't believe them."

"I don't think I do. Why would Amanda leave me a property she intended to sell?"

"Well, I'm pretty sure she didn't intend to die, either. The proceeds of the sale would be part of her estate regardless, so I'm not sure that argument holds water." He picked up his pen again to play with it. "Did she ever talk about the subdivision with you?"

I shook my head. "Only in general terms. She seemed to feel the subdivision was going to be built either way and wondered how that would affect her in the long run."

"So, she might have been planning to sell, and you didn't know it."

"Maybe." Darn it, Joe was making me doubt Amanda's intentions. "I think it more likely something changed in the last few days."

"Ms. Kelly's property is of a significant size that I doubt she'd have noticed much of a change. More traffic on the road, maybe. Did Riverside ever contact you about your land? It backs up to Ms. Kelly's estate, doesn't it?"

I sat up straight again. "I wish. I'd have sold it in a heartbeat. I'm never going to be able to build a clinic there, which is why I bought the property in the first place. And it's a decent size, even though it is long and narrow. But there's no view, and I guess that's what Riverside is looking for."

"Are you thinking of selling Ms. Kelly's land to them?"

"I've barely had time to think of it as mine to sell. And Brad intends to fight for it, that's for sure. But here's the interesting part." I pulled up my email on my phone and turned the screen so Joe could see it. "When I told them I wasn't sure about selling, they came back with a counteroffer within thirty minutes."

Joe's eyebrows reached for his hairline as he read the email. He gave out a low whistle. "They're offering double the original price?"

I took the phone back to stare at the screen. "Yeah. Seems a little anxious, don't you think?"

"Where were you the night before last?"

The question arrived out of nowhere so fast it nearly gave me whiplash, and it took me a second of frowning concentration to figure out what he was driving at.

"The night before last?" I repeated.

"Say, between six p.m. and three a.m., more or less."

"Is that when Amanda was killed?" It must have been, otherwise he wouldn't have asked. I wished I could take back the question as soon as the words left my mouth.

"The heated pool made it difficult to narrow down the time of death." Joe relayed that piece of information almost reluctantly and gave another glance at the recorder. "Your whereabouts?"

"You don't seriously think I had anything to do with her death, do you?"

A pained expression creased his brow. "I'm just doing my job."

We stared at each other a long moment before I said, "I finished up with the day's calls around six o'clock. I'm not sure of the exact time, but I had dinner at Sue's sometime around then. I probably still have the receipt." I made to root around in my purse for it, but Joe held up his hand, indicating that corroboration could wait. "Er, I got home a little after seven, maybe seven-fifteen."

"And then?"

"I'm thinking. The days all blur together after a while, you know." I snapped my fingers when I remembered. "Oh, right. I took a call from a non-client about a dog who'd swallowed a prescription medication, and I talked him through inducing vomiting at home. That took about twenty minutes or so. I didn't stay on the line the entire time, but called him back to make sure the dog threw up."

Joe made a faint grimace as he jotted notes on the legal pad. "After that?"

"At ten minutes to ten, I got a call from Dorothy Russell."

"You seem pretty certain of the time."

That made me snort. "I am because I was annoyed at how late it was. Normally, I try to be in bed by eleven p.m., so I looked at my watch when the phone rang." I'm sure my smile was rueful as I continued. "Dorothy's mother-in-law is visiting and her little Chihuahua, who hates everyone but her owner, ran into the bathroom and managed to get into the wall through a small gap under the sink."

Joe's pen abruptly stopped moving. "Say what?"

This time, I grinned outright. "You heard me. The Russells called in a panic. Her mother-in-law was sobbing in the background, and the kids were shrieking. Dorothy's husband was out—it seems he loathes the little dog—and she was freaking out about how to get the dog out of the wall before he got home. Dorothy put her daughter Kaitlyn on the phone with me. I guess she figured I'd be less likely to turn down an eight-year-old pleading for me to come help before her daddy got home."

Back in high school, Joe had been a huge fan of horror movies, something I could barely stand. But because I'd been crazy in love with him, I'd sat through his desire to watch what he called the "classics" of sci-fi horror, like John Carpenter's *The Thing*, when I would have rather watched *Practical Magic* or *Ever After*.

"Kaitlyn sounded all sad and pathetic. Remember that kid in the *Alien* franchise? The one who said the monsters came after dark?"

"Newt."

Of *course* he'd know the character's name.

"That's it. Well, that's what Kaitlyn sounded like. Please come and get Nan-nan's Pumpkin out of the wall before Daddy gets home." I imitated a small child pleading for my help in a small, soft voice.

"Barney has a reputation for having a short fuse. I can see the dilemma."

"Right? What else could I do but agree to help?"

Russell was known to be a hard man. There wasn't any evidence he was abusive, but I could understand Dorothy wanting to defuse a potentially volatile situation.

"What did you do when you got there?" Joe's smile invited inviting me to tell my story, as if among friends. For a minute, it appeared we *were* friends again. "The dog extraction must have taken a while."

"Not really. Dorothy led me to the bathroom. Can you believe it? The dog had found a space this big and squeezed through it." I held up my thumb and forefinger to show a distance of about two inches. "Pumpkin popped her nose out like a rat but dove back in when we entered the room. Dorothy began to wail her husband would *kill* her if they had to tear down the wall, and Mrs. Russell cried poor Pumpkin would starve to death like the guy in *The Cask of Amontillado*. You know how I said Kaitlyn was like Newt? Well, you'd have thought there was an alien in the wall when I shone a light in there."

All I'd been able to see was teeth and a gleaming eyeball. You'd have thought a demon was inside the wall from the sound of growling that emanated from such a tiny body. "I didn't want to be there when Barney got home, so I took the towel off the rack, wrapped it around my arm, and shoved it into the hole. When Pumpkin bit me, I dragged her out, latched onto my arm like a little shark."

Joe laughed at that. "You need your own TV show."

"Yup," I agreed. "*Ginny Reese, Chihuahua Hunter.*"

Too soon, the humor faded from his eyes. "So, how long do you think you were there?"

I shrugged. "I was home and in bed by quarter to twelve."

"Anyone able to vouch for that?"

The one time I could have wished for a late-night call from my mother, but no such luck. I shook my head.

Joe smoothly shifted gears. "Let's talk about this incident with your car last night. What happened?"

He sat in frowning silence as I recounted the events after I left Amanda's property. Then he made me go over the individual elements again and again. I finished with my assessment that the damage, while superficial, would probably cost a pretty penny to repair.

"And you didn't report it to your insurance company when you got home?" Somehow, his tone reminded me of my father in one of his stern disapproval modes, which made me defensive.

No point in telling him how much time I wasted looking for the sketch of Remy. "I was wiped out when I got home. It was dark, it was late, and I was still reeling from the reading of the will. I wanted a glass of wine and to read Amanda's letter, in that order."

The curve of his lips softened a bit at that. "Understandable, but how about this morning when you checked out the car? Why didn't you report this to the police?"

By police, he meant him. I sighed, barely refraining from rolling my eyes.

"Based on what? I didn't get a license plate. His headlights were in my eyes most of the time. I can't even give you a decent description of the car. And I hadn't decided on whether I'd file a claim yet." Besides, in the grand scheme of things, the dented fender was small potatoes. "Look, Amanda was using a pseudonym, and she was married to a guy named Derek Ellis, right?"

Joe's lips pursed in exasperation. "You know I'm the sheriff, right? This isn't my first murder investigation."

"Yeah, well, at the reading of the will last night, I met Amanda's agent, Laney Driver."

"We've spoken with Ms. Driver." Tight lips now, at least metaphorically. Not giving any details of the case away.

"So, Laney believes Amanda was hiding from Derek. I have to say, I'm right there with her on that one. He's an overbearing slimeball who seemed to think he was going to inherit everything and was pissed when he found out it was going to me instead."

The pen came back into play as Joe flipped it through his fingers. "Running you off the road wouldn't get him his inheritance back."

"No but trying to scare me might be right up his alley. When I first met Amanda, she told me Ming had broken his jaw in the past. It's difficult for a house cat who never goes outside to suffer that kind of injury by accident. If someone hurt Amanda, I'd take a hard look at her abusive husband."

"Rest assured, I'm taking a hard look at everyone involved in this case." He flicked a pointed glance at the still-running recorder on his desk before meeting my gaze again. "But you don't know he was abusive."

"Fine. Estranged, then." I folded my arms across my chest. "And before the reading at the lawyer's last night, I saw Brad Taylor having a meeting with some swanky woman at *Calliope's*."

"Pretty sure there's no law against that." The drawl was back now.

This time, I rolled my eyes. "Point being, he seemed to be showing her some of Amanda's art. Work he probably wasn't entitled to sell. Like the horses. Amanda left them to me outright, and when I asked Brad for my money back, he refused to even consider it."

Joe's eyes narrowed at that. "Good to know, thanks."

"I think he's hard up for money. You should look into the finances of his company. Amanda still got some dividends from it. What if she found out something hinky was wrong with Taylor Industries? That he'd misappropriated funds or something?"

He tossed down the pen. "Thank you for your cooperation, Dr. Reese. We'll be in touch if we have any further questions." He switched off the recorder and fixed me with a hard stare. "Don't get any bright ideas about being an amateur sleuth. I know you, Ginny."

"*Moi*?" I said, in my best Miss Piggy imitation.

"Yes, you. If it's a kitten in a drainpipe or a dog being kicked or a just cause of any sort, you're the first one to dive in the drain, so to speak.

You were the kid in middle school who collected over fifteen hundred signatures to protest the clubbing of baby seals."

"It was wallabies, not seals," I said stiffly.

"Right." His smile grew wider. "And as I recall, you confronted Mr. Burrows over his treatment of the neighborhood squirrels when you were only nine. Walked right up to him and told him to stop shooting them."

"He called me 'honey' and said he was just scaring them." I glowered at the memory. "I told him he was doing such a good job of scaring them, they were falling dead out of the trees. And he stopped shooting them, so there. Standing up to him was the right thing to do. What's so funny?"

"You think he stopped because some kid scolded him? More likely it was because you were covered in squirrels at the time. They popped out of your pockets and sat on your shoulders, cursing him a blue streak in squirrel-speak. He probably thought you were a witch or something."

I rubbed my nose to hide my embarrassment. "That was a long time ago. I'm not that person anymore."

He tilted his head to one side, as though he couldn't believe what he'd just heard. "No?"

I shook my head. That person, the one who believed in fighting for what was right? Life had beaten a lot out of her over the years. "No. I grew up."

I took on too many responsibilities. I got tired. More than tired. I was exhausted.

He shook his head sadly, a smile ghosting his lips. "That's not what I saw the other night when Taylor said he'd sold the horses to the slaughterhouse. Taylor saw it too. He was backing up when you climbed over that fence."

"Yeah, but that didn't stop him from accosting me on the street last night." I winced as soon as the words came out of my mouth. I hadn't meant to say that.

The playful look evaporated. Joe's eyes had gone still, like a fox noticing the rustle of a mouse in the grass. "What do you mean, *accosted*?"

"Bad choice of words." I waved a dismissive hand. "When I saw him at the restaurant, he came out and accused me of spying on him."

"Were you?"

"No!" Annoyed, I became defensive. "Like I said, I saw him through the window. He followed me to my car and got testy with me. Which strikes me as a sign of a guilty conscience, if you ask me. It wasn't a normal conclusion to leap to."

Joe sighed as he stood up and came around to my side of the desk, only to hitch a hip up and rest it on the corner.

"I understand Amanda was your friend. Someone killed her. You're going to want to stick your nose into the investigation; it's only natural."

"It's only natural." I repeated his words back at him, sensing a trap but not knowing where it lay.

"To someone like you. You're a puzzle solver. It's why you like medicine: the search for clues, asking questions to find out what happened, running tests to determine what's wrong... It's a lot like solving crimes. You're going to pick at this like it's a scab over a pocket of infection." The sense of camaraderie abruptly snuffed out. "But this is murder, not a case of what's wrong with Muffy. For your own sake, I'm telling you to leave it to the professionals."

Before I could tell him exactly how condescending he sounded, the noise of a commotion outside reached our ears. Joan said loudly, "You can't go in there!" just as the door flew open.

The woman in the doorway stood bristling with belligerence, like a pint-sized Annie Oakley about to enter a saloon. "Virginia Reese, not another word without your lawyer."

My mother had arrived.

Chapter Twelve

AT FIVE FOOT TWO, my mother had the delicate frame of a bird.

If that bird was a sparrowhawk, that is.

For over forty years, she'd run her classroom with an iron fist. She believed in rules and discipline, and the children in her classes had quickly learned she was not to be trifled with. She'd butted heads with parents and frustrated various administrations, but above all, she'd always put her students first. She'd gotten the best out of kids everyone else had given up on, and there were many adults now who could point to her influence and say she'd changed their lives for the better.

Most people bowed, if not cowed, to her dynamic presence.

Joe was not most people.

When my mother announced I was coming with her, I stood as though I were twelve years old again and she was picking me up from the principal's office for some childish infraction.

Joe was not finished with me, however. "Your time is still unaccounted for between midnight and three a.m. on the night in question."

I gave a helpless shrug. I was in bed, asleep. What more did he want?

"I said, not another word, Ginny."

"A shrug isn't speaking, Mom."

She opened her mouth to say something, no doubt cutting, but Joe intervened between us. Calmly, he faced down the cyclone that was my mother. "We'll be in touch if we have any further questions."

"If you need to speak with my daughter again, you can contact us through our lawyer." My mother's indignation brought color to her cheeks, or else it was the department-store rouge she favored. She pushed up the sleeves of her white cotton blouse. "Are you arresting her?"

"He's clearing me as a suspect, Mom." I shot Joe an apologetic look and was disturbed when he stood stony-faced without agreeing that was the purpose of the questioning.

After too long a moment, he said, "It's a mere formality, Mrs. Reese."

My mother harrumphed and said, "I'll wait for you out front, Ginny."

The look she leveled at Joe before leaving contained nothing but pure venom.

"Sorry," I muttered as Joe ushered me to the door.

"Don't apologize." He spoke lightly, as though it were of no consequence. "She hasn't changed much, has she?"

As he walked away, I couldn't help but wonder if my mother hadn't been a factor in his leaving me behind. If she was, then good riddance. I didn't need anyone in my life who couldn't stand up to my mother. Bad enough I kowtowed to her more often than not.

On the other hand, he could have been afraid I might turn into her one day.

Which, honestly, was a justifiable reason for dumping me.

As promised, my mother was waiting for me when I entered the main office. She pulled a moist towelette dispenser out of her cav-

ernous purse and handed one to me while glowering at everyone in
the sheriff's office who dared to look in my direction.

"Here. Clean your hands."

I could have used one of these yesterday after I got fingerprinted,
but I thought it wise not to mention that little detail. Why she felt I
needed to wipe my hands, I had no idea, but I'd learned long ago to
pick my battles wisely. I ran the wipe over my hands and dropped it in
the trash before following her out of the building. As soon as we hit
the sidewalk, she wheeled on me.

"I can't believe you spoke to the police without a lawyer present.
And when were you planning to tell me you'd inherited a fortune?"

She was indignant, but the sparkle in her eye was akin to that of an
old warhorse hearing the call of the bugle to battle. This was the most
exciting thing that had happened to her since her forced retirement,
and she was eager to put her energies to good use.

Which actually wasn't all that terrible of an idea.

"Do we even have a lawyer? Please don't say Ethan Burrows."

"Why not Ethan? He's handled all our affairs since your father and
I got married."

No use pointing out that forty-plus years of practicing law in a small
town didn't necessarily qualify him for the job.

"Lawyers specialize in different matters, Mom. Mr. Burrows is the
perfect man to go to for property matters and wills. But I don't think
he's ever handled a criminal case."

"Oh, pooh," my mother said inelegantly. "It's not going to come to
that. I'll say you were with me."

"Mom! You can't lie to Joe!"

"Why not?" She fixed a gimlet eye on me and I nearly caved.

Fortunately, I remembered I'd already answered Joe's questions regarding my movements that night. "Because I won't let you. Besides, I already told Joe I was alone that night."

"This is why you shouldn't have said anything." Her lips flattened into a thin line. "Don't you watch TV?"

That was rich, coming from someone who'd called television the "idiot box" when we were growing up and had put severe limits on everything Liz and I could watch. Apparently, retirement had introduced my mother to *Murder She Wrote* on the streaming platforms.

"So, when were you going to tell me about the inheritance?" She didn't *quite* tap her foot.

"Everything happened so fast, Mom. I had every intention of calling you this morning, only I had to come in for questioning." My stomach gurgled, and she shot it an incredulous look. "I only had time for a protein bar this morning. Let's go to Sue's for lunch, and I'll tell you what I know."

If that breakfast bar hadn't been so long ago, I'd have refused to eat lunch with her. As it was, everything I put in my mouth would fall under her scrutiny and criticism.

The short walk to Sue's did me some good, however. The air cleared my head, reminding me of the peace I'd experienced on Lizard Rock just that morning. As we walked, I filled her in on everything that had happened since I'd spoken with her the day before. Well, not *everything*. I left out the fact someone tried to run me off the road. She listened with frowning intensity. When I got to the part of how much money was involved, her opinion of my friendship with Amanda underwent a sea change. Suddenly, Amanda was no longer a peculiar woman but a savvy and talented entrepreneur.

I've mentioned I'm not a strong swimmer. I can get from point A to point B, provided the distance isn't too far. I confine my swimming to splashing around in a friend's pool and occasionally going to a lake. It's been years since I went to the beach. The idea of getting caught up in a riptide and drowning terrifies me. As usual, when things frighten me, I try to find out as much as possible about the risks and dangers of said thing so if I'm ever faced with that particular situation; I know how to act. One thing I learned about riptides was not to fight them. Try to swim across them until you're out of their pull.

My mother was a riptide.

I'd spent most of my life fighting her current. Today, I was going to swim across it.

As I opened the door to the diner, I said, "I need your help, Mom. I need someone who can make some discreet inquires, and you're the perfect candidate for the job."

Her eyes lit up. My mother fancied herself as intrepid and resourceful, someone not to be trifled with, and truth be told, she was all of those things. But she also believed she would have made an excellent spy, and John le Carré and Tom Clancy novels filled her bookshelves. After my father's death, she entertained the idea of applying to the CIA for work, like a modern-day Mrs. Pollifax. I wish I were kidding.

She practically beamed. "Because no one will suspect a little old lady in tennis shoes."

Heaven help me. I hoped this would not turn out to be a bad idea. "Precisely."

On entering, I immediately noticed Laney sitting at the counter, and a table of suits seated at a booth in the back. In a room filled with denim and flannel, the business executives stood out like show dogs at the pound.

I could have sworn one suit was the guy I'd seen shaking hands with Brad at *Calliope's*. His lunchtime companions didn't seem happy. In fact, all three of them wore expressions that ranged from disgruntled to disgusted. Perhaps Greenbrier's culinary standards weren't on the same plane as wherever these guys were from.

I led the way to a booth near them, giving Sue a little wave as we weaved our way through the mostly empty tables. The red faux leather on the seats was cracked, and the Formica tabletops were chipped, but I slid into the booth with an internal sigh of relief. You could rely on Sue's for excellent diner food. I was practically drooling at the scent of fried meat and potatoes.

After we took our seats, my mother leaned forward eagerly. "What do you need me to do?"

"Hang on a second." Sue's sister, Kim, was making her way to us with a pitcher in her hand and menus under one arm. "Let's order first, and then I'll tell you."

The suits tossed a few dollars on their table and passed us on the way to pay their bill. I might have been reluctant to gossip about the strangers, but my mother had no compunctions whatsoever.

"What are those sharks doing here in town?" she asked, as Kim filled our glasses with ice water and handed us menus.

For once, I didn't think my mother's imagination was running away with her. There was something about the way the men cut through the diner that was reminiscent of a great white moving through a school of fish. Cold, ruthless, and certain of their place on the food chain.

Kim looked over her shoulder at them as they took their receipt and headed out the door. "They're the developers. You know, Riverside. Been here for a few days now." She made a face. "You know the kind. Wants to know if the bread is gluten-free and if we have keto options. Think they're all that."

Which probably meant she'd flirted and been shot down.

"They didn't eat very much," my mother observed. Of course, she noticed what they'd left behind on their plates.

"I think they were kind of upset about something." Kim leaned in with a conspiratorial whisper. On catching her sister's eye upon her, she straightened and said, "Blue Plate special is flounder with green beans and mashed potatoes."

Decisions, decisions. Normally I'd get a burger or hot dog and some fries, but I loved a good piece of flounder, and I hadn't had anything green to eat in days. I settled on the special while my mother ordered a cup of coffee. No surprises there.

As soon as Kim left, I told my mother I'd seen someone I needed to talk to and that I'd be right back.

Laney looked up with surprise that turned into a pleased smile when I approached and spoke her name.

"Ginny! I'm glad I ran into you."

"Same here. I thought you were headed back to Atlanta, though."

Laney blew her breath out with a long-suffering sigh. "I thought so, too. That was before they determined Amanda was murdered and the sheriff called me in for questioning. I was told not to leave town."

I took a seat on a stool beside her. "They called me in too. I guess that means Brad won't be leaving anytime soon. Or Derek, either, depending on what time he got into town and if he can prove it or not."

"I'm sure you're right. I'd love to know where Derek was myself."

I caught her up on the incident with the car the night before and was gratified to see her eyebrows lift.

"You think it's connected to the will?" she asked.

"Seems awfully coincidental. Though my guess is, it was Derek venting his spleen. No matter what, he's cut out of the will, so it was probably just meanness on his part." I cast a glance back at the booth where my mother sat. Satisfied she wasn't about to join us; I leaned a bit closer. "Listen, I'm here with my mom. Do you want to sit with us? I have to warn you; my mother speaks to everyone as if they're in middle school."

Laney's laugh was warm and rich. "That's okay. I appreciate the offer, but I'm just getting ready to leave."

"Did you find out anything about Taylor Industries? What do they even do, anyway?"

She twisted her stool slightly in my direction. "That's a good question. They seem to have their fingers in a lot of pies. They've got civilian contractors in Afghanistan providing engineering support, as well as in telecommunications. They supply circuit boards to the airline industry and dabble in real estate on the West Coast as well. But word is they've lost some government contracts recently because of shoddy workmanship, and the stock value has fallen dramatically in the few years that Brad has been in charge."

"So, the notion he needs money isn't that far off the mark."

Laney shook her head with a fierce smile. "Especially since rumor has it, his marriage is on the rocks, and there could be divorce proceedings in the near future."

I digested that. "A divorce might force lawyers to look into his holdings as part of the division of assets."

"My thought as well. It could be he was hoping an influx of money from Amanda's estate would allow him to play a shell game a bit longer with his shareholders."

"Who do you think killed Amanda?"

Laney took a sip from her lemonade and then pushed the glass aside, as though she were through with it. "Honestly? I think Derek found her. He's the sort of guy that can't let go, and he'd never forgive Amanda for leaving him. If Brad were that desperate for money, I'm sure Amanda would have helped him out. Perhaps reluctantly, but eventually, yes."

"Even given the things she said in the will?" Something about the staging of Amanda's death scene bugged me. "Don't you think if Derek killed her, he would have been more vindictive? More violent? The coroner's office thought it was an accident at first. I think if Derek killed her, there would have been no doubt it was murder."

"That's a good point." Laney's face fell, and I recognized the look of regret that washed over it. "I just wish I'd gotten in touch with her the night I got into town. I called her several times, but she never answered."

"When was that?"

"The first call was right when I'd checked into the B&B. Around nine p.m. I'd say. I called again about ten o'clock, but when I didn't get her a second time, I gave up and decided to try in the morning. I wish now I'd gone out to her place anyway."

If she was telling the truth, then it was a possible timeline for Amanda's time of death.

I wasn't a touchy-feely kind of person, but I laid a hand on Laney's arm. "There's a good chance she was already gone by then. If you'd gone out there, you might have met the same fate."

Laney locked gazes with me. "Tell me you wouldn't have gone out there if you'd known. If you'd been worried about her safety."

She was right. If I'd thought Amanda was in trouble...

Laney must have seen something in my expression, for she said, "Yeah, that's what I thought."

Spotting Kim heading toward the booth with my lunch, I said, "I've got to go. Let's get together before you leave town, though. Maybe dinner tomorrow?"

Laney agreed, if somewhat unenthusiastically. Her next comment implied it had nothing to do with me. "Doesn't look like I'm going anywhere anytime soon."

I left her and rejoined my mother. I was surprised she hadn't bullied her way into our conversation already, but when I sat down, it was clear she thought she was already on the job.

"Is she one of your contacts?" my mother asked.

I managed to hide my smile by spearing a piece of crispy flounder and taking a bite. "That was Amanda's agent. Apparently, Amanda asked her to come up, only she died before the two of them could meet."

"So, she says," my mother said darkly.

She had a point. Was I wrong to trust Laney as much as I did? I tended to go with my gut when it came to reading people and animals. In the fifteen years since I'd graduated from vet school, I'd been bitten exactly twice, not counting my actively encouraging Pumpkin to bite me so I could pull her out of the wall. Once by a terrified cat who'd been abused, and once by a dog I'd just vaccinated without incident. They always say it's the ones you don't see coming. Point is, unconsciously or not, I pay attention to body language and the subtle cues animals give to show if they are comfortable. I always tell them what I'm about to do before I do it, like examine their ears, or open their mouths. I respect when an animal tells me they are unhappy or scared.

My gut told me I could trust Laney. That she was just as upset and angry over Amanda's death as I was.

But it's always the one you don't see coming.

Perhaps I should be a little more cautious in my dealings with her.

"You're right." A sentence I couldn't ever recall saying to my mother before. "I'm inclined to take what Laney says at face value, but maybe I shouldn't."

My mother straightened at my words, and a gleam entered her eye. Was it really that simple? I just had to pay heed to her advice?

My food was getting cold, so I dove into it. For once, she didn't criticize my choices at all.

"Before I forget, I have a drawing of Remy by Amanda that I need to have framed. Do you mind running it into Clearwater? I've already placed the order. I just need you to drop it off."

I suspect at any other time, such an errand would have taken a backseat to my mother's other activities, but as the drawing was tangentially related to Amanda's death, she was more than willing to help. Especially when she learned the sketch might be worth over five hundred dollars. It was priceless to me, but that didn't matter to my mother.

"Now this other task is only something you can do," I told her.

The narrowing of her eyes made me wonder if I was laying it on a bit thick, so I hurried on.

"See, I think Brad is hard up for funds." I glossed over the selling of the horses to Ringbolts. She would have been unhappy if she'd known how much I forked over to save them. Or would she? It was so hard to tell with her sometimes. Instead, I focused on the meeting with the art dealer from New York, and his reaction to my being named heir instead of him, winding up with the favor I wanted her to perform. "Rumor has it he was rude to Miss Ellie because she couldn't give him some piece of information he wanted. Could you go down to the library and see what it was about? Without seeming too obvious about it, of course. I don't want word to get out that I was asking about Amanda's brother."

Really, my mother was the perfect person to winkle this information out of Miss Ellie without raising any red flags. She seemed to know it as well.

Leaning back against her seat, she gave me a cat-got-the-canary smile and said, "You can count on me."

That's what I was afraid of.

Chapter Thirteen

As we were getting ready to leave the diner, my mother excused herself to go to the restroom. I took the opportunity to head over to the cash register and pay for our meal. To my surprise, Sue herself was manning the till.

The family resemblance between the Jackson sisters was strong. They both had blonde, curly hair and blue eyes, though Kim's hair was the stark white color that came from a bottle and had enhanced her eyes with colored contact lenses. Sue was a slightly older, less harsh version of Kim. It had been a while since I'd seen her last, and there were dark circles beneath her somewhat puffy eyes.

"Hey, Sue. I don't remember the last time I've seen you out front. You're usually back at the grill, making the best burgers in town."

"Given my competition is Mickey D's, I'd say you're trying to butter me up." She gave me a tired smile and pushed a strand of loose hair back behind one ear. "I'm hoping now that spring's here, some of the high school kids will be looking for part-time work. I can't keep any help."

I made a sympathetic noise as I handed her my ticket. "You'd think the perks of free food would be worth it."

She punched the numbers into the old-style register and rang up the total. "You'd think. But it seems no sooner than I get one set of teenagers trained, then they graduate and leave town."

A middle-aged man with skin tanned like shoe leather looked up from his BLT where he sat at the counter. "They got nothing to stay for."

Sue nodded. "That's true enough, Blair."

I hadn't placed him until Sue said his name, and then I recalled he owned land on the other side of Amanda's property. Blair Kendall kept beef cattle, and the one time he'd called about getting a rabies shot for his dog, he'd complained about my prices and said he'd get Doc Haskell to do it the next time he came out. Dr. Haskell was the large animal vet in the area. People often asked me why I limited my services to small animals, but the truth of the matter is that large animal work is brutal. You're out in the elements year-round, and because there aren't any emergency services that cover large animals, a livestock vet is on call 24/7/365 until the day you die or get too injured to work. I love horses and enjoy working with cattle, sheep, and goats, but I love sleep and intact bones more.

A sudden intensity flared in Kendall's gaze and he said, "You there. Is it true what they say? Did you inherit that artist woman's place?"

Amanda had been a neighbor, and he could only refer to her as "that artist woman." Oh yay. If things went as planned, he'd become *my* neighbor. So, I made the effort to be polite. "According to Ms. Kelly's lawyer, yes."

I had the attention of everyone in the diner now, from the couple seated at a nearby table to Kim, who paused in the act of loading dishes into a plastic tub. A large man sitting by himself wiped his lips with a napkin and got up from his booth. I realized with dismay it was Ed Linkous.

Great. Just what I needed. The de facto head of the Linkous clan. If there was a pie in Greenbrier County, Ed had his stubby fingers in it.

"You gonna sell?" Kendall growled as Ed made his way over toward us.

Not that it was any of his business. I faked an unconcerned laugh. "I haven't made any decisions yet. I'm still processing the information. I only found out last night."

Ed wasn't even pretending not to eavesdrop.

Kendall tossed some loose change down beside his plate and stood up. "You'd better decide soon."

"Excuse me?"

His manner was distinctly hostile, and I had no idea why.

"It's that new development." Sue took my card and ran it through the scanner. "They're looking to build all along the ridge there near Blair's farm."

She printed out a receipt and pushed it toward me to sign.

Kim brought her tub of dishes up to the counter and set it down to join in the conversation. "Not just a subdivision. Riverside is planning to put in a shopping center as well. Restaurants, a movie theater, department stores, the works. But only if the subdivision goes through."

"Which it won't if you don't sell." Kendall glowered at me.

At least the reason for the hostility was clear now.

"The truth is, Mr. Kendall, it will take some time for the will to go through probate—"

Before I could continue, he made a face and cut me off. "This town needs that development. The young people need a reason to stay. No one wants to be a farmer anymore, and I can't say as I blame them. It's hard work from sunup to sundown all year round, with precious little to show for it."

By now, Ed was close enough to insinuate himself into the conversation. A big man with a deep tan, he favored jeans, boots, and a cowboy belt buckle big enough on which to serve a Thanksgiving turkey.

"He's right, Dr. Reese. I know you've only been back in town a few years, but surely you can see how hard things are around here. Ever since the plant closed, we've had a tough time attracting new business to the area, and the local economy has suffered for it. We need an infusion of new blood into the town, or we're going to get wiped off the map."

Seeing as Ed's chief business was construction, and he subcontracted members of his extensive family as plumbers and electricians, his motives weren't entirely pure.

I tried again. "Yes, but—"

"No buts about it, missy." Kendall hitched his jeans up at the waist and took a step toward me. "That bleeding heart artist was holding out and if she didn't sell her tract of land, the whole deal was going to fall through, see? It wasn't right. She already had plenty of money. She could buy another place somewhere. The developers were going to do right by us."

I picked up my card and turned to face him as my mother came out of the restroom. "Are you saying that if Amanda had refused to sell her place, the subdivision was off?"

Sue cut a glance toward Kendall and chimed in. "Oh, they would have probably built somewhere else in the area. Just not in Greenbrier."

And by doing so, would cost Kendall the sale of his farm. Not to mention, the support of a lot of other residents in the area who might have embraced the idea of more development, more business.

"People would pay a pretty penny for that view," Kim added. There was a gleam in her eye that suggested she was enjoying Kendall's confrontation with me.

Her slight smirk disappeared when my mother joined me, and she busied herself with clearing Kendall's dishes and adding them to her tub.

"I want to know what you intend to do." Kendall demanded.

He'd reckoned without my mother, however.

"Is that you, Blair?" My mother rapped out in ringing tones, straight from the schoolroom. "I swear, I didn't recognize you. You've gained weight."

Kendall turned red in the face and screwed up his lips until he looked like a boiler about to blow. Ed's eyes grew wide, and he pulled his lips down in a heroic attempt to keep from laughing.

"Thanks for a delicious meal, Sue! Golly, look at the time. We've got to go." I grabbed my mother by the elbow and steered her toward the door, tossing Sue an apologetic glance over my shoulder.

My mother resisted being herded and seemingly had every intention of saying more to Kendall as her former student. I'd given up long ago trying to stop her from saying outrageous things in public, especially about appearances. Since she had no compunction about commenting on *my* appearance, it was a lost cause.

Instead, I leaned in and said as quietly as possible, "We've got another motive for murder. Act natural and come with me."

And she did, as meek as a lamb. If I'd known it was that easy, I would have played into my mother's spy fantasies decades ago.

We headed back to my car so I could give her the sketch to frame. I filled her in on what had happened while she was in the restroom.

"After I speak with Miss Ellie, I'll go down to the courthouse and ask to see the proposed development plans. That should generate a list of names of property owners who had a vested interest in seeing that Amanda sold her land." My mother nodded to herself as though it were a done deal.

It was an excellent idea, and the sort of research that would bore me to tears but that my mother would thrive upon. "I definitely think that's worth doing, but do you really think someone would kill Amanda over her refusal to sell? Look at the can of worms it opened, what with the will being contested and the likely delay to probate."

"I wouldn't rule it out just yet." My mother gave me a knowing tip of her chin as she lifted an eyebrow. "No one expected you to inherit. If you're right and he needs the money, that brother of hers would have sold in a heartbeat. Someone could have killed poor Amanda, thinking it would solve the issue of her being a holdout."

"I don't know." I shook my head slowly. "I could see someone pressuring her to sell. Maybe that's why her brother came to see her. But her death puts a monkey wrench into any sale until her will can be probated now."

We'd reached my car, and Remy popped up to drop his ears ingratiatingly as his whole body wagged side to side at the sight of my mother. As I'd parked in the shade and left the windows partly rolled down, he shoved his nose through the gap and tried to lick her. I ordered him to stay but allowed him to greet her as I rummaged through the car for the sketch.

"Maybe, maybe not." My mother fondled Remy's ears as he leaned out of the open door toward her. "If the developers knew Amanda's place would be available in a specific period of time, I bet they could be convinced to wait on the project six months or so if it were going to give them everything they wanted. From what you say, Amanda's property would make up a considerable chunk of any planned subdivision, especially combined with the surrounding farms such as

Blair's. And if her brother had been named heir instead of you, there's a good chance he would have been able to at least contract the sale on paper, which might have satisfied any creditors he might have. It's the fact that he intends to fight for it that makes it a problem."

I wondered if that made it more or less likely that Brad had something to do with Amanda's death? Contesting the will would drag the proceedings out for months, possibly years, if it didn't drain the estate dry. If he'd murdered his sister for her property, would he continue to fight tooth and nail for the inheritance if it couldn't come to him soon enough to put through the sale to the developers? Perhaps. Especially if he was desperate.

On the other hand, he could be fighting for her estate without having been the one to kill her at all.

"I'll speak to Ethan about it. He'd know what the law allows."

My mother's contacts were going to turn out to be useful after all.

I shut Remy in the car and handed the taped-together pieces of cardboard protecting the sketch to my mother. She took it, and then fixed me with one of her thoughtful expressions.

"Now that you're Ms. Kelly's heir, are *you* in any danger, my dear?"

It was a good thing I hadn't mentioned the incident with the car. She'd never believe the two weren't connected, and truthfully, I thought they were myself.

"Not to worry, Mr. Carter was very clear on that point in front of everyone last night. If anything should happen to me, the property goes to my heirs, no one else. That means they'd have to fight you."

I said it with a smile, but I didn't like the glint that entered my mother's eye. I could almost hear her saying, "Bring it on."

Instead, she asked, "What do you plan to do next?"

I blew air out of my lips. "I've got to see some appointments this afternoon, including the one I had to reschedule because they wanted me down at the station."

"I meant regarding Amanda's murder." My mother practically rolled her eyes at me, which was patently unfair.

"That's why I need your help. I've got a business to run. While you track down who might have been pissed off that Amanda was refusing to sell her property, Laney, the agent, is going to see if there's anything hinky with the art end of things—counterfeiting, illegal sales, that sort of thing."

"That's more like it." Clearly, she approved.

I glanced at my watch. "I need to hurry if I'm going to see patients. After that, I intend going to the town council meeting tonight."

This time she frowned. "I thought you said the issue with the dog licenses was flogging a dead horse."

Ah, she *had* been listening.

"I did. But as the potential owner of property being considered for development, I think I should be there for the meeting."

My mother pursed her lips and tapped the side of her nose. "Yes! Armed with the list of names I'll find, you'll be able to spot anyone who'd have a stronger motive than most for wanting Amanda dead."

"Maybe. That's the general idea, anyway."

I avoided pointing out that same person might aim their hostility at me next. What my mother didn't know wouldn't hurt her. Better yet, it wouldn't hurt anyone else, either.

Chapter Fourteen

I'D MADE GOOD TIME with my afternoon appointments and was pleased with my efficiency until I reached into my cooler and realized I didn't have enough doses of distemper/parvo combinations to vaccinate Lloyd Parker's litter of heeler puppies.

Using language that would have appalled my mother, I made an illegal U-turn and sped toward home, calling Lloyd on the way to tell him I'd be late. He took it in stride, and I ended the call to concentrate on my driving.

I pulled up in the drive with a little spray of gravel and hopped out of the car, telling Remy to wait as I dashed inside.

It was a good thing I left him in the car because the first sign something wasn't right was when I grabbed the doorknob, and it turned without me putting the key in the lock. Had I left the house this morning without locking the door? Not likely, but not impossible, either. I'd been distracted. I could have forgotten to lock the door.

But when I pushed it open and found a very disgruntled Siamese standing in the hallway lashing his tail from side to side, the depth of the wrongness was clear. There was no way I'd forgotten to lock up behind me *and* neglected to properly shut the door to the spare room as well.

I almost backed out of the door and headed to the car to collect the dog. Better to have backup before entering a home where an intruder might still be present. Even better to call the police and let them know you'd had a break-in. But by the way Ming was stomping around, it seemed unlikely that anyone was still in the house.

Cautiously, leaving the screen door latched to prevent Ming from escaping, I edged my way into the house and listened. I nearly jumped out of my skin when the refrigerator's wonky compressor gurgled, and I gave a breathless laugh at my fear. Any amusement died away when I saw the damage that had been done in the small living room. Someone had taken a knife to the cushions and slashed them until the cheap foam interior had spilled out in gaping wounds. The wall-mounted flat screen TV had a series of spider-webbed cracks across its surface, and the cast iron doorstop in the shape of a German Shepherd lay below it in front of the entertainment console. My beloved books had been swept from the shelves and some of them lay mutilated and torn asunder like murder victims.

A slow burning anger took me into the kitchen, where someone had ripped open boxes and bags of cereal, pasta, and dry goods and scattered them across the room.

Darn it. I'd just bought that box of Cap'n Crunch, and I'd only eaten one bowl.

I didn't go into the kitchen, but followed Ming down the hallway to my bedroom, where the damage was even more vicious. Clothes had been ripped and shredded. My favorite pair of boots had been scored with a sharp object. Drawers lay upended and emptied onto the floor. The crowning insult, however, was the damage to a photo of me and Major taken many years before on one of our favorite hiking trails. The frame was twisted into a pretzel, the glass shattered, and the photo itself torn. Pieces of the photograph lay scattered on my bed like rose petals from an obscene lover.

My pulse thudded in my temples so hard it was as if I'd mainlined an espresso straight into my veins. Nausea turned cartwheels in my stomach, and I had to put out a hand for balance along the wall as I continued my examination of the house.

The only room that had seen little damage had been the spare room which housed Ming. I looked down at him by my feet and met his cool, hostile gaze. "I'm guessing they weren't expecting to find you, were they?"

Ming, understandably, said nothing, but licked his paw to groom his face.

I finished my circuit of the house. It didn't take long. Glass crunched underfoot as I neared the bathroom, and there I discovered the intruder had used my special-occasions-only, expensive lipstick to scrawl hateful messages on my smashed mirror and gouged walls. The scent of my favorite perfume mixed horribly with the minty odor of the toothpaste that smeared the floor. Darn it, that perfume cost a bloody fortune. It was one of my few indulgences. When I caught up with whoever it was—and I had my suspicions—he'd pay for that. Oh, he'd pay.

On some level, I recognized that my obsession with stupid things like cereal and perfume was an attempt to wall off my emotions from the greater shock of having had my home invaded. Focusing on the minutia of the damage helped mitigate the feeling of violation. I took out my phone and began taking pictures with the detached dedication of a crime scene technician until it suddenly hit me that my home *was* a crime scene. I stuffed a protesting Ming into his carrier and set him outside while I went back and took dozens of photos of each room for insurance purposes. Only after I was done did I call the sheriff's department.

Predictably, Joe himself came out with Frank and Holly, along with a lab tech. He found me outside with Remy, photographing another scene of destruction I'd discovered: the perpetrator had found my supplies in the shed out back and scattered them to the four winds, smashing what could be smashed, and ruining everything else. Bandaging material, vaccines, flea and tick products, heartworm preventative—all destroyed. I tended not to keep a lot of inventory on hand, as most of my clients could order from my online pharmacy, but aside from what I had in my car, everything else was ruined. It represented a substantial monetary loss, and I'd been on the phone reporting it to my insurance agency as the entourage from the sheriff's office had arrived.

I don't think I'd ever seen Joe so contained and yet so angry at the same time. His fury was like a volcano. Slight indications of disturbance on the surface with the hint of dangerous lava and a possible explosion beneath. The tic of a muscle in his jaw suggested eruption might be closer to the surface than he'd care to admit, however.

"How are you doing?" He gave my arm a gentle squeeze that was at odds with his thunderous expression.

The image of the torn photo of Major came to mind, and I blinked furiously. I would *not* cry, damn it. Oddly enough, Joe's outrage had the effect of tempering mine.

"Okay, I guess. As well as anyone would be doing after such a violation. Whoever did this had an axe to grind. My guess is Brad Taylor or Derek Ellis."

My pragmatic response seemed to settle Joe, and his anger cooled into concentrated purpose. "No angry clients? No upset boyfriends?"

I snorted at the thought of my generating enough resentment to trigger a would-be lover into this kind of attack.

"Most of my clients appreciate that not only am I just about the only game in town, but I'm also doing my best. That goes a long way toward soothing even the most distraught client. As for boyfriends—" This time I couldn't help but laugh. "Let's just say that's extremely unlikely."

As in, I'd actually have to have one in the first place.

"Are you missing anything? What about controlled drugs?"

I nodded, already expecting this question. "To the best of my knowledge, about a hundred in cash that I hadn't taken to the bank yet. As for controlled drugs, I limit that to euthanasia solution and script the rest out. Whoever did this didn't find my safe—I keep it in the hayloft in the barn. I checked the contents, and everything is there." I hesitated and then went on. "However, I'm pretty sure the letter from Amanda that her lawyer gave me is gone. I left it on the kitchen table, and I can't find it anywhere."

"Well, *that's* not suspicious at all."

I welcomed the return of Joe's drawl. "Which is why my two favorite candidates for this are Taylor and Ellis. You might want to do a handwriting comparison between them and the messages left in the bathroom."

"Don't tell me how to do my job, Ginge."

"Don't call me Ginge."

Our exchange might have sounded acrimonious, but I think we understood each other. While he went off to examine the extent of the damage, I called Lloyd and explained I'd had a problem with vaccine spoilage, and it would be a few days before I could get more vaccines in. He took it in stride but reminded me the pups would go to new homes soon, and he needed to get that first vaccination done. I promised I'd let him know as soon as possible when the replacements had arrived and then called the distributor to beg for a rush delivery.

I could have told Lloyd what really happened, but something made me keep mum on the subject. Joe's people weren't likely to talk. It was best that the break-in stayed out of the local gossip network for now.

After what seemed like hours, Joe found me sitting under a tree, composing an email to my insurance agency, listing the damage and lost inventory as best I could. Remy jumped up to greet him with delight. I merely looked up at his approach.

He came to a stop to stare down at me. "The lab tech is just about done. We'll let you have copies of the photographs to share with your insurance agent."

As the quality of the photographs was likely to be better than mine, I thanked him.

"Chances are the perp wore gloves, but we can run any fingerprints we found through the system. We printed you the other day. Anyone else been in your house that we need to rule out?"

Well, *that* was an embarrassing question.

"My mother has been here a few times."

I hated to think about the fallout that would occur when she found out about the break-in and hoped her prints were in the system already as part of the National Child-Protection Act.

Joe's nod was very matter of fact. He took out a small notebook and pen. "Anyone else?"

I thought hard about who else would have been in my house and came up empty. "Er, no."

"No one?" The wrinkle on Joe's forehead proclaimed his disbelief. "You haven't had anyone over for dinner or… whatever?"

My cheeks couldn't get any hotter. "You've seen what a dump the place is. Even if I had the time and energy for socializing, I'd hardly invite anyone here. It's a real deal-breaker if I ever saw one."

His frown suggested he still didn't get it, so I elaborated. "Most successful professionals don't live in a broken-down double-wide."

The implication being I was *not* a successful professional.

When he spoke, there was no sign of a drawl whatsoever. "The people who measure the level of your success based on the kind of house you live in aren't the sort of people you should care about."

Easy for him to say. Or maybe not, considering at the moment he was camping in an RV. "Whatever," I said. "That doesn't change the fact I don't invite people over."

"No one?"

His gaze seemed to bore into me, asking all kinds of questions I preferred to leave unanswered. The best I could do was obfuscate. "If I want company, I go to someone else's house."

His eyes narrowed, but then he flipped the notebook shut and pocketed it. "I take it you'll stay with your mom tonight?"

"No way."

Okay, the words that came out of my mouth were more emphatic than that. At Joe's raised eyebrows, I hurried on.

"The last thing I want is for my mother to know about this. If I refuse to get a gun now, she'll arm herself like she's going to war and move in with me. I'll never hear the end of it unless I buy some darned assault rifle and enough ammunition to take out the entire town. Besides, I have this whole mess to clean up."

"Do you want help?"

His offer sucked all the air out of my lungs, and for a moment, I couldn't respond. I pictured the two of us working side by side; the company making short work of a miserable task. Maybe we'd order pizza. I'd open a bottle of wine (provided it hadn't been smashed) and we'd sit on the porch watching the sunset and talking about old times. I tried to imagine him picking through the detritus of my life—one in which I'd fallen short of all my goals—and the thought was unbearable.

"No, thanks. I appreciate the offer, but I've got this."

The look he gave me nearly pierced my defenses, but I knew I was making the right call.

I didn't hang about waiting for the lab techs to finish processing the house. I locked Ming in the large catio I'd had built onto the back of the house for the feral cats to stay while recovering from being spayed or neutered and took Remy with me as I drove into town for supplies. I'd have left him behind to watch the place, only there broken glass lay everywhere that I needed to get up first. I'd need lots of garbage bags, as well as a new mop and broom to deal with the mess, and I had to replace the ruined food, or no one would get anything to eat for dinner. I needed a few things to wear as well, at least until I could replace the bulk of what had been destroyed. As much as I hated the idea, shopping at the supercenter in Clearwater had to come first. As I made the drive, I could see where the convenience of a similar shopping center in Greenbrier might be considered worth it by many.

I returned from the store to discover the cleaning fairies had been busy in my absence. They had swept the kitchen. The flour, pasta, and dried cereal had been bagged, which now sat in neat rows beside the door. Someone had found my old vacuum cleaner and vacuumed up the broken glass. I'm surprised they got it to work. That Electrolux had belonged to my grandmother and was older than I was. An attempt had been made to remove the writings on the bathroom walls but had failed for lack of industrial strength cleaning agents. Chances were I would have to repaint it, anyway. The only room that had been left uncleaned was my bedroom, and for that I was grateful. No need for the cleaning fairies to poke through my ratty clothing and see for themselves that my fashion sense tended towards Early Thrift Store. In fact, if my mother got wind of this, she would stalk Goodwill for replacement items and the odds were high I wouldn't like her choices. For some reason, my mother bought me clothing that looked best on an eighty-year-old grandmother or a middle-aged farmer. Nothing in between.

But the generosity of the cleaning fairies had left me with very little to do. My mind boggled slightly at the idea of either Frank or Holly pitching in with the cleaning, but they must have. There's no way it could have been done that quickly otherwise. Even the remnants of all my medical supplies had been bagged and set aside for disposal. After I finished restoring order to my bedroom, I unlocked the chain from the catio and brought Ming back inside. Painting could wait.

I couldn't settle, however. In the morning, I'd call Doc Amos and see if he'd let me borrow enough vaccines to do Lloyd's litter. I'd replace them when my order came in. No point calling until then, however. Doc was probably long gone for the day. The thought of cooking dinner held no appeal. I didn't have a working television and reading only reminded me of the library of favorite books I'd have to replace. A big juicy cheeseburger from Sue's diner—the one I'd refused earlier today instead of something healthier—called my name. After that, I'd go to the town meeting.

My mailbox was at the end of my drive, and as I came level with it, I rolled down my window and collected my mail. Some flyers, some bills, but one plain white envelope was unmarked. Knowing clients sometimes left payments this way, I tore open the letter. Inside was a single sheet of paper.

When I unfolded it, the page bore a single sentence in New Times Roman created by anyone who had access to Windows Office and a printer.

If you know what's good for you, SELL.

Chapter Fifteen

SUE'S HAD BEEN CROWDED. I guess a lot of people had the same idea about grabbing a bite to eat before going to the meeting because the place had been jam-packed. Kim and Sue both looked run off their feet, and the food took longer than usual to arrive. I'd ended up taking a seat at the counter because all the tables were full. As soon as I'd eaten, I left a big tip and navigated the seated diners for the exit.

Because of the lack of a meeting room of sufficient size, the Town Council met in the library as a rule. It was a good thing I decided to walk because the library parking lot was full when I got there. People milled about the entrance to the building as I walked up. The heat inside was stifling, and I shed my coat as soon as I could. Experience told me it was best to hang on to it, so I folded it over my arm and made my way into the meeting.

It was already practically standing room only. Beth Ann Carlson and her husband stopped me when I would have made my way to an empty seat.

"Doc!" Beth Ann's hair was cut short in the back to angle down toward her chin, with tall spikes in the rear, and streaked in heavy bands of blonde and cinnamon. Her voice pierced the din of the room like a foghorn. "Is it true? Did you inherit all of Amanda Kelly's millions?"

I could never decide if Dave Carlson had little to say or if he figured it wasn't worth competing with his wife for airtime. His lined face bore the perpetual expression of a sad Basset Hound, and I'd been tempted in the past to offer him a dog biscuit to gauge his reaction. From the way he leaned forward to hear my response, for once he seemed interested in what his wife had to say.

"Millions might be stretching it a bit." Or not. I hadn't paid all that much attention to the extent of Amanda's holdings when I'd thought they were going to Brad.

"Then you *are*." Beth Ann's squeal would have made dogs howl in the next county. "What are you going to do with all that lovely money? Are you going to build a clinic? I think you should take a nice vacation. Someone said she had a villa in Italy. I'd love to spend a couple of weeks in Tuscany." She eyed her husband as if he would suddenly volunteer to take her.

I'm pretty sure I would have remembered an Italian villa.

Dave suddenly spoke up. "You should sell off that place of hers to Riverside. Too much for one person to keep up, and that land's worth more as part of a parcel than you'd ever get for it at any other time."

His gaze bored into me, and I recalled the Carlsons had land out toward Amanda's place. They'd bought it intending to build a house, but then the economy had been driven over a cliff, and their plans to build went on hold as everyone attempted to claw their way back out of the hole.

"I can't do anything at the moment until the will is probated—" I began, only to be interrupted when Jed Blankenship joined in the conversation uninvited.

"Well, how long is that going to take?"

In all the years I'd known him, Jed's grizzled chin was never entirely clean-shaven, nor did he ever grow a beard. Wiry gray hair had receded into a ring around his head, and his red-veined nose suggested he was fond of booze. There'd been a mousy-gray wife in the past, but she'd left one night without warning and no one ever asked about her. I'd been reluctant to see any of Jed's animals by myself when I first moved back to the area, but he'd contacted me early on about the best way to bottle raise a litter of kittens he'd found, and he'd been a good client ever since. Looks *could* be deceiving.

"I wish I knew." I held one hand palm up with a shrug. "You know how it is with lawyers."

They seemed to be the magic words because the others nodded and made noises of agreement. Beth Ann invited me to sit with them, but I saw Laney waving from a few rows up and she had an empty seat beside her. I thanked Beth Ann for the offer and made my way up the aisle to where Laney was sitting.

"I am so sorry. I forgot to call you about grabbing a bite to eat." Hastily, I explained about the break-in as she moved her coat to make room for me.

"That's horrible!" She leaned over my phone as I showed her some pictures. "There's some real hate behind this. What do the police say?"

Both our conversation and the photographs drew the unashamed attention of those sitting around us, so I put my phone away before our seatmates could join in the conversation and lowered my voice. "That I should go stay with my mom for a while. No thanks. What are you doing here, anyway?"

She spread her hands as if to say she didn't know and responded quietly as well. "Nothing better to do, I guess. I overheard someone talking about the meeting at the diner, and it occurred to me this land deal might have something to do with Amanda's death."

"Would she have sold, do you think?"

Laney leaned back in the hard plastic chair. "No, I don't think so. She loved that place. Loved the view, the sense of peace she had there."

"What if Derek had found her? You said you thought she might pick up and run again."

"Running would entail more than selling her home." Laney shook her head the more she thought about it. "She would have had to re-invent herself all over again, and her artistic style is—was—too distinctive to hide under another name. It would have forced her to give up painting altogether, and I can't see her doing that."

"Maybe she was thinking about confronting Derek. Divorcing him once and for all. What if *she* was the one who invited Brad to see her? What if she needed his help to get rid of Derek?"

"Given how shocked he was at the reading of the will, I can't believe Brad knew about Derek. If Amanda had told him about Derek at all, Brad would know how much she feared him, and that certainly would have come up at the reading if he thought Derek might get a slice of the pie. Are you looking for someone?"

Laney's question caught me mid-crane as I scanned the audience, and I grimaced. "Looking for Brad. I thought he might have had the same idea as you."

No sign of him. Or my mother, for that matter. Thank God. Hopefully, she wouldn't turn up waving printouts on the statistics of rabies cases in the county for the last fifty years. I did, however, spy the suits in the front row and pointed them out to Laney.

"See that guy up front? The one in the middle. I'm pretty sure he met Brad at the restaurant the same night he was there with that Markham woman."

Laney might have said something else, only the meeting was called to order.

If you've never been to a Town Council meeting, count yourself lucky. They tend to consist of interminable discussions of matters that hold little interest to the average person. Having sat through numerous meetings myself, I know in theory they deal with minor matters first so as to clear the decks for the main topic, but I suspect the real reason for the order of business is to bore the audience into leaving.

After a bit, Laney pulled out her phone and began scrolling through her various social media accounts. Though I wasn't big into social media—seriously, what would I post?—I checked my messages and saw that my mother had emailed me hours ago.

She wasn't big into email. In her typical, terse manner, with no opening salutation or explanation, she listed the names of property owners in the area of the planned subdivision, which included the Carlsons, Blair Kendall, and Jed Blankenship, among others, including several Linkous families. I wasn't aware Jed had land in that area, but lots of farmers had property that wasn't connected to their primary farm. My mother had also, bless her heart, included several maps of the proposed subdivision. She'd ended her email with CALL ME in all caps. I fired off a brief email thanking her for the information and reminding her I was at the town meeting and that I would call her when I got home before I silenced my phone. It surprised me she hadn't called already, and I didn't want her to interrupt the meeting.

"What's that?" Laney peered over my phone as I opened the first of the attachments.

"The planned Riverside subdivision. Look at this." I scrolled through until I hit designs of the housing blueprints. "These homes can't possibly go for less than three to four hundred K. Who exactly do they think is going to be living there? Four bedrooms and two baths on a postage-sized lot with your neighbors so close they can look in your kitchen window from their back deck."

"People tired of living in big cities, that's who. I caught a plane from Atlanta to Charlotte and then rented a car to drive up from there. Took me almost three hours to get here. But I could have paid extra for a commuter flight into Birchwood and driven from there, only I don't like prop engine planes. Still, what's that, forty minutes? An hour? There are people who'd rather drive an hour to work to come home to someplace pretty at the end of the day than have a shorter commute to live in town. Besides, Amanda told me that there are a lot of New York and New Jersey transplants here now because their money goes farther."

She was right. Several newest middle-aged and senior clients had sold their homes up north and moved into the area because the winters were kinder and they could buy land with a view for with the money they'd made on selling their little houses and apartments.

"They'll cut down every tree in sight and then name the streets after the wildlife that no longer exists there." I continued scrolling through the designs. The subdivision's plans covered a much larger area than I'd realized. And Amanda's land made up a prime portion of it. Without it, the subdivision would fall through, and Riverside would locate it somewhere else. Possibly not in Greenbrier at all.

I have to say one thing for the mayor: she ran a tight ship. When she opened the floor to questions and Tom Feldman stood to bring up the Riverside development, she quickly quashed him.

"Now, Tom." Her smile was polite, but firm. "You know we have other business to see to first." She lifted a placating hand when a murmur rumbled through the crowd. "And yes, I realize most of you are here to weigh in on the proposed development and what it might mean for Greenbrier. But first let me remind you that a Council meeting is not the same as a public hearing—"

The murmur rose in volume and developed an underlying tone of anger.

Mayor Austin cracked her wooden gavel on the desk in front of her. "Order, please."

The room fell silent, save for the restless shifting and occasional cough that went with any crowd of this size.

Mayor Austin passed her gaze over the room for a moment until she appeared to be satisfied with the audience's cooperation.

"That said, it is my intention to open the floor for public comment after the Council's business is done. The sooner we all take our seats and let us get on with it, the sooner we can hear what you have to say."

Laney leaned in to whisper, "So I take it there was a public hearing on the development already?"

"Late last year," I whispered back. "But that was before the additional planned development of a shopping center."

I'd ignored the notice for the hearing when it had landed in my mailbox. Subdivisions went up all the time. But to tie in the development of a planned subdivision with a shopping center was new. It made sense, though. The new residents would demand more choices than they could get at Bucky's grocery store, which closed at 9 p.m. every night except Saturday, when it stayed open until ten.

The Council finished their business at long last. I snuck a glance at my watch. It was getting on toward 9 p.m. The meeting couldn't last much longer. The lack of this being a formal public hearing meant the mayor could limit how long people voiced their opinions. I decided to stick it out a bit longer.

She held the floor open for a half hour. Most of the speakers were in favor of the subdivision, repeating themselves in pointing out that the land was largely unused and not particularly valuable, and the construction work would be a boon to the local economy. Several people nudged their neighbors and looked at me during these speeches. The weight of their collective scrutiny was enough to make me wish the floor would open up and swallow me. One woman expressed concerns about the nature of the new residents, and though she didn't come out and say it, you could tell she questioned whether they would be the "right sort of people." Judging by the murmur that went round the room after she spoke, she wasn't the only one.

Finally, the mayor stood. "Most of you know there is a planned development in the Potter's Ridge area outside town. That development has met with the Planning Commission's approval, and providing the sale of various properties goes through, building will begin in that area as proposed."

She leveled a cool look at the audience, and I could have sworn that last shot was directed at me.

"But there's much more at stake than just a few houses in a new subdivision." With a single flick of her hand, she waved away the thirty or so homes planned. "At long last, Greenbrier is growing again. I'm sure you all know with any change, there can be growing pains. But there are advantages to consider as well. The influx of new residents will attract a supercenter, which in turn will draw in other chain stores and restaurants. These same residents will demand entertainment, which means a movie theater, and more. A community center, complete with swimming pool, perhaps. Or a golf club."

She pointed to someone near the front of the room. "Becky. Just last week, you were telling me how hard it was to get anyone to work at your store. If there was more for our young people to do in the area, they'd be more likely to stay."

"Or these new stores could run me right out of business." Becky stood to make her point. I recognized her from the dress store downtown—a shop I'm sad to say, I'd never actually been in. "I'm having a hard enough time making ends meet as it is. I can't compete with a corporation."

Another ripple of agreement circled the room.

Mayor Austin shook her head. "You're looking at it all wrong. More residents mean more shoppers. More business means more money in the local economy. We could finally fund the new middle school we've needed for so long. Better school systems means a better chance of pulling industry back to the area. Believe me, I know things how tough things have been since the Baxter plant closed. But we stand a better chance of getting another textiles company to move in if we have something to offer them." She shuffled some papers and brought one to the forefront of her stack. "Anyone else? If not, we'll adjourn for the evening. A public hearing will be scheduled for the future planned shopping center as things proceed."

The pull to stand and say something was strong. Laney must have noticed because she said, "Are you thinking about speaking?"

Instead, I gathered up my coat. Around us, others stood and prepared to disperse. "What can I say? As a business owner, I should be behind the expansion and developments one hundred percent. The mayor's right. The kids need a reason to stay in the area after high school and right now, Greenbrier's got little to offer. If I object to the projects Riverside has planned, then it makes me look like I'm against progress, or worse, diversity. And if I refuse to sell..."

"You don't have to tell me. I've seen some of the hostile glances tossed this way."

Even as she spoke, a couple of the people nearest to us looked as though they wanted to say something to me. "I also got a threatening letter in the mail this afternoon."

"What?" Laney was shocked. "On top of the break-in? What did it say?"

"Shhh." I warned as the person ahead of us in the row toward the exit looked back at us. "I'll show you later. Ugh. I hate this. These are my clients. My neighbors. They're all looking at me like I'm getting into a lifeboat while the Titanic is sinking." I shouldered into my coat, taking care not to knock into anyone around me. "I wish Amanda had never made me her heir."

"I'm sure Brad would be more than happy to take her estate off your hands." Laney's voice was as dry as a Martini. "Oh, come on. Don't look at me like that. How about I buy you a drink?"

A drink sounded good. It had been a long day and I could use a little sympathy right about now. "You're on."

We made our way through the largely stalled out crowd, easing around clumps of people still talking to join the flow headed for the exit.

"Yoo-hoo! Dr. Reese."

I stopped to see the mayor making her way toward me with the man in the suit in tow. "There's someone here who'd like to meet you. Mr. Wainwright, this is the person I was telling you about. Dr. Ginny Reese. Ginny, Mr. Wainwright is with Riverside."

The suit thrust his hand toward me. "Please. Call me Steve."

I don't like shaking hands as a rule. Most of the time, I have to make sure mine aren't covered with some noxious substance. I also dislike the need to gauge the strength with which to respond. Many men offer a limp token shake, but there are others who are hand-crushers. Just Call Me Steve was of this variety, so when he gripped my hand as though he were Tiger Woods picking up a nine iron, I returned the favor with equal force. I had the pleasure of seeing Wainwright's eyes widen before I released his hand. "In a manner of speaking, we've met. I've received your emails, Mr. Wainwright."

"Quite some grip you have there, Doctor." He laughed as though he found this funny, but the amusement didn't touch his eyes. "Must be working with all those animals."

"Yes."

He waited to see if I was going to add to that statement, and the pause became slightly uncomfortable before he laughed again. "Er, yes. Quite." His expression sobered as if a switch flipped and he said, "I was so sorry to hear about Amanda Kelly's death. I understand the two of you were close."

I decided I'd make him work for it. "Yes."

This close, I upped the value of his suit to at least two thousand dollars. How could anyone spend what amounted to a house payment around here on an item of clothing? The narrowing of his eyes suggested he'd done his own assessment, and I'd come up wanting. His sharklike smile implied he'd eaten far tougher opponents for breakfast.

After a beat, I added, "This is Laney Driver. Ms. Kelly's agent."

Another round of handshaking. As Laney didn't wince, I presume he didn't treat her to the crush. After exchanging the usual pleasantries, Wainwright cleared his throat. "I know this may be a bad time to bring this up, but as Ms. Kelly's heir, I would very much like to talk with you about her property on Potter's Ridge. As you know from my email, we were in negotiations for the land before her death."

I exchanged a look with Laney before replying. "Do you have that in writing?"

I thought I managed a delicate balance between polite skepticism and outright disbelief.

His nostrils flared at my insinuation that he was lying. If he'd been a bull, I'd have been carefully making my way out of the pen right now. "As with all the landowners along Potter's Ridge, we'd had both informal discussions and made some formal offers."

"Making an offer is not the same as closing a deal, Mr. Wainwright."

"He knows that, Dr. Reese."

The mayor's disappointing tone weighed as heavily on me as if it had been my mother's, and I'm ashamed to say it took the wind out of my sails.

Wainwright pressed the advantage the mayor had given him. "Nevertheless, we'd verbally agreed on a deal. I believe Ms. Kelly had strong reasons for wanting to leave the area? Regardless, she intended to sell to us." Wainwright cocked his head slightly and gave me the smile among friends. He took a card out of his wallet and extended it. "Come now, Ms. Reese. I'm sure you want to honor your friend's last wishes."

I took a step back. "I'm not sure what those last wishes are," I snapped. "And I certainly will not be pressured into making a decision at this very moment."

Wainwright wasn't used to hearing the word no. Though ostensibly still smiling, his lips retracted to show teeth. When I refused to accept his card, he flipped it back into his wallet. "No one is asking you to decide right now. Merely to extend me the courtesy of a meeting. Riverside has a lot invested in this deal. I personally want very much to see it go through. I'm willing to offer whatever it takes to get you on board. The price I named before? Add another hundred thousand. Perhaps we could discuss it tomorrow?"

The mayor flinched slightly and skewed her head around to look at Wainwright as though she couldn't believe her ears.

There was no easy way to put it. "I'm happy to speak with you, but I feel it would be premature. The will must be probated first before I can make any decisions regarding the property."

"Of course. We understand." His shrug was very Gallic in nature. He lifted his shoulders with his arms open wide and his palms turned up. "When you're in the construction business, you get used to experiencing delays. Waiting a few months for the right piece of property is no big deal. However, a verbal commitment to the sale when possible would go a long way toward—"

"I'm sorry. I don't want to give you a false impression here. I don't know how long it will take to probate. You see, Amanda's brother intends to contest the will, and I'm told what should be a straightforward process might take years as a result."

"What?" Mayor Austin didn't *quite* screech.

Wainwright's expression turned thunderous. His nice-guy veneer cracked and revealed the ruthless man beneath. "I think you'll find I've been more than generous with you. If this is some hillbilly move in order to hold out for a better offer—"

Mayor Austin looked like an angler who thought his catch might break the line. "I'm sure this is just a temporary setback, Mr. Wainwright. Isn't that so, Dr. Reese?"

She pleaded at me with her penciled-in eyebrows, and I took pity on her. "The lawyer who wrote up the will assures me that Mr. Taylor doesn't have a case."

"There, you see?" The mayor spoke in a painfully cheerful voice, but it seemed to have a placating effect on Wainwright, who smoothed his tie and nodded.

"Judging from his reaction at the reading of the will, it might take Mr. Taylor some time to accept this fact." Laney spoke with bland unconcern. I glanced at her suspiciously. Nothing but innocence was writ on her face.

"Yes, well, we must be off. Nice meeting you, Mr. Wainwright. Laney, are you ready?"

"Quite," she said with a wicked smile.

Chapter Sixteen

"Are you really going to sell Amanda's place to that developer?"

We'd just taken our seats in the bar, and Laney hit me with the hard question right off the bat. With a sigh, I put my phone on the table between us and pulled up the maps my mother had sent me.

"See this?" I tapped on the image of Amanda's property. "That's a huge section of the proposed development. It's the best piece of property in the lot. How can I *not* sell it? Everyone in town will hate me if I don't."

The bar was crowded. It looked like most of the people at the meeting had decided to grab a drink before heading home. I spied the rest of the suits seated at a table near the window, and hoped Wainwright wasn't planning to join them.

"Who cares what everyone thinks?" Laney caught the attention of Ricky, the bartender, and he indicated someone would be over in a moment.

"*I* care. I can't run a business if everyone refuses to see me because I let the town drown in stagnation while I make out like a bandit with the inheritance."

"They'll get over it." Laney snagged a couple of pretzels out of the dish on the table and popped one in her mouth. "And if they don't, honey, you've got the money to go somewhere else, start over. Do whatever you want. Unless there's something keeping you here."

"My mom's here. She's getting on up there in age. Someone should keep an eye on her."

"Don't you have family? Are you the only one who can help her out?" Laney's arch look sliced through my objections.

She was right. I'd put in my time taking care of my dad when he needed it. Hopefully, it would be years before my mom would need that same level of care. In the meantime, I could get on with my life. Travel. Have fun. Meet someone. My days didn't have to be a constant battle to make ends meet, leaving me with no time or energy for anything else.

An image of Remy's forlorn face peering through the chain-link fence of a kennel sprang to mind. I couldn't just slam him and Ming into a boarding facility and walk away. Not for more than a vacation.

Not to mention Joe was back in town.

I made a noise of frustration and rubbed my hands over my face. "This would be a lot easier if I were a selfish witch who didn't give a rat's ass about anything except what I wanted. Or if I knew what I wanted. I love Amanda's place. It's ten thousand times nicer than the dump I live in and I'd be lying if I said I didn't envy her that lovely property. But it will always be Amanda's place in my head, you know?"

Laney twitched her lips to one side in sympathy. "Yeah, I hear you. But you could redecorate. Make it your own."

"It would be nice to have all my animals in one place for a change," I agreed. "Horses, cats, dog all under one roof. No more running all over the county to take care of critters."

"The mayor's wrong, you know. The development won't save the town. It will kill it off. The town will become something else, but it won't be Greenbrier. I'm not saying that's a bad thing." Laney rested one elbow on the table, her fingers eloquent as they shrugged for her. "But most of the people here are looking at the short-term."

"What else can they do? Most of the townspeople are desperate." I could sympathize. If it weren't for Amanda's wealth, I'd be in the same boat.

"We're talking about you, though. The thing about money is it gives you options. Maybe this little burg wouldn't seem as much of a ball and chain now." She tapped the table in front of me with one long, blue nail. "Your problem is you're a caregiver. It's hard-wired into you."

"You say that like it's a bad thing."

"Being a caregiver is bad if you never take time for yourself to recharge or if you try to carry the entire world on your shoulders. When the plane is going down, you have to put the oxygen mask on your own face first before you can help the others around you."

"Huh." I grabbed a couple of pretzels for myself. "How do you have me pegged so well, anyway?"

"It's no secret around here you came back here to nurse your dad through his last illness. Everyone knows you're a soft touch for stray cats or a hard-luck story." Laney ate another pretzel and lifted an eyebrow as if she dared me to argue.

I picked up my phone and adjusted the image before holding it out to Laney. "See that? My property abuts up to the planned subdivision. They even approached me about letting run-off from the division go through my land. If they'd made me an offer, I'd have snapped it up in a heartbeat." I explained the zoning issue that had made it impossible to open my planned practice there. "But once I realized I couldn't run a business there, I couldn't sell the place because after I bought my house, they changed the housing laws and my home doesn't meet the new criteria. It just missed getting grandfathered in, and I can't afford to upgrade it to pass. That would have been a moot point if the developers had offered to buy it. They would have bulldozed the house down, anyway."

"But the development didn't want it?" Laney craned her neck to look at the satellite map. "From the looks of this, your property is much better suited to building. You don't have the spectacular view, but you've got lots of flat land and most of it's already been cleared. Why on earth didn't Riverside want it?"

"Zoning." I sighed. "It's zoned agricultural. And believe me, I've tried jumping through the hoops in the county. The ordinances are a bear."

"Yeah, but you'd think with enough money..."

She was right. Riverside's deep pockets probably would allow them to get the zoning they desired. I shook my head. "I guess they really wanted land with a view."

Wainwright entered the bar. He paused at the entrance long enough to shoot a burning glare in my direction and then spotted his party. I hoped they'd stay put at their table.

One of the wait staff came to take our orders.

"I'll have a Cosmo," Laney said to the server. "What about you, Ginny?"

Normally a red wine kind of gal, I decided the day called for something stronger. "Whiskey sour."

"Jack, Beam, or Crown?" The server asked.

"Crown Royal, please." I preferred the smoother taste. As the server turned to leave, I called out, "Know what? Make it a double."

"Rough day." Laney's smile was sympathetic.

"You said it."

"Tell me about the threatening letter."

There wasn't much to tell. I showed her the scan I'd made of the letter, and she commiserated with me over the fact that anyone with access to a printer could have produced it. "Anyone who wants to see this development go through could have sent it," she pointed out. "Your inheritance was common knowledge at the diner this afternoon."

Our server returned with our drinks in record time.

"Who do you think was behind the break-in?" Laney removed the lime wedge from the brim of her glass and took a sip of her pinkish drink. "Someone looking for drugs?"

I knocked back a slug of my whiskey sour and appreciated the warmth it sent through me. Perhaps ordering a double had been a bad idea. It was stronger than I was used to. "I make it a point to keep as few controlled drugs in my inventory as possible and most people know that. As far as I can tell, none of my supplies were taken, just spoiled. The only thing I know is missing is some cash and the letter from Amanda."

"What letter?"

"Oh, that's right. Mr. Carter gave it to me after everyone else left. Amanda left me a letter explaining why she'd chosen me as her heir."

Laney looked expectant, so I gave her the highlights. Embarrassed when I finished, I took a big gulp of my drink and hurried on. "Anyway, no one but Mr. Carter knew about that letter, so it had to have been a theft of opportunity, but why take it? Who'd want it?"

Laney nodded. "Exactly. It wouldn't have meant anything to most people. There's also the extent of the damage. That was more than a break-in. There's a lot of hostility behind that kind of destruction."

"Which is why Brad or Derek get my vote for the perpetrators. What's the situation at Mossy Creek, anyway? Do they lock the doors at a certain time?"

Laney didn't quite make the leap. Confusion furrowed her brow as she answered my question. "The back door has a keypad for anyone who needs to come in after they lock the doors for the night. They change the code after anyone checks out. But what does that have to do with your break-in?"

"Nothing. I was thinking more along the lines of the night Amanda was murdered."

"Ah." Comprehension dawned. "Well, like I said, I didn't see Brad until the morning after I checked in. He could have been out or in his room, and I wouldn't have known the difference. I was beat, and after a glass of wine I fell asleep over a book in bed."

My mother's voice in my head added, "Or so she says..." but I ignored it. "What about sales of Amanda's artwork? Did you find anything out of the ordinary going on there?"

"It seems Brad attempted to sell one of Amanda's early works a few weeks ago. Under her real name, so probably something she'd painted for the family and left behind. He couldn't get nearly the amount of money he wanted without branding it as a 'primitive Amanda Kelly', and I know she would have blown a gasket over that."

"Hah. Maybe that's why he came to town. Maybe she demanded to see him." Another thought occurred to me. "Crap. If Brad forced the public connection, it's possible Derek found out about it, and he *did* know where Amanda was."

"Speak of the devil." Laney sipped her drink and nodded toward the door. "Look who just walked in."

Turning around to stare was probably stupid, but I did so anyway. Derek Ellis stood at the entrance to the bar, surveying the room like a lion on the veldt. We made eye contact, and his gaze bristled with hostility. I turned away to nurse my drink.

"Look out. He's coming over."

Laney's warning sent my blood pressure up, but there was nothing I could do but see what would happen.

"Well, well." Derek came to a stop at our table. "Two ... ladies ... out for a drink together. Guess Brad was right about you two."

I looked at Laney. "Does anyone really say, 'well, well' anymore? Who writes his dialog?"

Laney snorted into her drink.

"Heard there was break-in at your place. Hope nothing was damaged."

The malignant glee in his voice was impossible to ignore. He did it, all right.

I drained the rest of my glass in a long, single pull and leaned back in my chair. "Funny, that's not public knowledge. Which begs the question, how do *you* know about it?"

A lock of dark hair fell over his forehead. At any other time, with any other man, I'd have found it attractive. The only emotion I felt for Derek right now was a simmering anger combined with a need to get as far away from him as possible. Laney and I still had to get back to our cars, and this man posed an enormous threat to both of us.

"Oh, there are plenty of ways I could have found out. Maybe I have a police scanner. Or maybe I'm banging the dispatcher at the sheriff's office."

"Joan?" Incredulity cranked the pitch of my voice and I had to stifle a guffaw. "She's happily married with three grandchildren."

Amusement was the wrong tack to take with Derek. He wanted me cowering in my chair, and I wasn't sticking to the script. He placed one hand on the table and leaned in to growl at me.

"Or maybe I know who did it. Did you ever think about that?"

"Leave her alone." Laney's voice came out flat and angry, and when I flicked a glance at her, I saw she was videoing the interaction. To my dismay, she wasn't the only one. Several people had their cell phones pointed in my direction.

"Stay out of this if you know what's good for you." Derek didn't even spare her a glance.

"I *have* thought about it." My voice cracked when I spoke. Darn it, the last thing I wanted was for him to know his intimidation tactics were working. I cleared my throat and added, "I've shared my opinion with the Sheriff."

"Sheriff Donegan won't always be around to protect you." He brushed the side of my face with his free hand, smiling at the way I flinched.

"Hey!" Ricky called out from behind the counter. "You okay, Doc? Shall I throw the bum out?"

The hand that had just brushed my face sported a set of fresh scratches across the back of it. I recognized the pattern: four angry parallel lines that typified your average cat attack. He'd been in my house. He'd been scratched by Ming.

Before I could respond, Derek levied another bolt at me. "Unlike Brad, I'm not afraid of your dog, either."

What did he just say?

I lifted my eyes to meet his gaze full on. My heart thundered in my chest. "Are you threatening my dog?"

"Dog. Cat. Whatever." His smile said it all. I could almost hear the snap of Ming's jaw and realized the Siamese had a damn good reason for being standoffish and aggressive. "You'd better keep your mutt out of my way."

For a moment, I couldn't quite understand what he'd said over the booming in my head. His words became clear. I realized I was hearing my heartbeat.

Boom. Boom. Boom.

Derek sneered at me, his expression cocky and disdainful. He reveled in this moment, the one where I understood his intent and knew he'd found my weak spot and meant to exploit it.

You wanted my attention? Well, now you have it.

My hand shot out. My fingers connected with Derek's crotch and closed through his jeans with a vise-like grip. I stood, lifting him by his privates at the same time he pinwheeled his arms for balance and let out an unmanly screech.

"You're threatening my dog? You're threatening my *dog*?" The voice that came out of my mouth sounded more like Mark Ruffalo's Incredible Hulk than my own.

Derek fell backward on the nearest table as I continued to hoist him by his own petard, so to speak. Empty glasses careened to the floor in a shattering crash. He made a high-pitched keening cry as his arms flailed about.

"Get this straight. Don't you ever threaten me or my dog again, Derek Ellis," I snarled. "I can castrate a bull calf in under nine seconds, and I *don't* use anesthesia."

I might have imagined it, but I thought there was a collective wince and groan from the various onlookers, most of whom were now on their feet as well. At least one by-stander protectively dropped his hand to his groin. The three suits stood with their mouths open. I couldn't help it. I stared at Wainwright and curled a lip with a little tilt of my head.

I gave Derek a last squeeze for good measure, forcing another squeal from him before I let him go. My fingers were cramping anyway.

Derek lay sprawled on the table, gasping for air. Ricky had come out from behind the bar and stood next to me.

"What do I owe you?" I was proud of how calm I sounded.

Ricky cast me a glance, equal parts wariness and respect. "It's on the house."

"But—"

Laney took me by the arm. "He said it's on the house, Ginny. Come on, let's get out of here."

I made it halfway down the block before I had to bend over, hands on knees, and gulp several deep breaths of cool night air.

"Come on now. You can't collapse now." Laney tugged on my elbow. "Wonder Woman doesn't annihilate her enemies and then stand around pondering what havoc she's unleashed on Manhattan."

But I had to ponder. What had I just done?

Straightening, I said, "I seldom drink hard liquor."

"I can see why." Laney sounded admirably solemn, but amusement bubbled beneath her words.

"You're not going to share that video with anyone, are you?" I asked in a small, pitiful voice.

"I won't, but I can guarantee you, everyone else in the bar who filmed it has already uploaded it. Seriously, you were *amazing*."

I buried my face in my hands. "Darn it. I'm never going to get a date in this town again."

Chapter Seventeen

LANEY AND I HUNG out by our cars until I felt driving wasn't stupid. I hadn't had *that* much to drink. The confrontation with Derek had left me jittery and wired, as if I'd slammed back five or six espressos and then chased it with Jolt cola. A hard crash was in my future. I just hoped I'd be home when it hit.

Laney found a YouTube uplink titled "My Vet is a Bad-Ass" that already had two hundred hits and we watched it in my car. Seeing me drag Derek around by his crotch like *Xena: Warrior Princess* was appalling in a weirdly fascinating way.

"I don't see how you could do it. Lift him by his junk, I mean." Laney still sounded awestruck as she replayed the video a third time.

"A box of cat litter weighs forty pounds. A bag of grain weighs fifty." I thought about some of the other things I toted around on a regular basis. "A square bale of hay can weigh over seventy-five pounds." All winter long, I'd thrown bales of hay down from the loft at Amanda's and tossed them over the fence for the horses. "I cart around my tubs of medical supplies. I lift heavy dogs all the time."

"Still, I bet Derek weighs one-eighty, one-ninety, easy."

"Well, he had a vested interest in going in the same direction I was leading him."

Laney outright cackled at that. Her reaction was contagious and tugged laughter out of my tense, unhappy chest. It swept over us in waves, re-surging every time we looked at each other, until we finally subsided in snorts and giggles. I rubbed my eyes with the heels of my hands and contemplated the damage.

It wasn't good.

"This thing better not go viral. Oh my God. What if he has me arrested for assault?"

"Oh, you can count on it going viral." Laney's expression was hidden in the car's darkness, but the unspoken glee in her voice bubbled to the surface, anyway. "As for Derek pressing charges, he touched you first. That's clearly on video. Pretty sure the self-defense door is open. You were so darned fast." Her admiration was impossible to disguise. "It was like watching a snake strike."

"It was a bone-headed thing to do all the same." The more I thought about it, the less funny it seemed. "I humiliated him in public. I've made an enemy of him. If this thing goes viral, as you say, it will be even worse. Once he gets over the fact I stood up to him, he'll come gunning for me again."

I'd have to invest in an alarm system. I wouldn't be able to leave Remy in the car or put Ming in the catio. I'd have to warn my mother. Of course, if he came after *her*, he'd get what was coming to him.

"Or it might drive him to leave town. You never know. It could work in your favor."

"Only if he's allowed to leave town. Has Joe—the sheriff—said you could go home yet?"

"Joe, eh?" The headlights from a passing car briefly illuminated Laney's face, and her avid interest in my personal life was plain to see. When I didn't respond, she continued. "I asked during my interview when I could leave and all he said was not yet."

"Which means Derek has to stay as well. Great. A smart person doesn't smack a bear in the face without having an escape route planned."

"Oh, was that his face?" Laney said oh-so-innocently.

"Laugh it up. You were there to witness his humiliation. You clearly filmed the entire scene. He might assume you were the one who uploaded it. Don't be surprised if he comes after you, too."

"Okay, now you're scaring me."

"I hope so. Laney, I want you to be careful for the rest of your stay here. If anyone thinks you've been poking around..."

Eventually, my concern rubbed off on her and she stopped making jokes. We parted with a mutual warning to look over our shoulders at all times.

I couldn't bear the thought of speaking to my mother when I finally got home. I sent her a text saying I'd call her in the morning and crawled into bed.

I'm normally the lightest of sleepers. The patter of rain on the roof, the jingle of Remy's dog tags during the night, the hoot of an owl outside my window—any of these things would have woken me on a typical night. But the unaccustomed alcohol coming on top of several days of higher than usual stress must have hit me harder than expected and I was out like a light the moment my head touched my pillow.

I swam back to consciousness slowly and with great reluctance at Remy's persistent whining. "Five more minutes," I told him, pulling the pillow over my head.

He nudged my arm with his nose. When that failed to get me up, he punched me. Hard. You might think a dog can't punch a person, but believe me, when they drive their nose into you with the entire force of their body behind it, that's exactly what it feels like.

"Ow!" I sat up. "Damn it, Remy. Don't—"

In the faint light cast by the dial on my clock, I could make out a thick haze in the room. Remy barked sharply and began backing up toward the door, still barking for good measure. The scent of smoke, dense and suffocating, tried to smother me, and I brought my arm up over my face to quell a violent cough.

My house was on fire.

This was another one of those fearful scenarios that I'd tried to prepare for, like riptides. The key to surviving a house fire was to have a plan in place, and I had one. My brain just stalled out for a moment in confusion. Why hadn't my smoke detectors gone off?

And then adrenaline pumped my blood through my veins and my emergency plan kicked in. It didn't hurt that my emergency plan for evacuating from a fire was similar to my plan for taking the dog out in the middle of the night or answering a late-night call from a client. I slid my feet into my shoes, which were always by my bed. I grabbed my phone and car keys from the dish on my nightstand.

"Lumos!" I shouted into the phone.

The flashlight switched on.

Smoke filled the room. I had to get Remy, Ming, and myself out of the house. Now.

Holding the phone like a magic wand in front of me, I followed an anxious Remy out into the hallway. The smoke was thicker in the hall, and heat radiated from somewhere. I looked up and saw that the ceiling was on fire. Flames licked their way above me like they were following a fuse to a detonator.

A hammering at my front door made me gasp, which set up another violent round of coughing.

"Ginny!"

It was Joe. He beat on my door and bellowed out my name.

"I'm coming!"

I was. I just had to grab the cat first.

Remy beat me to the spare room door and began pawing at the carpet beneath it as if he could dig a hole inside. A flaming panel from the ceiling fell just as I reached the door and Remy yelped and jumped back. My cheap little trailer, all plywood and paneling, had caught fire like a straw hut. In the seconds since Remy woke me, the fire was already out of control. I had to find the cat and get out before the ceiling caved in or we succumbed to smoke inhalation.

The doorknob to the spare room was warm to the touch, but it didn't melt my skin, so I grasped it and opened the door into a scene from straight from hell. The walls were already alight. The blast of heat forced me back from the door. Ming was nowhere in sight.

Somewhere behind me there was the crash of breaking glass.

Another ceiling panel came down almost on top of me, forcing me to back up into the hall. I steeled myself to dash into the room, but a burning beam fell across the door like the warning guard at a railroad crossing. I couldn't get in this way. I'd have to go around through the window.

"Ginny!"

Joe's voice was much closer now. I tried to respond, but all I could do was cough. Suddenly, Joe's firm grip had me by the arm, and before I knew it, I was being guided out of the house. The fresh air outside was indescribable. It soaked into my parched lungs like water to a dying man in the desert. I gulped it down, coughing with the effort to breathe. Behind us, the house burned like a funeral pyre.

Remy was there beside us, shepherding us along as we stumbled away from the house.

"Ming," I gasped, turning back.

"No." Joe stopped me with a grip of steel on my arms.

Remy looked at me and then back at the house. Like an arrow, he shot back into the building like a heat-seeking missile. No hesitation. No sound. Just a sleek shadow as he bolted into the inferno.

"No!" I screamed and would have gone after him, only Joe held me fast in his arms.

I dropped my phone. I dropped my keys. I fought like a wildcat demanding release. "Let me go!"

"I can't let you go back into the house." Joe breathed in my ear, struggling to pin me down.

The sound I made wasn't entirely human. I clawed and scratched, twisting in Joe's grip. At one point, I even boxed his ears. "Stop fighting me," I shrieked as I twisted out of his grasp.

Panting, we faced each other against the backdrop of the burning house. His face betrayed his intent to prevent me from going after Remy. I turned and ran to the back of the house instead.

My poor, cheap mobile home burned like kindling in the hearth. It was worse in the back, and a still, quiet part of me knew that's where the fire had been started. Ming was probably dead. Remy might be dead, but not for lack of me trying to get him out. When I reached the window into the spare room, I looked about for something to break it. Spying a big rock, I pried it up and heaved it through the window.

Joe caught up with me as I was clearing the broken glass from the frame. He grabbed hold of my arm and neatly blocked the punch I attempted to deliver. "Let me," he said, short-circuiting any further protest from me.

"No." I'd deal with the flood of emotions surging through me at his willingness to lay his life on the line later. "You'll never catch Ming. Help me get them out."

There was a flicker of hesitation, and then he laced his fingers into a step, and I put my foot in his hands and sprang toward the window. I pulled myself inside and faced the inferno.

The scene in that room will be burned on my retinas as long as I live. The entire room glowed like a furnace. Flaming spars pulled away from the walls and fell to the floor. Fire licked up the walls like a living curtain. The heat was so intense, every exposed part of my body immediately went bone-dry. Blinking felt like dragging sandpaper over my eyeballs.

The cat carrier sat in the middle of the room where I'd left it. My goofy, knuckleheaded German Shepherd lunged at it in a silent, deadly dance. Two steps forward, one leaping step back. Two steps forward again. His head and neck were lowered and extended, his eyes intent on his target.

I dashed over and peered into the carrier. Through the suffocating smoke, I could make out the puffed-out form of a freaked-out cat hunkered down inside. My stupid, wonderful, brave dog was on genetic autopilot and had kept Ming from leaving the carrier. I slammed the door shut, snatched up the cage, and made it back to the window in three strides. Joe was there to catch it when I shoved the carrier out the window at him. Finding a strength I didn't know I had, I scooped Remy up and threw him out of the window, trusting him to land on his feet. I scrambled up to the frame behind him and jumped.

By this point, Joe had tossed the cat carrier aside and was waiting to catch me. I landed on top of him in an awkward spill of arms and legs that drove him to the ground on his back. He whooped for air, and I crawled off him to flip over on my back as well, coughing as I looked up at the night sky. The usual array of stars and planets were dimmed by the thick blanket of smoke coming off my house. In the distance, sirens shattered the night.

My house blazed out of control. I watched it burn, knowing that I would lose everything. Major's puppy pictures. The video of Scotty's first steps as a wobbly foal. The family photos I never got around to scanning. The award I'd won in high school for the State One-Act festival. My diplomas. My patient records. The necklace Joe had given me the night of the Prom. All the little markers of a life lived. Every little milestone that said my life mattered, if only to me. All gone. All ashes and dust.

If the break-in had been a violation, then this was total devastation.

And then Remy licked my face. I grabbed him by the ruff and kissed him. He reeked of smoke, and his fur felt crisped in places. The cat carrier lay on its side a few feet away, but within, Ming was safe, even if every hair stood on end as though someone had electrocuted him. Joe rolled onto his stomach and crawled toward me on his elbows.

"You okay?"

I was lying in a nightshirt next to my former boyfriend while my house burned, and I tried to cough up half a lung. Blood streamed down my arm; I must have cut it on the window. That had to be the stupidest question I'd ever heard. I put pressure on the laceration and grimaced. "No, not really."

Instantly, Joe reached for me. "Are you hurt? Burned anywhere? Do you need to go to a hospital?"

His hands patted my arms, as though he could find whatever ailed me.

Still holding my arm, I let myself fall dramatically back to the grass. "No. That's not it. You realize what this means, right?"

His face swam over mine and I squashed a hysterical urge to giggle as he stared down at me. "No, what?"

"I'm going to have to move back in with my mother."

Chapter Eighteen

MY MOTHER BLEW ON her cup of coffee and stared at me from across the table with narrowed eyes. I tried to figure out who she reminded me of, and then it came to me. Endora, Samantha's mother from that old TV sitcom, *Bewitched*.

"I guess that fire-safe doesn't seem like such a stupid Christmas present now, does it?"

Who says something like that to a person whose house has just burned down? *Gee, thanks, Ma.*

But deciding to act like a grown-up, despite the fact that sitting at the old breakfast table in the family kitchen made me feel as though I were in high school again, I let her have that one.

"You're right. It would be much harder trying to put my life back together if I also had to reproduce all my records and personal information as well."

I was dressed in some hand-me-downs from Betty, who, as my mother so kindly put it, was a "much bigger person than I am, dear." She didn't mean in terms of height, either. Poor Betty. My mother must have rousted her out of bed at the crack of dawn to bring me some clothes. The jeans I wore were too loose in the waist and too short in the leg. Betty's husband must have been a Louisiana State

University fan because my borrowed sweatshirt bore LSU's logo and garish colors.

I poked at my bowl of cereal. My mother believed that eating was a necessary evil to fuel your body, and that if you *must* eat, then you should get the most nutrition out of every mouthful. Ergo, instead of Cap'n Crunch, I munched on some sort of wheat flakes that tasted like the cardboard box they came in.

Remy lay at my feet, looking pathetic. He'd burned his pads in the fire, and now wore socks on three out of four paws to prevent him from licking off the burn cream. He also wore an inflatable collar to prevent him from taking off the socks and eating them. I'd gotten up early and cooked chicken and rice for him in lieu of dog food, however, so despite his woebegone expression, he'd received the hero's breakfast he'd deserved.

"What are your plans for the day?" My mother took her coffee black, and despite owning a coffeemaker, still used instant granules. I wasn't even tempted to have a cup.

"I need to go to the store and pick up some things. Clothes. A litter box. Pet food." My To Do list was frightening. "I have to call the insurance companies—both home and business." I'd decided not to tell her about the break-in that took place before the fire, or the confrontation with Derek, for that matter. As far as the fire went, she'd assumed it had started due to faulty wiring and had reminded me that when I'd purchased the place, she'd warned about its safety issues. "Ming is coughing. I started him on antibiotics and steroids for smoke inhalation, but I might have to take him down to Doc Amos for chest rads. I'm trying to decide if the stress of doing so is worth it."

My mother lifted a delicately penciled-in eyebrow. "Will it change how you manage him?"

I shook my head. "Not just yet. If he gets worse, he might need to go in an oxygen cage, though." That would mean driving him to Birchwood, and I hoped to avoid that. "I also need to call my distributors to see if they will temporarily ship my supplies to this address. So you see, I have a lot of things to do today."

"Including getting a decent haircut?" My mother suggested.

Remy wasn't the only one with burn damage. I'd gotten too close to the heat, and some of my hair had crisped up and melted. I'd looked at it dispassionately in the mirror that morning and lopped it off with a pair of dull scissors. Now I sported an uneven bob, the ends of my hair barely brushing my shoulders. I'd have to figure some way of keeping it off my face when I worked. Mentally, I added "buy hair clips" to my shopping list.

"I'll get around to it, eventually." I shrugged and took a bite of cereal, wincing at the pull of staples against my skin. The cut on my arm had proven to be short but deep. As I really, really hadn't wanted to go to the emergency room last night, I'd used the surgical stapler I kept for minor lacerations to close the wound and had bandaged it up.

The cardboard-flavored cereal had gone limp in the milk, and the entire mess was so unappetizing, I pushed it away. Desperate to talk about anything else other than the complete wreck that my life had become, I asked, "What did you want to tell me last night? In your email, you said you wanted me to call you right away."

"Oh, that." She took another sip of coffee and set her mug down. "I spoke with Miss Ellie and asked her what that Taylor man had said to her. Not in so many words, you understand."

I did. There would have been a song and dance that included the sharing of the latest local gossip before my mother had gotten down to business, which was precisely the reason I'd asked her to question

Miss Ellie instead of going myself. I indicated with a roll of my spoon that she should continue.

"Well, it was all rather mystifying. Mr. Taylor was looking for a particular book on the flora and fauna of the region. But someone had checked it out, and it wasn't available. He became quite steamed about that and badgered Miss Ellie to know who had it."

"Flora and fauna? You mean plants and animals? That doesn't seem to be Brad's kind of thing." I wondered what on earth he'd wanted with such a reference book.

"I'm afraid he was so rude he provoked Miss Ellie into a response she now regrets." My mother cast a knowing glance at me. "Miss Ellie told him if he was in such an all-fired hurry to have access to the book, he could go buy himself a copy."

That brought a smile to my lips, despite the events of the last twenty-four hours.

My mother, however, wasn't quite done. "The thing is, she told me that the person who'd checked the book out was Amanda Kelly."

"Huh. That's weird. Both his desire for the book, and the fact that his sister had it all along. But not weird Amanda had it in the first place. She sometimes used references to get the details of her drawings correct." I chewed over this information and came to a decision. "Thanks, Mom. I'll mention this to Joe when I see him next. It will be interesting to see if the book is still among her effects at the house."

"I thought so too. There's more. Wait here a second." She got up and went into the other room. When she came back, she brought a file folder, which she handed to me. "I had Betty go down to the courthouse and dig up anything she could find on the properties being bought by the developers."

I opened the file. Most of the papers comprised plot maps of the land in question, as well as the various filings for transfer of ownership to Riverside.

As I spread the papers on the table, my mother continued, "I spoke with Ethan yesterday. He said he couldn't give me specifics, as one or two of the properties in question were owned by his clients, but in general, Riverside included a clause in their purchase agreements that gave them an out if sufficient property couldn't be bought to build the subdivision, or if the land didn't perk."

A subdivision would have to have enough water to service it. Part of the problem with building on the side of a rocky ridge was how far you might have to drill for water. Not all the papers dealt with the proposed subdivision, however.

"What's this?" I asked as I pulled out additional maps.

My mother craned her head to see. "Oh. That. I thought it might be worth looking at the land around the Baxter plant. That's where they are planning to put the shopping center, if all this goes through."

"Who is Craigson, LLC?" I'd never heard of them, and they'd bought up almost all the land surrounding the old plant.

"That's the sixty-four-thousand-dollar question, isn't it? Whoever it is, they stand to make a killing if they build the shopping center there."

Remy made a subdued woof and went to the front door. A moment later, we heard the knocker. When I stepped into the foyer, I could see Joe through the glass panel at the top of the door.

"It's Joe," I called back to my mother.

"You answer it. I don't have my face on!" She called back.

Shaking my head at her need to maintain the illusion of perfection at all times, I opened the door. Remy nudged his way past in order to wag his entire body at Joe, who knelt to accept his greeting.

"Aw, man. He's not hurt too bad, I hope?" Joe had Remy's face in his hands and stared into his eyes as if the dog might answer him personally.

I blinked back the tears that came too easily these days. "Just singed in a few spots."

His gaze flicked upward to meet mine, and he stood. "You too, it would seem." He reached out and touched the ends of my hair where it brushed my face.

If I'd been close to tears before, I had to fight back the urge to bawl now.

"Hey." No lazy drawl, but concern made Joe's voice as smooth as whiskey. "You okay?"

"I'm fine."

"Even the arm?" The corner of his mouth twisted upward, and he shook his head in apparent disbelief. "I can't believe you made me hold the edges of your cut together while you *stapled* it."

"I couldn't hold the wound closed and staple it at the same time. I can't believe you almost passed out." There might have been a touch of smugness on my part.

"I did no such thing." His brows drew together.

"You were definitely green about the gills. Got a little light-headed, didn't you?" I was enjoying this far too much.

"I took in a lot of smoke." The smile that played about his lips said he knew he wasn't fooling me.

"Big City Detective, squeamish at the sight of a little blood." I practically sang the words.

The humor leached out of his face as though I'd pulled a plug. "It's different when it's someone you—someone you know."

The look he gave me was so intense, I was certain he was about to open up. Explain why he'd left. Why he'd come back. The shadow of stubble along his jaw suggested he'd been up all night, despite the crisp, brown uniform, which he hadn't been wearing when he burst into my house and forced me out of it. His expression shuttered, warning me this wasn't just a check to see how I was doing.

"Anyway, I'm doing as well as can be expected after the last couple of days." I gave a little shrug and then had to hitch at my borrowed jeans to keep them from falling down.

A reluctant smile tugged at one side of his mouth again. "Are you by any chance using bailing twine as a belt?"

"My mother doesn't have a belt big enough to fit me." The memory of her informing me of this soured my voice. "Nor clothes. I plan to go shopping later."

The steel door dropped down on his face once more. "I'm afraid it will have to be later. About the time your house fire started, someone tried to break in at Amanda's."

Just when I thought nothing else could surprise me. Remy pressed his head into my leg, and I dropped a hand on him to stroke his silky ears. "What? Did they get in? Do you think the two are related somehow?"

"Whoever it was triggered the alarm. They must have gotten spooked and left before my deputies arrived. But it's too much of a coincidence not to be connected in my book. Particularly following the break in at your place."

"You think someone is looking for something." I quickly relayed everything I'd found out so far about the subdivision and subsequent development plans. "You realize whoever tried to break in at Amanda's last night doesn't have the alarm code, so that means she must have known her killer and willingly let whoever it was into her house. Brad fits the bill for all of this. He wants her property. If I'm not around to fight him—"

"He'd have to fight your mother." Joe lifted a sardonic eyebrow. "Killing you doesn't solve the inheritance issue. Though we looked into his financials, and they are a mess."

"He hasn't met my mother. Maybe he thinks it would be easier to manipulate a little old lady in tennis shoes." I held up a hand to stop Joe from interrupting. "I know, she never wears tennis shoes, but that's how she likes to describe herself—someone to be underestimated."

"There's one problem with your theory." Joe's drawl returned, edged with a dark thread of sarcasm. "This morning, Brad Taylor was found dead in the garage at Mossy Creek. Car running, apparent suicide. Coroner says he died sometime between midnight and two a.m."

"Get. Out." My shock had me add a few more choice words that would have horrified my mother. "You're not buying that, are you?"

"We'll have to wait for the coroner's report, but no, I don't. There were signs of blunt force trauma, same as Amanda."

"Our murderer seems to be fond of trying to make it look like suicide. Of course, this means Brad isn't our killer. That leaves—"

"There's no 'our' about it. This is my investigation, Ginny, remember? You'd hardly appreciate it if I horned in while you were spaying a cat, now would you?"

"It's not the same," I said hotly. "For one thing, I don't do surgeries—not as a house-call vet. For another—"

"For another, you're a suspect. You need to come down to the station with me for questioning." He didn't quite sigh, but the sigh was implied just the same.

"Again?"

I must have sounded completely incredulous because Joe burst out laughing.

"It's not funny. When was I supposed to find the time to bash Brad on the head and stage a suicide? Before or after my house burned down? Or am I under suspicion of starting the fire, too?" My voice broke on the last sentence and I stuttered.

"Hey." He took a step closer, and I batted at his chest. He ignored me and swept me into his arms. I struggled briefly and then mashed my face into his shoulder as he stroked my hair. "It's going to be okay. This is just a formality. I know you didn't kill Amanda. I know you didn't kill Brad, either. You'd also never endanger your animals, but I was also watching your house last night. I know what time you came in and that you didn't leave until nearly four a.m. after the fire was out."

I lifted my head to look him in the eye. "I wondered how you just happened to be there last night."

"I was worried about you. There was a viciousness behind the damage at your house earlier that I didn't like." He let me go but didn't step back.

I was the one who put some distance between us. Running a hand through my lopped off hair, I said, "But you didn't see who started the fire?"

He shook his head. "Whoever it was must have come on foot through the woods." A grin peeped out from behind his grim expression. "The good news is you have a pretty unbreakable alibi for Brad's murder last night."

"And the bad news?" I gave him a watery smile.

"Well," Joe drawled, adding that lazy smirk I knew all too well, "apparently, my vet is a bad-ass."

I covered my face with my hands.

Chapter Nineteen

WHILE I WAITED FOR Joe in his office, I checked the video in question on YouTube. It had received over 40,000 hits since I'd watched it the night before. Someone had put it to "She's So Bad, She's Good" on TikTok and the dichotomy between the perky beat and the video made me snort despite myself. There was also a "You Threatened My Dog?" meme circulating on Twitter now. It would have been hysterical if it had happened to someone else—anyone else—but me.

I would never live it down.

I would have to move. Chop off the rest of my hair, dye it blonde, start wearing glasses. Move to another town. Upgrade my wardrobe. Out with the jeans and the fandom T-shirts. Wear heels, for pity's sake. Anything to wipe the old me off the face of the earth.

And then I remembered that someone had tried to eliminate the old me the night before, and suddenly going viral in an embarrassing video didn't seem so bad after all.

The interview with Joe had been brief and to the point. Once we reached the station, the only time his Representative of the Law mask had slipped had been when he asked about my whereabouts earlier the night before. When I'd relayed my movements regarding attending the town meeting and then having a drink with Laney, he'd said, "Yes, that corresponds with the statements of other witnesses."

And then his mouth had undergone a strange contortion that failed to contain the smile he'd been trying to damp down. It burst from him, and his eyes snapped with inner glee.

"Several witnesses," I added sourly.

"Several *thousand* witnesses," he amended. He at least had the grace to turn his snigger into a fake cough.

That was before he'd been called out of the office, and before I'd checked the video stats myself. Eventually, someone would mention the video to my mother. I cringed at the thought.

The door opened suddenly, and I flipped my phone face down in my lap.

Joe leaned in, one hand on the frame and the other on the knob, a fierce look of satisfaction on his face—much like a cat on spying a mouse moving in the grass.

"Frank and Holly picked up Ellis. I'm going to interview him now. Thought you'd like to know that his rental shows signs of damage on the front bumper. I'm betting the paint will match your car. Do I have permission to take samples?"

The air went out of me like a deflated balloon. I'd suspected either Brad or Derek had been behind the harassment, but suspicion wasn't the same as proof. The relief was overwhelming.

"Absolutely."

The expression on Joe's face was practically feral. "Good. You mind waiting? I've got a warrant on the way."

I glanced down at my hillbilly attire. The shopping could wait. "No problem."

"Excellent." Joe withdrew, and then paused to add, "I'll be in the interview room. You don't have to sit out front. You can wait here."

He flicked a quick glance at his desk and then back to me.

"Okay."

I'm sure I sounded confused and wary because the look he gave me tried its best to be reassuring. A tightening of the skin around his eyes in a not-quite smile combined with a barely perceptible nod. He shut the door behind him while I puzzled over what had just happened. Where did it matter where I sat while waiting?

I flipped my phone over and refreshed the screen. The number of hits on the video had jumped by another ten thousand views. How was that even possible? I closed the window and started to call Laney when I noticed a red light flare on the old-fashioned intercom on Joe's desk. Curious, I leaned over to look.

The device appeared to be a holdover from the seventies. Really, the sheriff's department was so small. If Joe wanted anything, all he had to do was open the door and shout. As it was, the intercom only had three of its many buttons labeled. Each button was paired with a silver bar that stood upright like a field of small flags. The first bore a sticker that read "FD" which I assumed stood for Front Desk. The second was identified only by a single letter "I". The third label said "O". The rest were blank.

The "I" button was lit.

I stared at it for a long moment, then glanced at the door. Still shut.

The red button called to me. On my shoulders, a small devil and her angel compatriot poofed into existence.

He left you in here on purpose.

The devil was quite compelling.

He didn't mean for you to listen in on the interview. That would be highly irregular.

Sadly, the angel had a point.

He specifically told you where he'd be. He practically pointed out the intercom.

I waited for the angel's rebuttal. After a moment of silence...

I got nothing.

If an imaginary angel could shrug, mine did. I flicked the silver switch.

Joe's voice came on mid-sentence. "—understand these rights as read to you?"

"I don't have to answer any of your questions without a lawyer."

"That's true." The lazy, amused drawl was in full force. I could picture Joe coming around to Derek's side of the interview table and hitching one hip up to sit on the corner. "Of course, you're not from around here, are you? So, I imagine you'd have to make do with a public defender. Now, we have a few in the area, but they're mighty overworked. And given that we're getting close to the weekend, it could be Monday before we can get someone out here. But not to worry, we'll set you up with accommodations in the local jail. Not private, you understand. Our jail's not that big. Just a drunk tank and a couple of cells."

"I know my rights." Derek sounded mulish and petulant, like a toddler refusing to take a nap.

"Not sayin' you don't." Somehow, Joe injected even more of Mayberry into his voice. "I'm in no hurry. We've got a warrant coming for your car, and I expect that will keep us busy for a while. Looks like you've been in an accident recently. Hope you bought the insurance policy on the rental."

Seconds ticked past, in which I imagined Derek sweating profusely. Would he give in or hold out for a lawyer?

His next words answered that question, at least.

"Look here. You call Brad Taylor and tell him I want a lawyer, pronto. This was all his bright idea, and I'm not taking the fall for this by myself."

"Well, now. I'd be happy to oblige only—" There was a delay, in which I pictured Joe rubbing his chin thoughtfully. "I can't do that."

An expletive burst from Derek's mouth. "Why the hell not?"

The sound of a chair being pushed back carried over the intercom, and I had to re-envision the layout of the room and the position of the players. "Brad Taylor was found dead this morning at the Mossy Creek B&B. The coroner suspects homicide."

"Dead?" Derek let out a squawk that made me smother a chortle.

The intercom picked up the whisper of shuffled papers. "Yes. So, you can see why we need an exact account of your whereabouts last night. Say, from about ten-thirty p.m. until my deputies picked you up. We know where you were before then."

The slightest pause and then the infusion of the last sentence with faint derision was masterfully done. No wonder Joe was so good at his job. Derek was still reeling from finding out that Brad had been killed, and Joe hit him with the one thing that was guaranteed to make Derek lose his cool.

And it did. If Derek's language had been blue before, it was practically indigo now. He called me several unflattering names that reflected on my status as a woman and a human being. Joe let him roll unchecked with his fury. After he called me an unspayed female dog for the second time, Joe interrupted with a short and bitter laugh.

"Tell me about it. I dated her in high school and had to move four hundred miles away to get free from her claws."

Had I not been alone in the room, I would have sworn I'd taken a punch to the solar plexus. All the wind sucked out of me, leaving me gasping for air. My mouth opened and closed several times, like the little bluegills on my hook when I went fishing with my dad the last year of his life.

Well, what did I expect? Joe *had* left all those years ago, and deep down, I'd always known it had been my fault. I hadn't given him much reason to stay, either. Too proud even then to admit how much the breakup had stung, I'd played it cool, agreeing with his decision by pointing out that high-school romances never survived broader horizons and that once we graduated, we'd be lucky if we kept in touch with more than one or two of our classmates down the line.

My hand trembled as I leaned forward to turn off the intercom switch.

Joe Donegan is an extremely talented interrogator.

Was that the devil or the angel who'd spoken? It didn't matter. I tried to reconcile the man in the interview room with the one who'd offered to take in the horses. Who'd been amused at the viral video. Who'd camped out watching my house because he was worried about me. Who'd risked his life to save me and my animals.

One of these doesn't fit with the others.

I sat back in my chair and listened.

"Okay, okay," Derek was saying. "Listen, I had nothing to do with Taylor's death."

"Hold on, now." Joe's concern was patent. "Are you waiving your right to a lawyer?"

"Yes, yes." Impatience made Derek harsh. "If anyone had a reason to kill Taylor, it would be your ex-girlfriend, not me."

"How so?" The creak of a chair made it appear Joe was making himself comfortable for Derek's story.

Derek quickly laid out the terms of the will, and Brad's reaction to the news.

"He was steamed, I tell you. After the reading, he caught up with me. See, I had even a greater right to Samantha's estate than he did, as we were still married, only she made damned sure to cut me out of her will. I had nothing to lose by helping Brad. He promised me a cut of the inheritance if I helped him win it."

"By harassing Dr. Reese? How could that help Taylor win his case?"

"By making her life so miserable, she'd give up fighting him." There was a pause, and then Derek added, "Yeah, I know. Who'd give up that much money without a fight? But he thought if she felt threatened enough, she'd take his offer to split the estate with him."

"I see." Perfectly neutral tone from Joe. "Sounds like Taylor was planning to divvy up the money quite a bit. You sure it was worth it to you?"

"It wasn't just the money Sam had, but what could be made as well. You know some developer wanted her property, right? Well, Brad thought he'd rake in the big bucks by getting the other property owners to agree to hold out for a bigger selling price."

A low whistle from Joe. "Sounds like he was taking a big risk there. What if the developer just backed out and picked a different site?"

"Taylor would have a lot of people angry with him. No skin off my nose."

A tapping sound came over the intercom, that I recognized as being Joe playing with his pen. "So, you tried to run Dr. Reese off the road the night the will was read."

"I wasn't *trying* to run her off the road." Derek's lie came easily, the confession of one man to another. "I just got a little too close, that's all."

"And you broke into her house. What was that about? Were you looking for the letter your wife wrote to her?"

"Huh? Nah, that wasn't it. I mean, I took it when I saw it, but that's not what Taylor wanted me to find. He was after some drawings Sam did."

Thank God, I'd sent the sketch of Remy to be framed after all.

"So." Joe drew the word out slowly. "The destruction to her house was because you couldn't find what you were looking for?"

"Taylor said to scare her, so I did."

I wanted to reach through the wires and wipe the smugness out of his voice.

"So, you went in her place and tore it up? I guess you wanted to make it look like a bunch of kids broke in."

"Yeah." Derek seemed to be rolling on his theme now, happy to let Joe feed him plausible excuses. "That way she wouldn't know who did it, right? But she'd wonder."

"Because of the nature of the damage." There was a thoughtful pause. "I see you've been scratched."

More vicious swearing about cats and how the only good cat was a dead one. My blood pressure rose steadily as I listened.

"I'm kind of surprised you didn't take care of that one when you had the chance. It was your wife's cat, wasn't it?"

Derek mumbled something that made Joe say, "I'm sorry, I didn't catch that."

"I said," Derek ground out, "I ran out of time. I didn't know when your ex was coming back, and it wasn't part of the plan for her to find me there."

"You ran out of time." Patent disbelief dripped in every word Joe spoke.

"Okay, I didn't know the beast was in the room. He came at me like some kind of demon when I opened the door. Seriously, I thought the bloody thing was rabid. I got out of there."

I really liked the idea of Ming getting some of his own back.

"What about the fire?" Joe asked oh-so-casually, in one of his abrupt change of subjects.

Derek went cagey. "You can't pin that on me."

"C'mon, Ellis. The whole town is talking about your altercation with Dr. Reese last night."

I winced and hunched down in my seat.

Joe continued in a friendly manner. "Jeez. She humiliated you in that bar. But if that wasn't bad enough, someone uploaded a video online. Last I checked, a couple of thousand people have seen it."

"A couple of thousand?" Derek snarled his rage. "Try more like *fifty* thousand. I'm a laughingstock wherever I go. And that's just here. I could lose business over this. I want her arrested and charged with assault."

"I don't know, man." Joe seemed amazingly sympathetic. "If all this stuff about you being paid to harass her came out, she might have grounds for a countersuit. A good lawyer could fry you on that. Give me something to hang her with." His tone hardened. "Give me an exact accounting of your movements last night. If you can't prove where you were during the time of the murder, then you're our number one suspect."

More cursing followed, but the rustle of paper made it likely that Derek had accepted a legal pad pushed toward him.

If only he knew his actions had provided me with an alibi.

Chapter Twenty

JOE FOUND ME READING my urban fantasy on the phone when he returned to his office. He cast a glance toward the intercom, but I was pretty sure I hadn't moved it when I turned it on. Besides, he'd wanted me to listen in, right?

"Good news." He parked himself on the edge of his desk, just like I'd imagined him doing when talking to Derek. "Ellis has confessed to the car incident, the break-in, and the fire. He draws the line at murdering Taylor, however."

Pretending I knew nothing about the interview seemed the safest course of action. "Did he say why?"

"Complicated plot to get you to cave in and accept an offer from Taylor to split the inheritance."

"Pretty sure Brad couldn't afford to rent an ice machine powerful enough to make snowballs where he is now."

"Taylor obviously didn't know you well." A flicker of a grin licked his lips and disappeared. "The important thing is you're safe now."

I frowned at that. "From Derek, maybe. But his setting my house on fire gives him an alibi for Brad's murder, doesn't it? And that still leaves us with a killer on the loose."

Joe pinched the bridge of his nose briefly with a grimace. "Derek's clear for at least part of the time, but there's no saying he didn't meet up with Taylor and kill him after he set the fire. Timing's pretty tight, though. I'd like to think these murders have something to do with the Taylor family itself, but I have a hard time tying that in with someone local. Still, I don't see how any of this can affect you now. There's no way anyone can gain from your death except your mother. By the way, Ellis said Taylor sent him to look for a drawing at your place. Did Amanda ever give you anything of hers? Or did you buy something?"

I told him about Remy's sketch and how I'd sent it to the framers via my mother. "But even if Brad had wanted to sell it, I doubt it would have fetched more than five hundred. A thousand, tops, according to Laney."

I pulled up the image of the drawing I'd scanned into the phone as a backup and showed it to Joe.

"Nice," he said, handing the phone back to me. "Charming. Whimsical, even. Really captures Remy's personality. But you're right. It hardly seems worth the risk of breaking and entering to steal it."

A thought occurred to me. "Did you ever find Amanda's phone?"

He shook his head. "No. Why do you ask?"

"Amanda was in the habit of taking photos of things she wanted to draw later. Things she had sketched too. I thought if you found the phone, there might have been something useful on it."

"Like the last person she spoke to the night she was killed." His voice brought up images of skeletons baking in the sun as tumbleweeds rolled by. "Let it be, Ginge. We've got our samples and our confession. Ellis won't be bothering you anymore. Why don't you go shopping?"

I stood up. You can take the boy out of the country, but you can't take the country out of the boy. I might have huffed a little. "You need to take a few minutes to realize just exactly how condescending you sound right now."

Joe rose to his feet as well. "Oh, come on. You know I didn't mean it like that. I know you have a lot to do and a lot to replace. I just meant that you were free to tackle the long list of things that must be on your plate today. With the peace of mind that comes with knowing Ellis is behind bars and won't be out there to hurt you anymore."

"I know exactly what you meant. You want me to go home like a good little woman and keep out of your investigation."

"Leaving it to the professionals—"

"I have every intention of doing that. I merely wanted to point out that while you may have access to her phone records, the photos she took wouldn't be accessible. If she had a Google account, however, she would have backed up her images to her laptop. At least, mine are. Well, the most recent ones, at any rate."

Not my older stuff. I thought of the lifetime of photos lost to the fire and closed my eyes.

Joe went on as though he was oblivious to my struggle with sudden tears. "We thought of that. But her laptop is gone too."

Amanda's murderer couldn't be very bright. How could her killer have possibly hoped to get away with making Amanda's death look like a suicide or an accident if these devices were missing? "She wouldn't have relied on only the laptop for storage. Not someone as organized as she was. She must have had a cloud account somewhere. Or an external hard drive."

"Nothing that's turned up, though we're still looking. Are you sure she didn't loan you anything? A book? Shared files?"

"Nothing I can think of." The mention of a book reminded me of Brad's run-in with Miss Ellie. I relayed what my mother had told me about the library reference and gave him the title.

Joe jotted it down but didn't seem impressed by the information. "I'll look into it, but I can't see how it relates. No more poking around in this investigation, Ginny. I mean it."

On that note, I spun on my heel and left.

I was staring at the window display of Becky's dress shop downtown when I heard someone call my name.

"Deb!" I turned to see her hurrying toward me, wearing a snowsuit to protect her from the biting March wind. It made sense for someone who worked outdoors, but had I chosen such an outfit, I'd have resembled the Michelin Man. The suit fit Deb like a glove. She looked as though she might go snowboarding any minute.

Normally phlegmatic, I'd never seen her so alarmed before. She grabbed my arm the moment she caught up with me. "Is it true? Did your house burn down last night? Is Remy okay?"

Trust Deb to get the priorities right.

"Yes, he's fine. Well, a little singed in spots, as am I. The house is a total loss, though. Hence the butchered haircut and the borrowed clothing." I flicked my hand up and down to indicate my appearance.

"What on earth happened? Let's grab something to eat and you can tell me about it."

She began steering me toward the diner, but for once, I had no appetite at all.

Even as she tugged on my arm, I dragged behind.

"I really need to buy some clothes." I glanced back at the window.

"Not from Becky, you don't." Deb tossed up a hand when I looked at her. "Oh, not that there's anything wrong with her merchandise, but it's mostly dresses. You're not a dress person."

Nothing like having your inner critic validated. "Gee, thanks."

Deb gave me the once over like I was a competition pony just pulled from the field and sadly in need of grooming. "You need to show off your assets. Dresses do nothing for you."

"And what, pray tell, would my assets be?" This I had to hear.

"Your arms, for one." Deb narrowed her eyes critically as she circled me on the sidewalk. How she could tell anything about my body while I was swaddled up against the cold, I have no idea. "You've got great arms and shoulders. The boobs, of course, go without saying. But you look better in pants than dresses. Riding horses gave you a butt. Flaunt it."

"Riding horses has also given me legs like tree trunks." I glanced down at my calves showing beneath my too-short jeans. The wind nipped at my exposed flesh. "You may be right about pants versus dresses."

Somehow, before I knew it, we were in a little boutique that had opened recently. Deb swept in the store and announced to the world at large I'd lost everything in a house fire before parking me in a chair and ordering me to sit. Sympathy rained on me from all sides as both patrons and the shop owner herself dropped everything to flutter around. Soon I was being plied with cookies and chamomile tea while Deb ruthlessly shoved clothing back and forth on the racks and brought me a growing pile of items to try on.

I had my doubts when Meg Bowers, the store owner, began helping Deb with the selections. She favored bold colors such as red and orange, and while her flamboyant style suited her dark coloring to a T, I knew such strong shades would clash with my hair. But she cast a practiced eye over me where I sat and steered Deb to a rack at the back of the store. Together, the two of them returned with an armload of clothing. It would have been rude not to try it all on.

One shopper, a woman I vaguely recognized but couldn't name, called out to me when I was in the dressing room. "Aren't you the woman in the bar last night? The one who threw that guy on the table?"

"Wait, what?" Deb was in the process of handing me another top to try on over the slotted door. "What are you talking about?"

"Oh honey," someone else piped up. "You haven't seen the video? Here. I'll pull it up."

The speaker turned out to be Sharon Bartlett, the middle school principal, a no-nonsense woman with steel-gray hair who bred and showed Border terriers on the weekends. She typed in the address for the video, and the other women crowded around, even those who had apparently seen it before. Penny Harris, a reed-thin woman in her sixties who thought nothing of driving to Pennsylvania or Georgia in a weekend to compete with her flyball dogs, pumped her fist in the air when Derek flew backward onto the table on screen. Even mousy little Amy Burdette, who rescued so many feral cats she lied to her husband about the total numbers, squeaked her approval as Derek floundered about in the video.

I stared at myself in the mirror. Despite the butchered haircut and the bandaged arm, I had to admit; I looked pretty good. The fitted T-shirt hugged my curves and the strong royal blue shade somehow made my eyes seem green. The black pants fit like a glove without binding. It was a dressier look than I normally maintained, and yet I didn't look like a total stranger, either. Several of the combinations that had been selected for me were things I'd have never chosen for myself, and yet somehow looked exactly right on me. I could get used to this personal shopper thing.

Meg tore her gaze away from the community phone. "Turn around," she commanded. When I did so, she gave a nod. "Nice. Boots next!"

She clapped her hands and moved off toward the shoe rack at the far end of the store.

Deb wiped tears of laughter from her eyes. "Oh, that was brilliant," she wheezed. She'd peeled the top part of her snowsuit back to reveal a black tank top, and no one seemed to think her outfit was strange at all.

"He threatened my dog." I folded my arms across my chest defensively.

"He had it coming then," one of the other women said, and a murmur of agreement went round the room.

"He burned my house down." A wave of exhaustion swept over me, pulling at my arms and legs with lead weights, and I sat down abruptly.

Exclamations of shock and outrage followed. Pastor Bogg's wife, Mary, dug around in her enormous tote and pulled out a notebook and pen. Making notes as she spoke, she said, "Right then. You'll need dishes, bedding, linens, and food. We'll start a drive at the church this Sunday."

Guilt assailed me. I seldom went to church, preferring to find my sanctuary on a windswept mountainside instead of in a building. Helplessly, I began, "Oh, I couldn't—"

"Don't be silly," Mary said, frowning over her pad. "Now, if you'll give me your measurements, that will eliminate you from getting things you can't use."

"But—"

"Clothing's on me," Meg announced, and then grinned when I gaped at her. "I insist."

"No, you can't." I knew how hard it was for anyone to make ends meet in Greenbrier. "I'm relying on your sense of style and expertise as it is. I *have* money."

Well, at least in theory I did. When it would actually be in my bank account was another story, but until then, there were credit cards.

Meg bristled up as though to prepare for battle, but Deb interrupted. "How about you accept a pair of boots? Everyone wants to chip in to help you. You do so much for us, Ginny. Let us do something nice for you in return."

I stared at the crowd of women surrounding me, their faces shining with the pleasure of doing a good turn for a neighbor.

All this time, I'd been resenting this community to a certain extent. Seething over having had to come back to the one-horse town and its small-minded denizens. Railing against the work and the responsibility that kept me chained here. Only to find that here, unlike anywhere else, I'd found my people. My tribe.

I was going to build the best darn clinic they'd ever seen. They deserved it.

Reaching out, I stroked the soft gray suede boots Meg held in her hands. Too pretty for work. I doubted I'd have many opportunities to wear them. But I said, "They are lovely. Thank you."

I wound up leaving with several new outfits, the pair of gray suede boots, and an attractive navy-blue pea coat as well that was as warm as any parka without making me look like the Stay-Puft Marshmallow Man. I carried the clothes I'd borrowed from Betty in a shopping bag. Deb made me promise to take her with me if I did any more clothes shopping—who would have thought someone so practical and utilitarian when it came to clothing would have such an eye for fashion? I took my leave with gratitude and drove out to the supercenter to pick up underwear and socks along with pet food and cat litter.

While in Clearwater, I found myself standing in hesitation outside a new hair salon. Perhaps just a trim to neaten up my ragged edges. I went in intending to do just that, fully expecting to wait to be seen, but the only stylist present was thrilled to see me. Having just opened, business was slow. Somehow, she talked me into a pixie cut, and I sat in shocked disbelief as she tugged a razor blade through my hair and chunks fell to the floor.

"You're going to love it," she said as she worked. "It won't just get rid of the damaged bits; it really flatters your bone structure."

"My mother has a pixie." My words sounded flat and unhappy, even to my own ears.

"You shouldn't avoid a style for fear of looking like your mother." Linda, the stylist, put the finishing touches on my hair and spun the chair around so I could face the mirror. "Take it and make it your own."

I turned my head from side to side. The cut was striking, that's for sure. I sat in stunned silence as Linda whisked off my protective gown and brushed hair off the back of my neck.

"You look like an elf-princess." Linda's eyes sparkled as she held up a hand mirror so I could view the back.

"I love it," I said with all honesty.

I felt ready to take on the world.

It was nearly dark when I returned home. I'd almost gone to Amanda's to feed the cats first, but I knew Remy needed to go out and my mother lived in a subdivision. Remy would have to be leashed to walk there, and I had visions of him dragging my mother across the lawn at the sight of a squirrel. Thankfully, my mother was out when I got in, otherwise I'd have to hear her opinions on my shopping expedition and the new look. By the time I'd unloaded the car and fed the animals, I was starving myself. My mother's fridge was even more empty than mine had been—no surprises there, as I often wondered if she merely fed on the energy of those around her—so I ended up wolfing down a peanut butter sandwich.

Ming was breathing better when I gave him his meds, but after I set up his litter box, my nose told me he'd gone somewhere in the spare room. Thankfully, it turned out he'd left me a present in his cat carrier, which was easy enough to clean. I pulled out the old piece of carpet and threw it away. It was a simple matter to find some newspaper to line the crate with, but when I knelt to stuff the paper within, I realized there was already cardboard inside the carrier.

Two pieces of cardboard, to be exact. Taped together and wrapped in plastic. Much as I'd done with the sketch of Remy.

I pulled out the cardboard and broke the tape binding. Between the layers of cardboard were half a dozen exquisite drawings of a small pond. Surrounding the pond in one picture were insets of flowers and animals: a ladybug crawling on delicate Queen Anne's lace, a bee bumbling about a purple thistle flower, a toad on a lily pad, and the tiniest turtle you could ever imagine. Amanda had sketched it sitting in her palm, and it scarcely was as big as her thumb. She'd drawn the faintest smile on its reptilian face, and the whole thing was adorable.

How on earth had these drawings ended up in Ming's carrier? And why? Amanda must have hidden them there, but surely, she'd known how vulnerable to soiling they'd have been.

She hadn't planned on using the carrier. She thought it was the safest hiding place.

It was the only plausible explanation.

Chapter Twenty-One

I THOUGHT ABOUT AMANDA's drawings on the drive out to her place to feed the cats. Why hide those pictures in particular? Though lovely, there was nothing special about them.

A ladybug, a bee, a toad, a turtle.

Queen Anne's lace, thistle, a lily pad, the palm of her hand.

It felt almost like a riddle offered by Gollum to Bilbo in *The Hobbit*.

Collectively, in light of her death, they might be worth a couple of thousand dollars. To someone like Brad, so desperate for money that selling his dead sister's horses for slaughter seemed like a good idea, the drawings would be worth stealing. But someone killed Brad. It seemed unlikely there were two killers running around Greenbrier. Who else would Amanda have hidden her sketches from?

Laney.

The wheel twitched when I gripped it convulsively, and I nearly ran off the edge of the winding road until I regained control of the car again.

Instinctively, I rejected the notion Laney could be the killer. I *liked* Laney. A lot. She was fun to hang out with, and I'd nearly called her to join in on the shopping spree earlier. Could the woman who'd videoed me destroying Derek in public have killed one of my few friends in town?

Setting aside the fact that I liked her, what did Laney gain from Amanda's death? Twenty-five thousand dollars was nothing to sneeze at. Maybe not enough to consider killing someone over, but I knew nothing about Laney outside of what she'd told me. She could have a desperate need for money that had driven her to kill Amanda, though if she knew anything about probating wills, she'd have known it could be a long time before she saw the cash. Besides, she stood to make more money as Amanda's agent, particularly if Amanda was her biggest client. If nothing else, she could have asked for a loan. As generous as Amanda was, she would have offered the money without hesitation.

But what if the two of them weren't on good terms? What if Laney had been about to be fired? What if that was the reason she'd been invited to Greenbrier for a face-to-face meeting? What if her chumminess was simply to cultivate a friendship with me so she could continue to manage the artwork?

Nope. That didn't work. The will was only a few weeks old. If Laney had been about to get fired, surely someone as organized as Amanda would have called Mr. Carter and added a codicil to the will changing both her praise of Laney and altering the bequest. And why hide the drawings from Laney? There would have been no need. There had to be something about those pieces in particular that made them worth hiding.

The sun had almost set as I bumped over the cattle guard and drove up to the barn. Dark pink and orange streaks lit up the clouds, but dusk was closing fast. With the inflatable collar on, Remy couldn't shove his head between the seats as he normally would have done, but he whined and pressed his nose against me.

I'd almost left him at home, as I didn't relish the thought of him getting his bandages wet and muddy, but he'd been unusually anxious and clingy when I returned from my shopping trip. He'd stayed pinned to my side almost like an obedience champion ever since I'd come home, and he'd chewed up one of my mother's shoes in my absence—something he hadn't done since he was a puppy. Better to take him with me than let him do more damage at the house.

"You stay here," I said as I got out of the car, using my stern voice. He whined unhappily but remained in the back seat where he sat as upright and rigid as a Buckingham Palace guard. The fire must have upset him more than I realized, and I wondered if doggy tranquilizers were in his future. I'd have to talk to Deb. Though she worked primarily with horses, she was a phenomenal trainer in general. She'd know what to do.

All three cats were waiting for me when I carried the food out to their stations. Harley wound around my legs, doing his best to try to trip me, while Blackjack sat on a stump and cried piteously. "I'm coming, I'm coming. Keep your fur coat on."

Solomon slipped into the bushes like a wraith, but his white bib allowed me to spot him in the gathering gloom. By the time I'd fed the ferals and disposed of the empty cans in the trash can inside the feed room, dusk had fallen.

I was about to switch off the light when a thought occurred to me.

The hidden drawings were all centered around a pond, one that looked very much like the pond on Amanda's land. I'd only been out to it once last spring; the path to it was overgrown with greenbrier, mountain laurel, and wild azalea. Once we'd hacked through the thorny brush, the blooming wildflowers had been stunning. If I closed my eyes now, I could hear the piercing trill of the redwing blackbirds as they sang their mating songs. Amanda had talked about graveling the trail and building a little gazebo out by the water. It would have been a lovely spot to read a book or draw if I had the talent.

She had the resources. She could have easily built the gazebo over the summer, but she hadn't.

She'd hidden a packet of drawings in her mean cat's carrier. Her phone—including the gallery of images she'd taken to paint later—was missing, as was her laptop and anything where she might have stored her photos. She'd checked out a natural history book from the library her brother had demanded to see. She'd changed her will and called her agent to come for an urgent meeting.

Maybe her death was connected to those drawings.

Joe had asked me to turn over my key, but I knew where Amanda hid a spare. And, unless the police had changed the alarm, I knew the code to that as well. What if there was a connection between Brad's interest in finding that reference wildlife book and the drawings Amanda had hidden in Ming's carrier? There was no other word to use—you don't stash valuable drawings in a crate where you know your elderly cat might pee on them unless you're desperate to keep them away from prying eyes.

I reached up on the shelf in the feed room and pulled down the half-rusted coffee can there. Dumping it onto the counter, I sorted through the contents: several hoof picks, a couple of pens, a broken pill cutter, a padlock, and Amanda's spare house key.

I drove to the top of the hill and parked in front of the house. Someone had murdered Amanda and Brad. To be on the safe side, I let Remy out of the car. He glued himself to my side as we went up the porch steps.

The key turned without hesitation in the lock, and as soon as I opened the door, the panel on the alarm turned red and began a beeping countdown. Hastily, I punched in the code to deactivate it, praying that it was still the same and that I'd entered it properly.

The warning counted down for several seconds after I entered the code, and then it shut down, the panel turning green again.

Remy took off down the hallway at a trot, his booted feet making scarcely any noise as he went looking for Ming, no doubt. Even his tags were silent for once, as the inflatable collar prevented them from jangling together.

I had no issue with him disappearing to check the place out. He'd return when he was done. I had explorations of my own to do. Unlike the dog, however, my best bet for success was likely to be Amanda's studio.

I'd been inside the main part of the house a couple of times before, though usually when I came over, the door to the studio was shut. It felt like an intrusion to enter Amanda's private sanctum without her, but if she could look down on me acting on her behalf, I'm sure she would have approved.

Large plate-glass windows filled the far wall, revealing the last streaks of purple and orange that painted the sky over the valley below. When I flipped on the switch, the view vanished, to be replaced by stark black panes. Someone I didn't recognize stood reflected in the glass, and my blood froze in my veins until I realized I was looking at myself. Between my short haircut and the new, snazzy leather jacket, I could have been the cover model for one of those intrepid female detectives from a gritty crime series. Once I got over the shock of seeing myself in the glass, I took a deep breath and looked around.

The starkly furnished room seemed almost bare in the harsh overhead light. French doors interrupted the bank of windows to lead out onto what I knew to be a deck that overlooked the valley. A large easel faced the windows, along with a workbench covered with a paint-spattered drop cloth. Brushes and pigments lay aligned in a neat row along the cloth-covered surface, and several paintings appeared to be drying there as well. The completed paintings were the bread and butter beach scenes that Amanda abhorred but that I found peaceful. Dune grass waving in the breeze. Light shining through the brilliant green water of a cresting wave. That sort of thing. The drawing on the easel was the barest of sketches, bold strokes of charcoal that outlined the recognizable form of horses grazing in the fields. Amanda's last work. Never to be finished.

The view must be incredible during the day. Facing west as it did, the room probably stayed cool until well into the afternoon during the summer. It was the perfect workspace for an artist.

It was a place of work, however. Aside from the armless chair that stood in front of the easel, there was no other seat. Another landline phone sat on the bookcase standing just inside the doorway that also contained books on art and technique. There was a gorgeous compilation of works by John Singer Sargent that I would have loved to pore over, as well as many books on animal anatomy, watercolors, oils, and acrylics. My heart skipped a beat when I came across some identification books on plants, birds, and mammals, but none bore a library sticker.

Remy padded into the room, mouth open in an ingratiating grin, ears at half-mast and tail wagging. He thrust his nose into my hand, and after I absentmindedly patted him, began an exploration of the room.

Where was the library book, darn it?

Obviously not here. I'd have to check her sitting room, and if that failed, her bedroom. Always providing the killer hadn't taken it with them, which would assume that the book was the key to everything and that somehow, the killer had also known that. It felt like a stretch to me.

I gave the room a final once-over as I reached for the light switch.

I could picture her as she might have been that night. Long blonde hair pulled back in a sloppy ponytail. She'd changed out of her painting gear and into the clothing that she'd been wearing when I found her: dark blue boot cut jeans and a burgundy wool sweater. She'd opened a bottle of wine—perhaps she'd expected her visitor? No, more likely she'd opened the wine for herself, and then got interrupted. And something about her "guest" concerned her enough that she'd hidden her drawings. The cat carrier normally resided in the hall closet; she must have found an excuse to shove the drawings in there if she hadn't already done so before her visitor arrived, that is.

A trash basket sitting beside the workbench caught my eye. It was filled to the brim with paint-covered rags and old newspaper. What if she'd hidden the library book as well?

I crossed over to the basket and picked it up. It was heavier than I expected. Curiosity made Remy join me, and he followed me to the workbench, where I shoved the beach paintings aside and dumped out the trash onto the floor. It took a firm shake to dislodge the library book from the bottom of the can.

Some powerful need must have driven Amanda to risk damage to the reference book by placing it in the trash. As it was, a daub of sky blue marred the cellophane surface of its cover. I wiped at it with my thumb, but the paint had dried.

I scarcely noticed when Remy lay down at my feet. I opened the text, hoping it would fall naturally to the page I needed, but with no such luck. Instead, Amanda had used little slips of paper as bookmarks, and I had to check each one. I'd hoped for enlightenment, but the photographs were so ordinary. Nothing special. The same bugs and flowers I saw every day. An alphabetical listing of weeds and mushrooms. Of birds and animals. I paused for a moment over a photo of an endangered salamander, a species that existed only in the Shenandoah Valley, and remarkably, had a twenty-five-year life span. Interesting, but not particularly useful information.

Yet Amanda had hidden the book. Why?

I selected another bookmarked page and saw it: the reason Amanda had died.

I didn't need to look up the photos of Amanda's drawings I'd taken on my phone. I remembered the whimsical little turtle she'd drawn in the palm of her hand.

It matched the description of the bog turtle, a tiny reptile that rarely grew more than three and a half inches long and preferred wetlands and ponds. Favored by reptile fanciers for its small size and ready adaptation to captivity, it was also known as the red-necked turtle. It was also endangered.

And it lived on Amanda's property.

For a split-second, I thought of Ben and his cages of reptiles, but Ben loved his charges and wouldn't do anything to threaten their safety. No, the problem lay because this small turtle had the power to stop the development cold. Amanda's land was the centerpiece of the subdivision. Without her property, would Riverside even want to pursue building in the area?

I refilled the trash basket while I thought about who benefited the most from keeping the existence of the bog turtle a secret. Amanda must have known how upsetting this information would be, or else she wouldn't have hidden the sketches or the library book. She must have told someone as well, someone who couldn't afford to let the development fall through.

But who? The possibilities seemed endless. Any one of her neighbors, desperate to sell their land at a hefty profit, had reason to stop this information from getting out.

I was still mulling that when I picked up a folded newspaper that hadn't been balled up like the rest. It was a copy of the *Greenbrier Gazette*, a weekly paper put out with more enthusiasm than information by Ted Eastman, a former journalist for the *Richmond Times Dispatch*. It wasn't his fault the *Gazette* rarely had anything of interest to report, and was considered mostly a gossip rag. I nearly tossed it aside, but for the fact it was the only newspaper that was practically in pristine condition. The side facing me contained a large advertisement for a pre-Christmas sale. I turned the paper over and saw a photograph of the mayor at some ribbon cutting ceremony I didn't remember.

In the photo, Mayor Austin held an oversized pair of scissors, as she paused for effect before cutting through a large ribbon in front of a store. A group of people clustered around her. The caption beneath the picture read: *Mayor Austin at the Grand Opening of Kirkpatrick Pharmacy. From left to right: Jim Kirkpatrick and his wife, Selma. Mayor Austin, her husband Wilbur, and their son, Craig.*

Below the article was a small posting notifying creditors that Linkous Construction had filed for Chapter 11 bankruptcy. That surprised me. Though things had been tight for some time in Greenbrier, I would have thought that the interconnected Linkous businesses would have kept the flagship afloat. I checked the date on the paper. Last November. About the time the planning commission authorized the subdivision. Ed must have counted on the new construction to shore up his business. An environmental impact study investigating the turtles would have killed the project.

I opened the paper and Steve Wainwright's smiling face met mine.

"I'm making it my personal mission to see that this development succeeds," I read aloud. Wainwright has said something similar at the town meeting. How important was this subdivision deal to him? How much of a personal stake did he have in its success? His fury over hearing about the possible delay to probate wasn't the reaction of a man who wanted to wait years to move ahead on a special project. Add an endangered species to the mix...

I punched Joe's number on my contact list and muttered, "Pick up, pick up," as the phone rang.

"Ginge." His smoke and whiskey voice almost made me cry with relief.

"Listen, I know why Amanda was killed." I spat out the words in rapid staccato. "Amanda found an endangered species on her property. It would have shut down the subdivision. Without the development, Riverside would never have put in the shopping center."

"What's that? You're breaking up."

Joe broke up as well, and I cursed the poor reception in the mountains. I moved closer to the windows.

"Can you hear me now?" I sounded like a parody of one of those cell phone ads, but I didn't care.

"A little. What did you say?" Static interrupted his words, but for the most part, I could make them out.

I repeated myself and added, "An environmental impact report would have shut down the development, possibly for good. Too many people had too much at stake for that to happen."

"I only got part of that." His frustration came through loud and clear, however. "Where are you?"

"I'm at Amanda's. Look, I found proof. She'd made a drawing of a bog turtle—that's the endangered species. The pictures were hidden in Ming's carrier. I—"

Remy lifted his head. A low growl rumbled through his chest, and his hackles raised like a Mohawk along his shoulders.

I froze, listening hard like a rabbit who might have caught the soft-footed pad of a fox. The sound of the front door closing carefully caught my ears.

Crap. I hadn't locked the door when I came in. I hadn't reset the alarm for intruders. "Joe." I whispered desperately into the phone. "Someone is here in the house with me. At Amanda's. Do you hear me? Someone is in the house—"

The phone went dead. The signal was lost.

Remy got to his feet. I grabbed his collar and forcibly dragged him back from the door. Shoving him under the workbench, where he was partially hidden by the drop cloth, I took his face in both hands and looked him in the eye. "If you love me, you'll stay right here until I say otherwise. Got it? *Stay.*"

I made my hand like a wall in front of his face and let the cloth fall to obscure him from view. Had he been Major, I would have trusted him to stay wherever I'd left him, however long it took for me to come back. Remy's stay, on the other hand, was wobbly at best.

Tonight, I needed his best.

It's odd how fast your brain can work when you need it to do so. In the seconds before whoever it was entered the room and discovered me; I went through my options. I could have gone through the French doors onto the deck, but there was no way either Remy or I could survive a thirty-foot drop without serious injury. With any luck, Joe had hopped into his car and was, even now, driving like a bat out of hell to reach me.

I prayed Joe was on the way.

"Hello!" Dulcet tones, merrily bright, rang out from the hallway. "Anyone home?"

That voice was so familiar. My brain went nuts trying to figure out who it was.

Answer or not? Stalling for time and hoping Joe showed up was my best option, if not defusing the situation altogether. Whoever it was had seen the lights, and probably my car as well. They knew I was here. My best bet was to pretend there was nothing wrong, and that Joe was already halfway here.

There are prayers, and then there's common sense. I picked up a palette knife and tucked it into my palm.

I snapped the switch on the table-side lamp and flicked off the overhead light. A gentle glow replaced the stark white brilliance of the previous lighting. Now there were shadows, and it would be easier to overlook Remy's presence if you didn't know he was there. Just the same, I moved to stand in front of the workbench so I might obscure any slight movement he made.

"In here," I called out, adding a quiet but firm, "Stay."

The faintest jingle of dog tags indicated Remy had shifted position but hadn't gotten up. I should have removed his collar. Too late now.

The click of heels down the hardwood floors was as loud as thunderclaps. They paused outside of the studio for a moment, and then Mayor Austin popped her head through the open door. Her bright expression had the hard, plastic look of a doll, forced forever to smile at everyone she met.

Mayor Austin? How could I have gotten this so wrong? Okay, maybe I wasn't wrong. Maybe I was overreacting.

"Ginny! I'm so pleased to have caught you here."

Trying not to read too much into her words, I went for pleasant confusion. "Mayor Austin. What a nice surprise. What brings you here?"

"I could ask you the same." She stepped into the room, blocking my exit by filling the doorway. "I happened to be passing by and saw the lights on up here. I'd heard there had been an attempted break-in, so I thought I'd check in."

Lie.

The house lights could hardly be seen from the road. The mayor would have had to have already been on the property to know there was anyone up at the house.

Stall for time. Keep her busy until Joe gets here.

Why Mayor Austin? Other than the prestige of presiding over the town's revival, she could hardly have a major stake in whether Riverside built in Greenbrier. Was it all for the glory? Or were there kickbacks involved with Wainwright?

"Gracious," I said. "How intrepid of you. My first thought would have been to call the police."

The fixed smile never faltered. "Well, but you see, once I reached the house, I recognized your car. The personalized plate is a nice touch. VET4PET. Cute." Her glance flicked about the room and came back to rest on my face. "I guess I shouldn't have been surprised to find you here."

I managed what I hoped was a sad nod. "You heard about my house fire, I take it?"

She was wearing black slacks paired with a black long-sleeved sweater, and the frilled cuffs of a white shirt peeked out around her wrist as she pressed an open palm to her chest. "I *did*. How horrible. I heard it was a total loss. I hope your animals got out okay."

Her concern seemed genuine, and I relaxed a fraction.

"A little singed around the edges, but no serious damage done. Like me." I made a rueful grin and tugged at my newly shorn hair.

"Ah. That explains the drastic change. I thought you were just going for a more... practical... appearance." A smirk then, as her hand fell back to her side.

Hah. She thought she'd wounded me with her little dig. As if I hadn't been fencing with my mother my entire life.

"Well, you know what they say. No hair mistake is permanent." I gave a little shrug. "Anyway, the police released the crime scene and told me I didn't have to be escorted to feed the cats anymore. I guess I couldn't help coming up here and looking around."

"I imagine you'd want to escape your mother's house as soon as possible. So, when do you gain control of the property? Are you planning to stay here?"

I bristled a bit at her comment about my mother. It was one thing for me to resent my overbearing, irritating, control-freak of a parent, but it was quite another for someone else to disparage her. Still smiling, Mayor Austin slipped her hand in her pocket.

"Hard to say. Now that Brad is no longer around to contest the will, perhaps sooner than—" I broke off, disconcerted. Slapping myself on the forehead would hardly be the smooth move to make, but suddenly Brad's death made sense now. Of course, he had to die. He would have held up the probate.

The image of her cutting the ribbon in front of the pharmacy flashed back to mind, as well as the caption under the photo. Mayor Austin had a son named Craig.

Craigson LLC had bought up land around the Braxton plant in anticipation of the shopping center being built there.

Who else would Amanda have called first when she realized there was a problem with the development?

The mayor, that's who.

Her smile became a little pinched at the corners, and her eyes narrowed at my sudden stillness. Her attention sharpened, like a hawk sensing movement in the grass. "You were saying?"

My heart thudded for three long beats before I could wrap my tongue around a reply. "Oh, that sounded bad, didn't it? Like I was glad he committed suicide. I didn't mean that. Still, with Brad out of the picture, Mr. Carter assures me probating the will won't be an issue."

I tore my gaze away from her face and allowed it to rest pensively on the sketch on the easel. "I don't know that I would ever feel at home here, though. Amanda would haunt this place, I fear. I picture her the way I found her, at the bottom of the pool..." I gave a theatrical little shudder.

The tension seeped out of Mayor Austin's shoulders at my words. "Oh yes. I can see that. So, you'd be selling then? I imagine the sale of this property, plus whatever you gained from the estate, would allow you to set up wherever you'd like to go. Why, you could even leave Greenbrier." Her eyes practically glowed as she warmed to her theme.

"You know, you're right." I spoke slowly, as though the thought hadn't occurred to me. "I guess I should contact Riverside. I probably need to contact Amanda's family as well and see what they want me to do with her things."

With my free hand, I gestured toward the door, as if inviting the mayor to head out before me. I'll never know if it was the movement that was the mistake, or if something in my voice sounded off to her, but she glanced at the workbench behind me, and then her smile turned hard and cold.

"I see you found the library book. I was hoping to take that away before anyone noticed it."

Stall for time. Play dumb.

"Excuse me?"

"The reference book on the local flora and fauna. Can you believe it? All this fuss over a stupid turtle." She indicated the trash can, still on its side, with a nod of her head. "I tried to reason with her, you know."

"What?" Involuntarily, my gaze was drawn to the items in question, and like an idiot, I'd left the book open to the page on the rare turtle. Yeah, kind of hard to deny that one now. I turned back to the mayor to do just that, only to stare down the barrel of a 9mm semi-automatic.

My blood went to ice, and then rebounded with a hot, frightened pulse.

"I don't understand," I stuttered.

"Oh, I think you do. Please don't waste my time pretending you don't." She held the gun with a confidence that spoke of time spent on a firing range. That didn't bode well for my chances of making a run at her. "I tried to tell Amanda, but she refused to listen."

She's a dangerous dog that I need to calm down before she attacks. I can do this. I can play cool until Joe arrives. If he arrives.

"You don't need to do anything rash." I shrugged, as if killing your neighbors and constituents was no big deal. "Like you said, I *want* to get out of town. I was hoping you didn't know about the connection to the turtle, because then I wouldn't be able to sell."

"You see?" Her gun hand lowered slightly. "When I suggested the same to Amanda, she pointed out that an EIR would discover the existence of the turtle and shut down the project anyway. But the impact study wouldn't stop the project if there were no turtles to find."

"You wanted to kill the turtles?" I couldn't keep the incredulity out of my voice.

"I offered to move them first." Mayor Austin frowned slightly. "Were we really supposed to put the welfare of a couple of turtles over the entire community? Over jobs and a new school building? Over a significant improvement in our economic base?"

She'd chosen those things over the lives of two people. Three, counting me, and I was pretty sure she was.

Going for casual, I said, "So we relocate them, then. No big deal. Everyone wins."

Her gun dropped a fraction lower.

"Oh, Ginny. I'd really like to believe you're on board with this, but I know you. Everyone here does. You were the Squirrel Girl." Regret thrummed in her voice as she lifted her weapon back into firing range. "Believe me. I have no choice. We've invested every penny into buying up land to sell to Riverside. We even took out a second mortgage on the house. If the subdivision falls through, we'll be stuck with worthless tracts we could never sell. So you see, I'm in too deep to back out now."

She raised her gun hand.

"Wait." I threw up my hands as a poor shield. "You know killing me won't solve anything. The property will just go to my mother. You have no guarantee she'll sell. I'm telling you, I'll sell! Give me that developer's number. I'll call him right now."

I made as if to reach for my cell phone, still lying on the workbench.

"Stop. Don't move." Her aim wavered the tiniest bit, and she lifted a hand to rub at her temple. "Let me think."

I held my breath. For an instant, I thought she'd go for it, but she shook her head slowly, as though having an argument with herself. Her gun hand steadied, and she focused on my face once more.

"No. Sorry. I can't risk it."

"You'll have to deal with my mother," I warned.

To some people, that would have been an effective argument.

Mayor Austin, however, laughed. "Oh, please. As if your mother will be an issue. Without you, she'll have no reason to stay in Greenbrier. God, if killing you will rid me of her as well, it would be worth it for that alone. Do you know what a thorn in my side she's been all these years? She thinks she's so tough, but she's just another delusional old woman. And if she refuses to sell? Well, I actually *know* how to shoot a gun."

Her smile was that of an apex predator, content in its supremacy.

Stall. I had to stall for time. What could I possibly say that wouldn't have her shoot me on the spot?

"Won't shooting me be hard to pass off as a suicide?"

I cringed even as I spoke. Perhaps reminding her of her failed cover-ups wasn't the smartest move.

"Ah, but someone has already tried to burn your house down. Obviously, someone has it in for you, Dr. Reese."

"Fine." My words came out cool and flat. "But I have proof you killed Amanda and why."

"The drawings? Nothing links those scribbles to me." The look she gave me was almost pitying. "You've got nothing. And without this book, the sketches you found will simply be the last works Amanda Kelly ever drew."

"I'm not talking about the drawings. I mean real evidence. DNA evidence."

That shook her. "What are you talking about?"

I indicated her long sleeves. "Every time I've seen you, you've been covered up as though it's twenty below outside. Normally, you're the first person to break out your spring suits. Ming scratched you the night you killed Amanda. I took samples."

I saw the gears spinning as she processed that bit of information. Where the hell was Joe? Even if he was already back out at his place, surely he would have sent one of the deputies here by now. Had I been cut off before he heard anything I'd said?

All too quickly, she'd evaluated the threat and dismissed it. "If you had anything on me, you would have turned it over to that ex of yours by now."

I *would* have if he'd listened to me. Thinking fast, I said, "I collected the sample—your skin under Ming's claws—and called him. I was supposed to take it to him this morning, but with the fire and everything, I forgot."

Her lips narrowed into a thin line as she pressed them together. "Your house burned down. Any evidence you have against me has been destroyed."

Hah. My old fridge had held up better to the fire than expected, but she didn't need to know that. I was about to make my mother proud. I smiled my own shark-like smile. "Firesafe."

She sucked in a breath between her teeth. "Well, then. You and I are going to take a little drive. You're going to take me to your safe and open it."

Hurry up, Joe! Get here already.

"Move." She stepped aside to wave me toward the door. "Count yourself lucky you didn't bring your stupid dog with you for once. I'd have shot him in front of you."

In the silence that fell between us, a faint whine could be heard.

"What the—" Her head whipped toward the sound.

I was out of time.

"Okay, Remy!" I commanded.

Remy exploded out from under the workbench with a thunderous volley of barking, his hackles raised in a sharp ridge down his spine, his tail upright and flagged behind him. All ninety pounds of him sprang forward like a bear coming out of a cave. Even I was taken aback.

Mayor Austin screamed and brought her weapon around to this new threat. I drove the palette knife into her shoulder, forcing her arm down even as she pulled the trigger. The sound of the bullet cracked with deafening loudness in the small space, and Remy yipped.

The gun fell to the floor with a clatter. I kicked it aside. Austin screeched with rage and pain and turned toward me with fingers curled like claws.

I rammed the heel of my hand straight up her nose. Cartilage gave way and blood spurted everywhere. Austin's face contorted in an extraordinary grimace as her hands flew up to her nose. But I wasn't done yet. I hooked my foot around her ankle and swept her feet out from under her. She fell backward, and I followed her down with an elbow strike to her solar plexus in a move worthy of a professional wrestler. When I crawled off her, tears streamed down her face and she whooped for air.

"Remy!"

He was nowhere in sight. Blood spatter was everywhere. Surely all of it hadn't come from Austin?

"Remy!" I lifted the drop cloth and found him cowering beneath the workbench, eyes dilated into black pools. "Oh, honey. It's all right. Did that loud boomy scare you? Are you hurt?"

I dragged him out by the collar to see if the bullet had struck him. But as I ran my hands over his fur, he began licking my face, and I took a moment to bury my nose in his ruff. He was okay.

A shuddering groan from Austin made me turn back toward her. Her face was splotchy, and her nose was a wreck, but she was catching her breath.

"I'll take that," I said, pulling the palette knife out of her arm.

She squealed and sobbed.

I pocketed the knife and stood. The nice thing about landlines was the phones usually came with lots of cord. I jerked the silver cable out of the back of the phone and made several passes around the mayor's feet, binding them together. Then, over her curses and protests, I flipped her onto her stomach, bound her hands together, and tied them down to her feet. I trussed her tighter than a rodeo calf when I was done.

Remy, who'd been watching me with keen interest, now lifted his head and gave a muffled bark.

"Police!" Joe announced from the hallway, sounding mean and authoritative in a way I'd never heard before. "Come out with your hands up!"

My help had finally arrived. About bloody time.

Chapter Twenty-Two

FRANK PAUSED EVERY FEW seconds as I recounted my story to shake his head.

"You busted the mayor's nose."

"She tried to kill me, Frank. What part of murderous intent do you not get?"

"She'd already committed two murders. I think Doc here was justified in defending herself." Holly hitched up her belt in solidarity with me as I gave my statement.

"I get that." Frank gave his partner a hairy eyeball before staring at me as though I were some sort of alien shapeshifter living in their midst. "But the EMTs think she may have broken some of the mayor's ribs, too."

We'd relocated to Amanda's living room. I sat in an overstuffed chair. The light from the reading lamp beside me cast a gentle glow around me. Remy lay on top of my feet. He was quite heavy, but every time I tried to move, he shifted to drape himself over my boots again. In the surreal half hour that had passed since the arrival of the police, the mayor had been checked out by the EMTs, then handcuffed and sent to the hospital with a State Trooper to watch her until they could transfer her to a jail cell.

How could Frank possibly be that dense?

"She threatened to kill my mother."

Frank's brow furrowed in consternation. "I thought you didn't like your mother all that much."

I don't know what he saw on my face, but he took a step back. Remy lifted his head, a low rumble emanating from his throat. Before I got to my feet, Joe had placed a hand on my shoulder.

"Here. Drink this." He handed me a cold soda, the sides damp with condensation. To Frank, he said, "For better or worse, you don't mess with family."

"You don't mess with Doc, period." Holly may have spoken quietly, but the grin on her face shouted volumes. She gave me a small thumbs up when I glanced over at her.

I accepted the soda with shaking hands, like an addict reaching for a much-needed fix. The cold, sweet, bubbly drink was like nectar to me. I recalled Amanda never touched the stuff and realized she must have stocked it in her fridge just for me. I mentally toasted her.

This one's for you, Amanda.

"Popeye, spinach," Joe murmured as I sipped, and I choked on my soda. I swear he timed his comment with that effect in mind. He waited for me to stop sputtering and added, "Personally, I thought hogtying her with the phone cord was a nice touch. You can take the girl out of the country, but you can't take the country out of the girl."

"Where'd you learn to fight like that? The Mayor looks like she went three rounds with Mike Tyson."

"Self-defense course paid off, I guess." Carla, my instructor, would be proud.

"Who taught the class?" Frank demanded. "*Charlie's Angels?*"

Joe snorted as I reached down to brush Remy's head. "She tried to shoot my dog."

"Well, now," Joe drawled in that oh-so-familiar manner that warmed me in a way that was hard to explain. It was a shared joke among friends, the recognition that someone got you in a way you'd forgotten could happen. "That's just plain crazy. She must not have seen the video."

"What video?" Frank asked.

The noise Holly made *could* have been a cough, but I doubted it. She gave Frank a pitying smile. "I'll show it to you later."

When I made eye contact with Joe, it was like a lock and key effect until I dropped my gaze back to Remy again.

"I can't believe the mayor is a killer." Frank was really having a hard time taking this in.

"According to her, she sank a lot of money into buying land around the old Braxton plant through a corporation she created to hide that fact." Exhaustion threatened to pull me under, so I focused on filling in the blanks.

Joe scratched the side of his face thoughtfully. "All on the assumption Riverside would buy the land to build the shopping center and movie theater to complement the new subdivision. I've seen the plans. We're talking high-end stores, shops, and professional suites for doctors, dentists, and the like."

"Yeah, but you're telling me all of that would have been stopped by a *turtle*? C'mon, they're a dime a dozen around here." Frank shook his head.

The sugar and caffeine from the soda sang in my veins. The shakes stabilized. My brain felt sharper, and the explanations came easier.

"Not just any turtle. A protected species. Even if Amanda had been inclined to sell before, she never would have done so once she found the bog turtle on her property. And the discovery alone might have scuttled the development. Performing the studies to determine the risks to the environment, even if Amanda's land was eliminated, could have taken months, even years, to go through."

"The mayor probably came over to discuss Ms. Kelly's find." Joe took over the summation. "Something she said must have raised Amanda's suspicions, so she hid her original drawings. The mayor probably killed Amanda, thinking her brother would be easier to deal with." He addressed his next comment to me. "You were right about his financial situation. He'd embezzled from his own company. His impending divorce would have triggered an audit, and he was desperate to replace the funds he'd stolen."

"So why kill Taylor then?" Clearly, none of this made sense to Frank. He was still stuck on the fact all of this hinged on a turtle.

Holly snapped her fingers. "Of course! Taylor thought he'd inherit. But when Doc got the money instead, his plan to contest the will was going to delay any potential deal further and increase the likelihood Riverside would build somewhere else."

Joe picked up the threads once more. "Exactly. If Taylor had inherited, he could have signed a contract offering the land to Riverside once probate went through. Under those circumstances, Riverside probably would have been content to wait before breaking ground. After all, they were in discussions with other landowners but hadn't purchased anything yet. It's one thing to wait for a will to be probated. It's another to hold out on a deal without the certainty it will go through in the end. I spoke with Mr. Wainwright. Riverside was waiting to see if Amanda would sell before buying the other lots. Taylor was greedy, though. According to Ellis, he planned to get the other owners to hold out for more money. Given the problems popping up left and right with the deal, the odds were high Riverside would look somewhere else to build. Wainwright told me Taylor's plan to contest the will was the last straw as far as he was concerned. He intended to take his plans and move to another area. In the mayor's eyes, Taylor had to go."

Frank shook his head. "That's just cold, man."

After I'd finished giving my statement, Joe walked me to the door. Remy remained pressed close to my side as we went down the hallway. Joe steered me with one hand on the small of my back.

"Remy's pretty rattled," I said, as I paused on the front porch. "I think I might need to put him on anti-anxiety medication for a while."

"What about you?" Joe looked at me with quiet concern. "You've been through a lot these past few days. I'd drive you home, but I'm going to be tied up for a while yet."

A simple move on my part would have made him open his arms and take me in. The temptation was strong; stronger than anything I'd ever felt before. Instead, I said in a brisk tone, "I'll be fine. Besides, if you drove me and the dog to my mother's, I'd just have to get a ride back out here to collect my car in the morning. Anyway, the most important thing for you do to now is nail the mayor."

He blew his breath out with a long sigh. "As far as tonight goes, you know it's going to be her word against yours. Thanks to your suggestion of where to look, we'll be able to prove she was buying up the land around the plant, but a good lawyer—and you know she'll have the best—will point out there's no law against that. I've seen this happen again and again, Ginge. The powerful always manage to walk."

A bleak shadow crossed his face. There was a story there. This wasn't the right time to ask about it.

"Short of a confession, I've got nothing to connect her to the murders. And she doesn't strike me as the confessing type."

The corners of my mouth turned up in what had to be a wicked grin. "But you *do* have evidence. Remember what I told you about Ming's claws? I collected the material caught in his toes and saved it."

Joe's eyes narrowed as he pulled his head back slightly. "Your house burned down."

"Mayor Austin said that too." Was I being smug? If so, I didn't care. "But I'm betting it survived the worst of the fire. I stored it in my fridge. If the sample contains the mayor's DNA, won't that prove she was scratched by Ming prior to Amanda's death?"

"A good lawyer can make short work of that." Joe's expression became sly and made me glad we were on the same side. "But with that piece of evidence, Judge Fowler won't be able to refuse to issue a search warrant, as I'm sure he otherwise would. He and Wilbur Austin are golf buddies. Maybe we'll get lucky on the search. You're brilliant, you know." He leaned in suddenly and brushed my cheek with feather-light lips.

The scent of him coming back to me after all these years, combined with the faint rasp of stubble against my skin, made me close my eyes.

When I opened them, he was petting my dog. "I'll talk to you in the morning. Like the hair, by the way. It suits you." As he went back inside, he began to whistle.

It took me a second to recognize the tune as "She's So Bad, She's Good."

Three days later, I lay on my back, staring up at an impossibly blue sky. White, fluffy clouds scudded across my line of sight, and the ground smelt fresh and earthy. Cold mud seeped through the back of my jeans, soaking me to the skin, but I didn't care.

I was being mauled to death.

By a litter of puppies, that is.

My shipment had arrived by special delivery, and I'd rescheduled my appointment with Lloyd Parker to vaccinate his pups. One look at the bunch of chubby puppies waddling toward me on fat little legs, and I was doomed. I rolled over in the mud and gave in to my fate. Puppies swarmed my body, licking my face and leaving adorable little paw prints on my polo shirt. The temperatures were in the sixties, spring was in the air, and I was in short sleeves to celebrate.

And I was covered in puppies. Laughter bubbled up as they whined and pawed at me, some tugging at my hair. If Laney had seen me then, she would have given me a knowing smile and said, "I knew it. Puppies and kittens. Being a vet is the best job in the world."

Just then, I wouldn't have argued with her.

Laney and I had said our goodbyes over breakfast at the diner the day before. With Amanda's murderer in jail, she was free to go home, and she was more than ready to leave Greenbrier.

"I'll never forget this trip, though," she'd said when she gave me a hug on leaving. "What a roller coaster! I'll think of you every time I hear 'She's So Bad, She's Good.'"

I'd covered my face at that. Given her handling of Amanda's artwork, I knew we'd stay in touch, but more than that, I'd made a friend.

I giggled as one of the puppies snuffled in my ear.

Lloyd looked down at me with a bemused expression, as if he wasn't sure I was quite sane. Bushy grey eyebrows and hair provided stark contrast to his dark, weathered skin as he shifted his pipe from one side of his mouth to the other.

"Them pups are getting you filthy."

"I don't mind." I sat up, causing a cascade of puppies to tumble into my lap. The nine-week-old blue heeler pups were as cute and clumsy as a litter of panda bear cubs. One little female with a black patch over one eye and ear tugged determinedly at my bootlace.

Lloyd's heeler bitch, Candy, wasn't particularly well-socialized, but she threw well-built, healthy pups with a natural drive to work cattle. His pups were prized as working dogs, and he had a long wait list. Raising puppies was just one of many ways Lloyd worked to make ends meet, but as a responsible breeder, he had me examine and vaccinate the puppies before he sold them when he could have gone down to the feed store and purchased crappy vaccines to give them himself. Because Candy barely tolerated my presence, and certainly not around her puppies, Lloyd had locked her in the barn. Remy lay on his belly beside me, gently mouthing the puppies that clambered over him.

Remy still wore a protective boot on one foot, but the rest of his injuries had healed. His physical injuries, that is. Mentally, he was still spooked and unwilling to leave my side. But despite the enormous difference in size, he played with the puppies as carefully as if they were made of glass.

"He doing okay?" Lloyd indicated Remy with his pipe.

Regretfully, I rolled to my knees and brushed off the back of my jeans. The puppy with the patch continued to worry my laces as I stood and went over to my cooler where I kept the vaccines and I dragged her along with me as I moved.

"Mostly. Loud noises bother him. More than they used to. I have a feeling the thunderstorm and fireworks season is going to be tough on him now." I wasn't looking forward to the next few months. Clashes between cold and warm fronts made for spectacular thunderstorms in the mountains, and the 4th of July wasn't so much as a holiday weekend as it was an excuse for a weeklong display of fireworks in all forms. Not to mention the year-round target practice that took place in many neighborhoods.

Lloyd nodded and clamped his lips around his pipestem again.

We got down to business. Remy kept the puppies occupied while I pulled up the vaccines and a round of dewormer for everyone. Lloyd kept the records, while I caught puppies one at a time. He'd put different colored collars on them, which made things easier. I examined each puppy, weighing them on a baby scale, taking their temperatures, listening to their hearts, checking their eyes, making sure they didn't have any gross abnormalities and that the boy puppies had both testicles descended, and then gave each a distemper/parvo vaccine and a dose of dewormer. A dab of canned squeeze cheese kept the puppies happily occupied while I poked and prodded them. After I finished with a pup, I marked a front paw with a cattle grease pen so that I wouldn't accidentally vaccinate the same puppy twice.

It wasn't our first rodeo. Lloyd and I worked our way through the litter in no time flat.

Remy was the consummate babysitter.

"You pay that dog a salary?" Lloyd asked when we were done with the last puppy.

I laughed. "I should. The only problem is he's lousy at paperwork."

The sound of an engine coming up the drive made me turn my head. It was one of the new vehicles from the Sheriff's department. Lloyd and I watched in silence as the SUV pulled up into the graveled parking space in front of his trailer.

Somehow, it didn't surprise me when Joe got out of the vehicle and walked in our direction.

Still, I asked, "What is he doing here?"

Lloyd spoke slowly, as if considering my question. "Mayhap he's looking for you."

I shot him my best "oh please" expression, and Lloyd's lips curved into a smile.

"Or it could be he's here for a puppy."

I levied a sharp glance at Lloyd before switching my focus to Joe's approach. Though he'd made eye contact with me briefly when he'd gotten out of the car, his attention was all on the puppies now. The litter, spotting a new attraction, followed Remy over to meet Joe. As I watched, Joe got down on his knees and the puppies swarmed him, even as Remy's entire body wagged from side to side. He stroked Remy's head and greeted each puppy as though they were being introduced at a party.

When he stood, mud caked his knees. He nodded in greeting. "Doc. Lloyd."

"Pup's all ready to go. Just got her first shots and wormer. Needs a booster in three weeks, and then three weeks again after that. But you can take that up with Doc here. Let me go get your paperwork." Lloyd left us to go into the trailer for the puppy's papers.

"You're taking one of the pups?"

Duh. Nothing like stating the obvious here.

"Yeah." Joe smiled, and it was like the sun coming out from behind the clouds. "The little female with the patch over her eye."

Of course.

As we watched, Remy flopped over on his side in an invitation to play, and the heeler pup with the patch pounced on him.

"Got a name for her yet?"

"Toad."

I laughed. Toad was the perfect name for her. She looked exactly like a fat little toad with her wide frog mouth and round little body as she threw herself at Remy's neck.

Automatically, I shifted into my puppy spiel: what to watch for post-vaccination. How often to feed her. The best way to housebreak her. What was normal and what was cause for alarm over the next few weeks until she finished her vaccine series. Joe could have interrupted to remind me this wasn't his first dog, but instead, he nodded and listened.

Toad seemed to know we were talking about her. She left Remy and her littermates to trundle over to Joe. The look on his face as he fondled her ears was one of pure love.

He used to look at me like that.

Getting a dog was a big deal. Finding a place to live in the city with a dog wasn't easy. Adopting Toad implied Joe planned to be here for the long term, even more than building a house from the ground up.

"Why did you leave Greenbrier?"

The words came out of me so unexpectedly, I practically gasped. That was *not* what I wanted to ask him.

His laugh was resigned. "Why do any of us leave? No jobs, no future, no potential for growth. The same old same old every day. We all thought about leaving before we graduated from high school. Even you, Ginge."

He was right. I'd brushed the dust of Greenbrier off my boots the second I'd been accepted into college. From college to vet school, and from vet school straight into a busy, high-volume practice. I wouldn't have returned had it not been for my father. I'd been telling myself that story for years. Was it true?

Somewhere nearby, a mockingbird broke into a heartbreakingly beautiful song.

"Why did you come back? Your parents aren't here any longer. They're living the high life in Boca Raton."

He scooped up Toad and waggled his fingers in front of her before answering. She nipped at his hands, and he gently pinched her lips until she let go. My caution about letting her mouth him died unspoken when I saw he was handling the situation appropriately.

"Why did I come back?"

I saw the weariness then, like Atlas, the weight of the world upon his shoulders; Sisyphus pushing his boulder up a hill, only to have it roll back down again. It was there in the timbre of his voice, in the shadows within his eyes.

"I thought I was going to make a difference. To be a force for good in this world. Instead, I learned that what is good and just means less than who has the power to make things go away. I came home to lick my wounds."

"Oh."

That sounded so unbearably sad. So defeated.

"And," he added, as almost a casual afterthought while he played with his puppy, "maybe I came home because of the people here."

Oh.

Well, that certainly gave me something to think about. On the one hand, Joe had been incredibly cool about letting me park the horses at his place on short notice. He'd also been there for me the night of the fire. But I couldn't discount the fact occasionally he still behaved like a condescending jerk or that we'd tried the relationship thing once before and it hadn't worked out.

That was, of course, assuming that any of this conversation was aimed at *me*. For all I knew, he'd come back to Greenbrier for someone else. Presumptuous, much?

Yes, I was attracted to him. Who wouldn't be? But perhaps that was the problem. Good-looking guys like Joe were used to having women fall at their feet.

I wasn't the same girl I'd been in high school. Was I? Sure, the fundamentals were still there, but I was older and wiser now.

Joe broke the silence abruptly. "The D.A. offered a deal, and Mayor Austin took it. Plead down to second degree murder in the case of Amanda's death, and first degree in Brad's. Time served consecutively, with the possibility of parole in fifteen years. We found nothing incriminating in her home or office, but Rusty remembered Wilbur had a hunting cabin. We hit the jackpot there. Found Amanda's phone and laptop."

It didn't seem like enough jail time, but I knew we were lucky to get that. "She should have gotten rid of them."

"Yeah, if she'd tossed them out the car window on a mountain road, we never would have found them. She probably wanted to be certain she'd tracked down every photo or drawing of the turtles before she did." Then, in a sudden change of subject, he asked, "What's the status of probating the will?"

"Um, Mr. Carter seems to think under the circumstances, I'm within my rights to take possession of Amanda's estate early. Her father isn't competent to handle any legal affairs, and without Brad to contest the will, there shouldn't be any problem with my moving in within the next couple of weeks."

Which wouldn't come soon enough for me. The night I'd returned home from nearly being killed by the mayor, my mother had taken one look at my new haircut and said, "You're lucky I didn't shoot you. I thought you were some strange man breaking into the house."

Joe still played with his puppy. "Then I guess you'll be moving the horses back at some point. I've been to look at that blue roan Deb mentioned, and I like him. But as you know, you can't keep just one horse. They need company. If I decide to buy him, can I send him along to your place with the others?" He looked up then, as something occurred to him. "You *are* keeping Amanda's property, aren't you?"

I blew out my breath in a low whistle. "That's a tough one. I've been getting a lot of pressure to sell. Most people couldn't care less about the bog turtle or the ramifications of doing an environmental impact study. Especially once we found out Brad had poisoned the pond."

At some point, Amanda must have told Brad about the turtle situation. While he still thought he was inheriting, he'd snuck onto the property and poured hundreds of pounds of rock salt into the little pond, destroying everything within it. The environmental guys had found no evidence of the bog turtle on Amanda's land, or anywhere nearby, for that matter. I didn't know what was worse: the thought that Brad might have killed the turtles, or that Amanda had been mistaken about their existence in the first place.

No point in telling Joe about the messages on my phone that ranged from pleading to downright threatening. I never did figure out who'd left me the nasty letter in my mailbox, though I'd lay odds it was Blair Kendall.

"But when I spoke with the people at Riverside, they were already backing down on Amanda's property. I think they're afraid any kind of investigation will turn up reasons not to build the development at all."

Joe nodded, rotating his free hand and splaying his fingers as if to say this made perfect sense to him.

"So," I continued slowly, "I made Riverside a counteroffer. Instead of Amanda's land, which was problematic because of the possible existence of the bog turtle, I suggested they buy my property instead. It backs up to the planned subdivision, and while it doesn't have the views that we get up on the ridge, my land has the advantage of being both flat and mostly cleared. It would also give them another access into the subdivision. Mr. Wainwright seemed interested. He said he'd get back to me after he spoke with his partners."

"But why didn't they offer to buy your place initially when they planned the subdivision?"

I gave a little shrug. "I guess they were set on those mountain views. They can get a lot more money for a house overlooking the valley than one backing up against the ridge."

"So you're telling me you'll get to keep Amanda's place and make some money off selling your land, which was an albatross around your neck even before Ellis burned your house down?" Joe pursed his lips with a slow nod. "Sweet."

It was, actually.

Lloyd came outside with papers in hand, as well as a zip locked bag of kibble. He handed both to Joe, who tucked them under one arm while he struggled to hold the wiggling puppy.

"Her papers, including her vaccine information," Lloyd said. "And some of the food I've been feeding. If you decide to change brands, mix the new stuff in slowly so you won't upset her stomach."

Joe thanked Lloyd, and with a smile aimed at the both of us, made his way back to his car.

"I guess I'll be seeing you in three weeks for puppy shots," Joe said over his shoulder as he walked away.

"Three weeks," I agreed, holding Remy by the collar so he didn't follow Joe.

Joe turned to face us, walking backwards as he held the puppy close to his chest. "Or sooner, as the case may be."

He winked at me.

"Any time of the day or night," I felt compelled to drawl, a slow, lazy version of my usual way of speaking.

Joe's eyes lit up, and he laughed as the puppy licked his chin.

The End

Chapter Twenty-Three

HYPERTHYROIDISM IS A RELATIVELY common disease in senior cats. The vast majority of time the cause is a benign tumor of thyroid origin that results in an excessive production of thyroid hormone. In rare cases, the tumor is a malignant adenocarcinoma. The cause of hyperthyroidism is not known, but they theorize that certain fish-based diets, as well as exposure to chemicals such as flame-retardant upholstery, may contribute to the disruption of the thyroid gland function and promote this condition.

Middle-aged and senior cats with hyperthyroidism typically present with weight loss, despite a strong appetite, and frequently drink large amounts of water and urinate excessively. They can be hyperactive and become unkempt and matted. Sometimes their nails grow excessively thick as well. Some will also exhibit vomiting and diarrhea. Uncontrolled thyroid disease can result in increased blood pressure, which can lead to retinal detachments and strokes, as well as cardiomyopathy.

The good news is hyperthyroidism, if caught early, can be one of the more treatable geriatric cat diseases. Your vet can diagnose this condition with bloodwork and initiate the best form of therapy based on your cat's overall health and response to treatment.

Chapter Twenty-Four

M.K. DEAN LIVES WITH her family on a small farm in North Carolina, along with assorted dogs, cats, and various livestock.

She likes putting her characters in hot water to see how strong they are. Like tea bags, only sexier.

Under the name McKenna Dean, she has penned several books in the award-winning Redclaw Origins and Redclaw Security series. If you like your mysteries with a paranormal flair, check out McKenna Dean's books as well!

If you enjoyed this story, please consider leaving a review on the platform of your choice. Reviews help with visibility, and therefore sales. Likewise, be sure to recommend it to your friends. Every recommendation means more than you could know.

If you want to follow M.K. Dean on social media, be sure to check out her linktree account: . All important links are there, including how to sign up for her newsletter, follow her blog, or find out when the next Ginny Reese book is coming out!

Chapter Twenty-Five

BISHOP TAKES KNIGHT (REDCLAW Origins Book 1)

Bishop's Gambit (Redclaw Origins Book 2)

The Ginny Reese Mysteries

An Embarrassment of Itches

The Dog Days of Murder

Barking All the Way

Made in the USA
Monee, IL
17 October 2024